# *Bennett's*
# TRIALS

## KAREN D GRANT

 FriesenPress

One Printers Way
Altona, MB R0G 0B0
Canada

www.friesenpress.com

ISBN
978-1-03-914759-1 (Hardcover)
978-1-03-914758-4 (Paperback)
978-1-03-914760-7 (eBook)

1. FICTION, ROMANCE, SUSPENSE

Distributed to the trade by The Ingram Book Company

# CHAPTER 1

Lilia Bennett knew that this would be the last day she would wake up hating her job. Her resignation letter was already written, printed, and burning a hole in her purse. She couldn't wait to put it in Melinda Kent's hand. A partner at Hale, Cross & Associates, Melinda treated all the clerks and executive assistants like they were her servants. And she treated Lilia worse than everyone else, although she had no idea why. She had made her two years as a law clerk at the firm a living hell, and Lilia couldn't take it anymore.

Working full-time, Lilia was also attending law school and taking correspondence courses. She had hoped she would complete her law degree while working and articling at the firm and then get hired as an associate, but Melinda was making that impossible. She almost had her law degree and was looking forward to practicing law, but she didn't want to do that anywhere near Melinda Kent.

Hale, Cross & Associates was a predominately Black law firm that had been started by two lawyers, Chris Hale and Shawn Cross, about ten years ago. The story was that Chris and Shawn had been best friends in law school and decided to begin the firm together shortly after they graduated. As their firm grew, they took on a lot of high-profile cases, gaining prestige and fame after representing a well-known actor, Rich Lane, who had been accused of murdering his estranged wife, Cynthia. Rich Lane hired them as they were the only lawyers that truly believed in his innocence after one meeting. With a celebrity as their client, Chris and Shawn were able to take on an investigative team, led by a childhood friend of Chris's, John Benning. The law firm received both intense scrutiny and media attention when they uncovered the true murderer, Clay Prince, who had been an obsessed fan of Rich's.

As the firm got more attention and high-profile cases, they hired two additional associates: Melinda Kent and Warner Reid. Expanding their firm allowed them to fulfill Chris's desire to help those from low-income communities, where he'd grown up. They took on pro bono cases, defending and fighting alongside those whom they believed were innocent, but that wouldn't be able to afford their services otherwise.

What the general public didn't know was that Hale & Cross also gave back to the communities by investing in programs that inspired, motivated, and kept children engaged after school and on weekends. Lilia had been familiar with the firm, hearing about them and being inspired by them more as she decided to pursue law as a career. She found out about their advocacy for the community when she began applying to firms two years ago, as she wanted to not only learn from great lawyers, but also be a part of giving back, as she wished she had access to these types of programs when she was a child.

As Lilia stared into her bathroom mirror, she wished that she had gotten the position that was available in Warner Reid's office instead. But at the time she was looking forward to working with a Black female lawyer and had hoped that her new boss, Melinda Kent, would recognize her potential and take her under her wing.

Warner seemed to respect all clerks, mentoring them, and taking the time to assist anyone that needed it. Melinda respected no one. Over the last year, Melinda became more critical, belittling everyone who was her subordinate. In addition to his regular cases, Warner always took on pro bono cases. Melinda turned down cases if they didn't seem like an easy win. Warner often took his team out for dinners after winning a case. Any assistance Melinda received from the clerks and assistants went unacknowledged.

As Lilia begrudgingly got ready for work, she recalled the incident the day before, which was the event that made her decision to give her two weeks' notice so easy.

*Lilia rushed into work that morning as she had to ensure she arrived before Melinda. Bracing herself for whatever mood Melinda was in, Lilia watched as she arrived in the office. As soon as she looked at her, she knew that Melinda was not in a good mood.*

*As Melinda passed Lilia's desk, Lilia said, "Good morning Ms. Kent."*

*And, as she did every morning, Melinda walked past her without acknowledging Lilia at all. After a few moments in her office, Lilia watched as Melinda's office door opened and Melinda walked out striding quickly to Warner Reid's office, walking through the open door and closing it loudly behind her. Shortly after that, Melinda returned in an even more foul mood—if that were possible.*

*She stopped immediately at Lilia's desk, looked at her with disdain and said, "Why can't you dress more professionally? Your clothes are sloppy. Your desk is disorganized."*

*Lilia sat in shock as Melinda continued, "Never mind your work. If you don't want to work here, I can make changes, so you don't. Do you want to look for a new job?"*

*Melinda didn't wait for an answer, as she turned, and called on another law clerk to follow her into her office.*

*Coming out of her shock, Lilia looked around and noticed that all eyes in the office were on her, full of sympathy and pity. Lilia looked down, grabbed her purse, and got up muttering to the receptionist as she passed her, "Excuse me, I'm just... rest room."*

*Once in the restroom, Lilia washed her face, looked in the mirror, and said to herself, "You will not cry. You will get through today." When the door to the restroom opened, interrupting her quiet, Lilia straightened her back with dignity and went back to her desk.*

As Lilia finished getting dressed and made breakfast, she began to wonder, what am I going to do? She needed to find another job, and soon. She had her condo to maintain, the bills to pay, and student loan payments to make. Lilia was on her own—she had no family to turn to. Lilia's parents, Joe and Lisa Bennett, had passed away in a car accident ten years before. With no siblings or extended family, Lilia had learned to rely only on herself.

Lilia's parents had raised her to be a very independent person. As a child, they encouraged her to solve problems on her own and were examples of this for her. She never wanted for anything, as her parents always ensured that she was fed, clothed, and had a roof over her head. She never recognized that anything was wrong, but she got older, she became more aware that her parents went without to always ensure that she had. She remembered at dinner time, eating first, and then her parents having what was left over. Once she recognized what they were doing, she began to eat less, so they would have enough.

Both of her parents worked hard, her dad working days and her mother nights, to make sure someone was at home with her. As soon as Lilia was old enough to work, she did, despite her parents' protests around her juggling work and school. Friends, movies, and parties were not even a thought for teenage Lilia, as she was either working, at school, or studying. She needed to be successful so that she could take care of her parents as they had taken care of her. That, sadly, would not happen. Joe and Lisa Bennett died before Lilia received her letter of acceptance for law school.

As they passed away so suddenly, they hadn't told Lilia that they both had life insurance policies. It was enough money so that after paying off bills and their funerals, she was able to put a down payment for her condo, and pay for most of law school, with the remainder of it diminishing monthly. Once she was working full time, she would financially be okay. She just had to pass the bar, and the exam was in less than two weeks. ⸙

As she thought about how much her life would change in the next two weeks, Lilia left her one-bedroom condo and took the elevator to the parking lot. Driving to work, having stopped at a traffic light, she pulled the resignation letter out of her purse, resolving to give it to Melinda as soon as she came in. Pulling into the firm's parking lot, Lilia started to feel joy for the first time in a long time.

When she arrived at her desk she peeked into Melinda's office. She wasn't there. Lilia placed her letter on Melinda's desk. Cowardly, Lilia decided she didn't want to be around when she read it.

Lilia started to get anxious as the hours passed and Melinda still hadn't arrived. She wanted the ensuing drama that was sure to come to be over and done with.

Just after noon, Chris Hale, one of the founding partners, passed by Lilia's desk, greeting her politely, and walked directly into Melinda's office. Lilia saw him pick up her letter, read it, then pick up the files on Melinda's desk. He then walked out of Melinda's office straight towards Lilia's desk.

"Lilia, I read your resignation letter. I hope it isn't too late to discuss this."

"I'm sorry, Mr. Hale, but my decision is made. Please know that I have enjoyed working for you and Mr. Cross, but unfortunately I can't stay."

"Does this have anything to do with what happened yesterday?"

"What do you mean?" Lilia began to feel nervous.

"I would like you to meet with Shawn and myself in my office in about ten minutes, okay?"

"Yes, sir. I will. Thank you."

Lilia sat there as Chris walked away and let out the breath that she had been holding since she saw him pick up her letter.

When she gathered up her nerve, she walked to Chris Hale's office, took a deep breath in, and knocked on the door.

When the door opened, Lilia was greeted by Chris Hale, Shawn Cross, and Warner Reid.

"Please come in and have a seat Lilia," Chris said

Lilia sat down at the edge of her seat quietly, "Thank you," and crossed her legs, clenching her hands in her lap.

"Lilia, Chris told us about your resignation. Is it directly related to Melinda's treatment of you yesterday?" Shawn asked, not one to mince words.

"How did you know about that?" Lilia asked, surprised at his candor.

"I told them," Warner Reid interjected.

"H-H-How did you know?" Lilia stuttered.

"I was there. I saw what happened. What's been happening," Warner said.

"Lilia," Chris interjected, "Melinda is no longer with this firm. Due to performance issues and her behaviour, we let her go this morning. Warner has been informing us about how she has been treating the staff."

"In saying all this, Lilia, we hope that you will change your mind and stay with us. We have been very happy with your performance." Shawn said.

"We know you did most of the groundwork in preparing Melinda's cases, and over the last two years we've been keeping track of your work. We were discussing offering you a position with us after you got your degree. You've already completed the ten-month Articling placement. Now, upon you passing the Bar and being sworn in, we would like to offer you the position that has become available." Chris stated.

At Lilia's stunned silence, Warner stated, "I have agreed to oversee all of Melinda's open cases. You would continue to do the research and prep and I will take them to trial, until Chris and Shawn feel you are ready."

"Well, Lilia, what do you think?" Shawn asked.

"Well, I'm very honoured. I thank you very much for the opportunity and I would like to withdraw my letter of resignation." Lilia replied.

"Accepted," Shawn declared, "Now that that is said and done, let's get back to work." Shawn stood up and reached out to shake Lilia's hand.

"Thank you, sir," Lilia said, "thank you," as she stood and shook both men's hands.

"No more sir," Chris replied. "It's Chris, Shawn, and Warner now."

"Thank you, sir. I mean Chris," Lilia floated out of the office to her desk when Warner approached her.

"You should start moving your belongings into the office."

"I still feel as though I'm dreaming. What did you tell them? How did you know? Not just about yesterday, but how she treated me, us all? And about my work?"

"I noticed at first that she would always take the credit for the research on her cases, taking all of you for granted. I saw you and the other clerks doing the work, though, and told Chris and Shawn. She would sometimes make comments about the law clerks not working hard enough. I saw that she was overly demanding, and critical, but at that point I really didn't know how harmful she was being."

"That's how it began." Lilia said thoughtfully, "Then she would pull us aside and berate us in private. She eventually stopped caring who was around."

"I spoke to her about it. I thought she was creating a negative workspace, and I told her I was going to speak to Chris and Shawn if she didn't change. She blamed it on your, all of your, bad performance. That she couldn't trust you to do your jobs. She didn't stop and I couldn't stand by and allow it to continue. I went to Chris and Shawn, who already had concerns and begun to keep abreast of all of her cases. They had already decided to let her go when she yelled at you yesterday."

Warner continued, "She used to be such a great lawyer. I used to admire her. I don't know what happened."

"When I heard I would be working with her I was thrilled to be working with someone so esteemed. I wanted to learn so much from her."

"Hopefully she takes this as a wake-up call, and she can have a fresh start. Just as it is for you," Warner continued, "You take the Bar exam next week, right?"

"Yes. I've been studying as much as I can."

"I can't believe you've been working full time and going to law school," Warner said incredulously.

"That's why it's taken me so long," Lilia said with a small smile.

"Well, let me know if you need help with anything. I need to go over the cases with you, the ones that you're already familiar with. Can we meet now about the ones coming up?" Warner asked.

"Yes, I'll get them for you."

"Actually, I already have them. Chris got them from Melinda's—no, your office this morning, before we spoke with you."

"Oh yes—I saw him. Shall we go to your office then?"

They worked on the cases in Warner's office for the remainder of the day.

Once Lilia got home from school that night, she was tired but elated—even though she still had more studying to do before she could go to bed. As she got undressed and got into the shower, she wished she had someone to tell. She wished her parents were still here to share in her joy. It may have taken her longer than most, but she almost had everything that she had worked so hard for.

Standing under the stream of hot water, she realized tears were running down her face.

# CHAPTER 2

I n her car on her way to the office the next morning, Lilia felt a sense of apprehension.

"Oh, what did I do?" she said to herself quietly. *Why had she accepted the position? Was she ready for this?* "Oh dear," she sighed.

Working with Warner yesterday had really made her respect him as a person and a lawyer. He never once spoke down to her as Melinda had. Even though he challenged some of her research, he never once made her feel inadequate. He treated her as an equal.

She arrived at the office and began organizing her new office space, when she heard the sound of knocking at her open office door.

She turned to see Kathy, one of the law clerks and office gossips standing there.

"Hi, Lilia. I just wanted to say congratulations. I heard the news, and I am so happy that you got rid of Melinda.

How did you do it?" Kathy didn't give her time to answer: "I heard that you stood up to her and then told Hale and Cross that it was either her or you, and they chose you. Is that really what happened?"

At that, Lilia was stunned into silence. She didn't know whether to address the incorrect gossip that was flying around the office or Kathy's audacity in being so nosy. They were both startled at the sound of someone clearing their throat behind Kathy.

"Kathy," Warner said, "do you not have anything more productive to do than to repeat idle office gossip? I'm sure that there is a case or two that require your..." Warner paused, "research."

"Oh yes, Mr. Reid, I certainly do." Kathy gushed, blushing, "I'm working on the Weitzman case right now. I was just congratulating Lilia on her promotion."

"Well, I need it by the end of today so we can go over it. Thank you, Kathy." Warner said, politely dismissing her. He then turned to Lilia.

"Lilia, do you have a couple of minutes to go over a few documents?"

"Of course, Mr. Reid."

"Warner," he said.

"Pardon?" Lilia asked, confused.

"Remember, it's Warner. You're an associate now."

"Oh yes, Warner," Lilia said shyly. "And I'm not an associate yet," Lilia smiled, "I have to pass the Bar first."

"Don't worry, you will." Warner replied surely. "So, how do you like the office?"

"I'm not sure yet." Lilia beamed, "I've only just started to organize myself."

"Are you planning to take some time off before the Bar so you can study?"

"No I wasn't. I requested this week and next week off from Ms. Kent, but she denied my request. She stated that my first priority was to her."

Warner shook his head and mumbled something under his breath that Lilia couldn't make out. "She's no longer your boss, and you are going to take the time." Warner stated.

"B-B-But…" Lilia stuttered not knowing what to say.

"No buts. Clear your schedule today and tomorrow and then catch me up on all of the impending cases. As it's already Wednesday, I don't expect to see you here on Friday," he said. "Now that's cleared up. When exactly is the exam?"

"Next Thursday and Friday, six hours a day," Lilia stated.

"Good, so we'll see you the following Monday then."

"Thank you, Mr. Reid, I-I-I mean, Warner."

"Don't worry about it. Melinda should have given you the time off. Anyways, what's done is done. If you need any help next week let me know. I'll check in with you at some point to see how you are doing."

"Oh, that's very generous of you, Warner. Thank you, but it's not necessary. I wouldn't want you to go out of your way."

"I wouldn't have offered if I minded. One thing you'll soon learn about me, Lilia, is I don't say things that I don't mean." Warner stared right into Lilia's eyes at that.

"I-I… thank you," Lilia stuttered quietly.

"Okay, that's settled. Let's get started." Warner motioned for her to sit down in her new chair and then sat down in the chair in front of her desk, opening the first file.

Lilia and Warner worked closely going over only one case file for several hours, when Lilia's office phone rang. Lilia answered it without thinking saying "Hello. Hale, Scott & Associates, can I help you?"

"Lilia Bennett?" said the person on the other side of the phone.

"Yes?"

"This is Mary, from Mr. Reid's office. I'm sorry Ms. Bennett but is this not your office extension?"

"Yes, it is. Sorry, Mary, I guess I'm just not used to answering the phone yet." Lilia said, slightly embarrassed.

"That's alright," Mary said, "Is Mr. Reid still in your office?"

"Yes, he's here. We're working on a case file."

"Would you please let him know that Mrs. Reid is here for their one o'clock lunch appointment?"

"Yes, I'll tell him." Lilia said. "Thank you, Mary." Lilia hung up the phone.

"That was Mary," Lilia said, "She said your one o'clock lunch appointment is here."

"Oh yeah. I forgot Wren was coming." Warner said more to himself beginning to stand up. "Can we continue once I get back?" Warner asked as he moved towards the door.

"Of course."

"What will you do for lunch?"

"Oh, I always bring my lunch to work."

"Alright, I'll see you around two thirty." Warner stated and then walked out of Lilia's office.

Wren Reid, Lilia thought to herself. She hadn't known that Warner was married, nor had she noticed that he wore a ring. *Oh well, some married couples choose not to wearing rings*, she thought, and even if he wasn't married, she wouldn't be interested. She had far too much on her plate to even think about trying to add the complications that came with a relationship to it. Lilia then turned her thoughts back to the work at hand. She got her brown lunch bag out and began to eat as she opened the next case file. She wanted to make sure that she had everything organized upon Warner's return.

Hearing a curt knock on her door, Lilia looked up to see Warner.

"Sorry I'm late. I lost track of time."

Lilia glanced at her clock, seeing he was only fifteen minutes late. "No problem. I was just finishing up anyways. I hope your lunch was good?"

"It was very good, thank you," Warner replied, "Shall we get to work?"

"Absolutely," Lilia said and pushed the case file they were working on to his side of the desk.

They worked steadily for the remainder of the day when Lilia noticed the time. "Oh my, it's after seven. I didn't even notice anyone else going home."

"I know. Sorry about that. We were working so diligently on the case; I didn't notice how late it had gotten."

"At least we got a lot done."

"What are you doing for dinner?" Warner asked as he packed up the files.

"I have some leftovers at home waiting for me, while I get some studying done."

"Yes, of course, the books," Warner said with a smile, "you work so much, don't forget to play sometimes too."

"Unfortunately, I don't have much time for play right now; I barely have time for sleep. But at the end of the day, it will all be worth it if I pass the Bar."

"WHEN you pass the Bar." Warner stressed.

Lilia smiled and looked at Warner, "Yes, when."

Warner picked up his suit jacket and placed it over his arm, "Wait for me here so I can walk you to your car. I'm going to get my things." He walked away not waiting for a response.

Lilia stood there for a moment while she debated waiting for him as she wasn't quite sure she liked being directed. She was used to counting on herself. As she got ready, she decided she would rather wait for him to walk her to her car than to walk through the dark parking lot by herself.

Just as Lilia finished packing up her things, Warner came back into her office. "Are you ready?" he asked.

"Yes," Lilia said, "thank you."

"I kept you late, I just want to make sure you're safe." Warner said as he followed her out of the office.

"Well, you didn't have to, but I do really appreciate it. I certainly would have been nervous walking out here by myself."

"The parking garage is too far from our office building, and not well lit. I've been meaning to speak to Chris and Shawn about it, but usually I'm the only one here late. We should do something about it though."

"I try never to stay in the office too late. I leave when Jeff is locking up." Lilia said as they approached her car.

"Jeff?" Warner questioned.

"Jeff Sanders… the nighttime security guard," Lilia answered, "He's the last guard on duty."

"Oh…" Warner stared at her thoughtfully.

"Thanks for walking me to my car," Lilia stated, pulling him out of his thoughtful state.

"Goodnight, Lilia. Drive safe," Warner said, opening her car door for her.

"Thanks, you too. Goodnight, Warner."

Lilia started her car and drove towards home thinking what a gentleman Warner was.

"Get it together, Lilia," she whispered to herself as she drove, "you have far too much to do than to think of a man—a married one at that." Lilia resolved to make it through the night without having another thought about Warner.

# CHAPTER 3

The next morning, Lilia arrived early. To her surprise, Warner was already sitting at his desk, working. She walked over and stood at his door. He was so involved in his work he didn't even look up. Lilia cleared her throat and knocked. Warner looked up at her.

"You beat me." Lilia said.

"I wanted to look things over before you came in. As it is your last day, I just want to be prepared for the Wilkins case as the arraignment is Monday. I don't understand why Melinda had the client plead not guilty. The evidence against him is overwhelming. It would have made more sense to plead guilty and take his chances with a judge instead of a jury. What was she thinking?"

"I can't explain it. I provided her with all of the evidence that the prosecutor presented. I researched the precedents and gave her those statistics as well."

"Didn't you go with her?" Warner asked.

"She told me not to."

"I see she also requested an order to exclude the witnesses so that they would not be privy to the others' testimony, which was denied. What would make her think she could get that before the first appearance?" He sat back in his chair and shook his head.

Lilia didn't answer. It didn't appear as though he was looking for an answer and she had the same questions. As Warner buried himself in the paperwork about the case, Lilia made her way to her office to get to work. There was still lots for her to do before the end of the day.

The case would be a difficult one to win. Warner would have to try to convince the client to change his plea before the arraignment so they might negotiate a lighter sentence. Why would Melinda take the case? It was an impossible win. And Melinda took cases that made her a winner, not cases like Wilkins.

Luke Wilkins had been charged with four counts of murder and eight counts of aggravated sexual assault. The evidence against him was damning. Two of the four surviving women identified him as their attacker and were going to testify. There was also DNA evidence, that all eight of the victims provided, in and on their bodies. They had all been violently beaten and raped. The women that had survived spent several weeks in the hospital recovering before they were even able to give their statements to the police. The last four victims had died from asphyxiation, with the bruises of their killer's hands around their throat.

Once Chris and Scott had met with Luke Wilkins, reviewed the evidence, and accepted the case, it was Melinda's prerogative to accept it. Initially, both Melinda and Lilia met with Wilkins, and Lilia's instincts told her he was guilty as she felt an instant disdain for him. She felt as though he were leering at her, seeing through her clothes to her body beneath. Lilia didn't mind when Melinda had boldly told her that as Lilia was useless anyways, she couldn't attend any more meetings with the client.

As a woman, Lilia found it difficult working on behalf of an accused rapist and murderer, especially when the evidence was so overwhelming. But the lawyer and advocate in her knew that everyone deserved the right to a fair trial and to a strong defence—no matter what; guilty or innocent.

Lilia worked throughout the morning and just before lunch Warner knocked and walked into her office.

"Can we break for lunch?" he asked her.

"I was actually about to." Lilia replied.

"Great. Let's go."

"I brought my lunch, thanks, so I'm fine. You go ahead." Lilia stated, wondering why he would want to eat with her. "How did the meet go with Wilkins?"

"That's exactly what I want to discuss with you. Over lunch. My treat." He stated.

"I'm not very hungry, so I can just nibble on my lunch."

Just then, Lilia's stomach chose to betray her and growled loudly.

"Oh," she said with an embarrassed look on her face, "I guess I'm hungrier than I realized."

"And as time is ticking away on your last day, I would like to tell you about the meeting while we eat. Can we go now? I'll drive." He stated as he walked out of the office assuming she would follow.

Lilia begrudgingly collected her purse and coat, slowly following him out the door.

"What did Wilkins say? Did you ask him about the plea?" She asked as Warner held the door open for her.

"He was extremely agitated that I had taken over the case and he was demanding that Melinda be put back on his case. I explained to him that she was no longer employed by Hale & Cross. He then demanded that you were his lawyer and I explained that you were not an esquire as of yet. All in all, it was an extremely unproductive meeting."

Lilia paused before she responded, waiting for him to get into the driver's side of the car after he had opened the passenger side door for her to climb in.

"He didn't want to change his plea, did he?"

"He refused."

As they parked in the restaurant parking lot, Warner opened her car door and asked, "I trust you like Italian food? This is a very good restaurant. I come here all the time. The chef creates great Italian dishes quickly."

"I do like Italian." Lilia said as they walked into the restaurant.

"Mr. Reid," the attractive hostess greeted them, "welcome back. We are always happy to have you at our establishment."

"Thank you. Can we have a table for two? Secluded please." Warner requested.

"Yes, certainly. You and Mrs. Reid would like some privacy today?" the hostess inquired. Lilia looked at her, startled at her forward behaviour.

"I am not Mrs. Reid. I am his colleague, and we have business matters to discuss." Lilia said quickly, slightly annoyed.

"Oh, of course. My apologies. I am so sorry for the assumption, Mr. Reid." The attractive hostess stated as she strategically placed her hand on his upper arm. "Please follow me to your table."

The hostess walked in front of them to their table putting an exaggerated sexy wiggle in her walk. She stopped at their table and handed them their menus after Warner held her chair and sat in his seat.

"Thank you." Warner and Lilia said in unison.

"What do you feel for?" Warner asked Lilia as he perused the menu.

"I'm still thinking," Lilia stated, wondering why she suddenly lost her appetite. She hoped the hostess wouldn't be their waitress too.

"I told you the food is great. I don't know why I'm looking at the menu. I always get the same thing—seafood fettuccini in a white wine sauce."

"That does sound good." Lilia said.

"Do you want to get it too? Once we order we can talk about the case."

"Okay—sounds good." Lilia said.

Just then the waitress came over. "Hi, Mr. Reid, welcome back to Buca Terroni." She turned to Lilia, "My name is Lisa, do you already know what you'd like to order? Or do you need more time?" Lilia was pleased that this new waitress was not openly flirting with Warner.

"We're ready," Warner stated.

"Seafood fettuccini in a white wine sauce for you, Mr. Reid?" the waitress said knowingly.

"Yes—two please—for my guest as well." Warner replied.

"Anything to drink?"

"Water, please." Lilia said.

"Two waters." Warner stated and the waitress walked away.

"You weren't kidding when you said you always get the same thing. How many times have you been here?"

"I really don't know. Once or twice per week for as long as I've been at Hale & Cross."

"Okay—so what else happened with Wilkins? Did you get him to agree to change his plea?"

"Not at all. He was so focused on Melinda and you that he dismissed anything I had to say and demanded that you be present for all meetings."

Lilia was shocked and puzzled, which she didn't hide from Warner. "Why does he want me there? What did you say?"

"I said that unfortunately you would not be able to make it to the next meet or arraignment but that you could be my second at the trial. It will be a good experience for you."

Just then the food arrived, and Warner immediately began eating. The food looked so good that Lilia's hunger returned, and she began eating as well.

They ate in silence for a minute, pondering their own thoughts, before Lilia spoke again. "Alright. As much as I detest the man. Innocent until proven guilty and all of that."

Warner laughed, and Lilia realized it was the first time she had ever heard him laugh. She liked the sound and smiled.

"Yes, well, with all of that evidence I would be shocked if any jury or judge found him innocent. I explained to him what all of the evidence was, and he still wouldn't change his mind. Melinda said nothing to you about her reasoning with this case?"

"Not at all."

They finished their meal. Once the waitress brought the bill, and, out of habit, Lilia reached for it at the same time as Warner. As their hands touched, Lilia felt a fluttering in her chest, and she looked up at Warner suddenly to find him looking right back at her.

*Had he felt it too?* she thought.

"Sorry," he said while still looking into her eyes and yet not moving his hand from on top of hers.

Lilia quickly pulled her hand out from under his. "Sorry" she said, breaking his hold on her gaze.

"I told you it was my treat," Warner said.

"I forgot. I'm used to paying for myself."

"Only child?"

"Yes," Lilia smiled, "You?"

"I have an older sister," Warner stated.

"Are you close?"

"Yes, to her, her husband, and my four nieces and nephews." Warner signaled to the waitress his desire to pay. "Do you have close family?"

"No, there's just me. My parents passed away several years ago and they had no siblings either." Lilia didn't know why she was willing to share so much personal information. She wasn't close to anyone at Hale & Cross.

"That must be hard, especially when you've got so much on your plate like law school. You definitely need a support system while you're going through it."

In that moment, Lilia decided not to offer any more information to Warner unless he asked her directly. She was already confused by the different feelings she had been experiencing around him, and she didn't want to confuse herself more by getting to know him on a personal level.

Once the bill had been paid, they returned to Warner's car, and headed in the direction of the office.

"Have you wrapped everything up? Is everything organized for the other associates to take over next week?" Warner asked her.

"Almost," Lilia replied, "I will definitely be finished today. But if there are any questions about any of the cases, please contact me. I can come in. I am very grateful for the time off, but I'm sure it's hard without Melinda there."

"You have worked very hard to get where you are now, Lilia. Do not risk it by being kind. The next week is going to be hard for you without work as well." Warner said sternly.

Lilia looked at Warner not knowing what to think. Once Warner heard her silence and felt her looking at him, he glanced over at her while trying to keep his eyes on the road.

"Is there a problem, Lilia?"

"No problem. Thank you, Warner."

Once they got to the firm, they both went to their offices to finish off their work for the day. After working for what seemed to be a few hours, Lilia closed the last file. Getting ready to leave, she noticed the office was empty, so she glanced at her watch at the time, shocked at how late it had gotten. Walking into the hallway she noticed the light in Warner's office on.

"Ready to go?" Warner asked, seeing her standing out in the hallway.

"Yes, I am," Lilia stated slightly confused about why he was still there.

Warner got up from his desk and gathered his things to leave.

"Are you leaving now too?"

"Yes—I was ready about a half hour ago, but I noticed you were still working so I decided to wait and walk you to your car," he said matter-of-factly as he led her out of the office and down the elevator. "You finished the files?"

"Yes," Lilia stated, "they are organized and placed by level of urgency for each associate."

As they walked to her car Warner stated, "When you return, you must let... Jeff, is it? Know when you are leaving, so he can leave with you. I don't know how he has been allowing you to leave with me this week."

Lilia stopped walking and questioned, "Why should it matter to Jeff whether I leave with you or not?"

"Aren't you and Jeff—" Warner started.

"Oh no!" Lilia interrupted, "Jeff's wife and children wouldn't be too happy to hear that! Why would you think that?"

"Sorry—I just assumed you were—as you know so much about him."

"His name, his shift, and the fact that he has a family is all I know of Jeff." She stated.

"I'm sorry for assuming. I don't know everyone in the building, and I didn't think that you would," Warner said as they arrived at Lilia's car.

Warner opened her car door and said, "Good luck next week. If I can give you any advice at all it would be to relax. You know it. If you need any help let me know,"

"Thanks. And I mean it when I say that if anything is needed about any of the cases just let me know. I want to help if I can."

Warner smiled, "Goodnight."

Lilia got into her car and once it was started and her doors were locked, Warner walked to his car. She waited until he got in and started his car, waved, and then pulled out of the parking lot. She drove home trying to make sense at the feelings of loss she felt at the prospect of not seeing him for more than a week.

*I am being absolutely ridiculous*, she thought as she pulled into her condo's underground parking lot. *You're going to miss going to work each day, now that you've actually begun enjoying it since Melinda left.* Lilia went to her unit and put all thoughts of work and Warner out of her mind so she could settle in for a peaceful night.

# CHAPTER 4

For the next two days, Lilia went to the law library very early in the morning so she could make the most of her day and get a hold of all of the books and publications she would need. She would only break to eat and use the washroom, and then it was back to studying.

By Monday, Lilia could no longer lie to herself. She was getting distracted by thoughts of Warner. Every man she passed on the street or in the library either looked like him, or had his scent. Lilia finally acknowledged that she missed him. She resisted the urge to contact him, even though she also wanted to know how the arraignment went. She didn't know the exact time frame, thankfully, or she was sure she would have called him two minutes afterwards.

To make herself concentrate, Lilia decided to go to the library for the rest of the day. Lilia was annoyed with herself. After she placed her phone down on the kitchen table for what seemed like the one hundredth time, she decided to leave her cell phone at home.

She lost herself in the books, until she heard an announcement on the PA system that the library would be closing shortly. Lilia gathered her things to head home; the time had passed so quickly.

As she pulled up to her condo unit, Lilia noticed a car that looked exactly like Warner's. As quickly as the thought came to her mind, she quickly dismissed it. *Now I'm seeing his car? Get a hold of yourself.*

She pulled into the parking garage and went up the elevator to her unit. As she got to her door, she could vaguely hear her cell phone ringing. She tried to get the key in the lock quickly to catch it, but it had stopped. Before she could lock the door, the phone started to ring again. As she picked it up, she saw a number she didn't recognize. She hesitated, but then curiosity got the better of her.

"Hello?"

"Lilia! Where have you been? I've been trying to get in touch with you for hours!"

It was Warner. *Had she conjured him up by thinking of him all day?*

"Warner? Are you okay? You sound upset."

"Lilia, I need to speak with you. I'm in the lobby of your building. Can I come up?"

"You're here? I thought I saw your..." Lilia paused, "What are you doing here?"

"I need to see you, speak with you, know you're safe."

"What are you talking about? Of course I'm safe."

"Look, I'm downstairs, please buzz me in. I need to speak to you."

"Oh… um, okay". Curious about the urgency in Warner's voice, she buzzed him in.

*How did he get her number and address?* She'd ask him when he came up. At that point she noticed the twelve missed calls, all from the same phone number—Warner's.

The knock on the door startled her. Lilia went to open the door and as soon as she opened it, he stepped inside.

"What's going on Warner? How did you get my number and address? What are you doing here?"

"I got both from the office. Where were you? Why didn't you answer your phone? I was worried when you didn't answer."

"I was at the library. What's going on?"

"Can we sit down?"

"Sure—sorry. Of course. Sit anywhere." She answered gesturing at her sofa. "Do you want a drink?"

"No thanks. Let's sit." Warner took her by the hand and led her to the couch.

Lilia was baffled. *Why was Warner acting like this? Why was he holding her hand?*

"I have something I need to tell you."

"Is it about the arraignment? How did it go?"

"Never mind the arraignment for now. It's about Melinda."

"What about Melinda?"

"Her body was found today." Perplexed Lilia asked, "What? What do you mean 'her body'?"

Warner took her hand in his again, and paused before saying, "She was murdered."

"Murdered?! What are you talking about? Are you sure? How do you know?" Lilia stared at Warner stunned and at a loss for words.

"Her neighbour found her over the weekend and the police confirmed today that she was murdered. They came to the office. I found out after the arraignment."

"This can't be true…" Lilia's voice trailed off.

Warner reached up and wiped a tear from her face. Lilia hadn't even realized she was crying. He left his hand cradling her cheek as he said, "I can't believe it either. You know better than anyone that she was not a kind woman, but no one deserves…" Warner paused, "I'm sorry to have to tell you. I knew you'd be upset, that's why I came over. Are you going to be okay? Do you want me to stay for a while?"

"Oh, no." Lilia pulled her hand out of his, realizing she was taking too much comfort from him, remembering that his wife was probably waiting for him to come home. "I'm okay. Thank you. I don't think it would be appropriate."

"I just don't want you to be alone when you're so upset. I know we work together, but I would never abuse my authority. I'm not like her." Warner stood and began to stride to the door.

"Warner, wait. I just meant that you should be home. If your wife knew Melinda, she may want to be with you."

Warner smiled and turned to her shaking his head slowly, "My wife? Where did you meet this wife of mine?"

"At the office, your assistant said that Mrs. Reid was waiting for you. At least, I just assumed it was your wife. Was I wrong?"

"Yes, you were wrong. Mrs. Reid is my sister, Wren." He explained, "Mrs. Wren Hunter Reid, who has not changed her maiden name, is not my wife and I had a fabulous lunch with her. The position of Mrs. Warner Reid hasn't been filled yet." Warner stared at her, holding her gaze.

Lilia stared back silently for a moment before shaking her head and breaking their locked gaze.

"Oh, I'm sorry. Not that you're not married—for assuming. Sorry." Lilia stuttered.

"Don't worry about it. Now I ask again. Do you want me to stay for a while?" Warner said, placing his hands on her shoulders and reattaching their gaze.

"Thank you. I'm okay though. I think I'd like to be alone. I still can't believe it."

"Can I check on you tomorrow?"

"I'd like that. Thank you, Warner. Get home safe." Lilia walked Warner back to the door.

Warner smiled, "I will, thank you."

"Will you call me… or text me? Just to let me know you're home safe?" Lilia explained, "under the circumstances I just want you to be okay."

"Of course. I'll text. Goodnight, Lilia." Warner smiled again and headed out the door.

With Warner gone, Lilia was alone with her thoughts. She locked the house and got ready for bed, alone with her thoughts.

*Who murdered Melinda? Why? Could it have been an accident? A break-in or something? Who had a reason to kill her?* In bed, Lilia began to cry again thinking of Melinda and the pain and fear she must have felt. She thought about Melinda's family as Lilia was sure someone had to miss her.

Her phone buzzed, interrupting her thoughts and alerting her to a text message. It was Warner. *I'm in. Call me if you want to talk.*

Lilia texted him back, *Thank you. I'm going to see if I can get some sleep. Talk tomorrow?*

*I'll call you.* Warner responded quickly. *Goodnight.*

On Tuesday, Lilia had originally planned to spend the whole day at the library, but she could barely get herself out of bed. Looking at her swollen puffy eyes, she recalled that she had spent a lot of the night crying. Lilia washed her face and did what she could to make herself presentable. Just as she'd finished, she heard her cell phone ring. *Who's calling so early in the morning?* Picking up her phone, she smiled.

"Good morning, Warner," Lilia greeted.

"Good morning, Lilia," Warner said, "How was your night?"

"I didn't get much sleep. I couldn't stop thinking about Melinda. Her poor family..." Lilia's voice trailed off.

"I had some trouble sleeping too. I'm still in disbelief. Hoping I'd get a call saying they were wrong."

"You've known her for a long time Warner. I'm really sorry." Lilia paused. "Have you spoken with Shawn and Chris? How are they doing?"

"I saw them briefly in the office yesterday. They were a mess. Everyone was pretty distraught, not saying much. Shawn and Chris told everyone to go home for the day, but no one did. Before I left, I got your information from Shawn. I wanted to be the one to tell you. Make sure you were okay."

Lilia smiled softly, "I'm glad you were the one that told me." Lilia continued, "What about family? Friends? Was anyone close to her?"

"She had no family that I'm aware of." He answered. "I don't know any of her friends. Maybe Shawn and Chris do. Are you going to the library today?"

"Yes, I should be…"

"Will you let me to take you to lunch? I can pick you up from the library then take you back after we eat."

"Oh…" Lilia paused. She wanted to say yes, but she felt as though she was getting too attached to him.

"I still have to tell you about the arraignment." He stated.

"Right. I meant to ask you about that."

"Okay. I'll pick you up from the library. About one? That should give you a good amount of time to get your research done. I'm in the office now so I'll check in with Shawn and Chris, see if they know anything more about Melinda before I leave."

"Okay. Please let them know that I send my condolences. Actually, never mind. I'll send them a note or pop into the office later." Lilia said thoughtfully.

"Okay—that would be nice."

"Chris and Shawn have always been kind to me. It's the least I can do."

"You better get moving before I'm picking you up at your house instead of at the library."

"Right." Lilia said, looking at the time. "See you later." Lilia said.

"See you."

Before Lilia knew it, she was at the library and it was nearing one o'clock. She began to pack up to wait for Warner outside when she heard her name gently called behind her. She turned around to see Warner.

"Hi, you got here early." Lilia said.

"Yes, I came inside to help you carry your books." Warner put out his hand to take her full bag of law books from her.

Lilia handed it over to him without complaint, "Thank you. How was everyone at the office?" She asked as they walked towards his car.

"I'll fill you in once we get in the car." Warner said ominously.

Once they were both settled, Lilia asked, "What happened?"

"Right after I got off the phone with you the police came in and asked if they could speak with the staff. I spoke to them right after Shawn and Chris. They asked when the last time I saw Melinda was and wanted to know if I knew of anyone who wanted to harm her. They also wanted to verify my alibi for the day and time of her murder."

"Oh my." Lilia was shocked.

"Before they left, they requested a list of all the staff missing from the office, so I wouldn't be surprised if they contact you soon with the same questions."

"Okay, thanks for letting me know."

"If you want me there when they interview you, just let me know."

"I will. Thank you." Lilia continued, "I feel like I'm always thanking you for one thing or another."

"You don't have to thank me." Warner stated as he pulled into the restaurant parking spot, and then locked eyes with her. "One thing you'll find out about me is that I don't do anything I don't want to do. Now let's go eat." Warner got out of the car and walked around to open her door for her.

"I'm not used to people doing things for me." Lilia said while getting out of the car.

"Well, you'd better get used to it." Warner said with a smile, "Okay—no more talking until I have a big plate of fettuccini in front of me please."

Lilia laughed, "Why don't you try something new?"

"What's the point? When you find something you like, stick with it." Warner said seriously.

Lilia laughed again as they walked inside.

"Mr. Reid," the same hostess greeted them. "So nice to see you again, with your colleague," she stated in a flirtatious manner.

"Good afternoon. A table at the back please. Secluded." Warner said in a dismissive tone.

"Of course, Mr. Reid."

Once they were seated alone at the table, Lilia said, "I know I agreed not to say anything until you're fed but… you must notice how the hostess flirts with you. Why do you act like you don't notice?"

"I'm not interested in flirting with her or doing anything else with her." Warner said looking directly at Lilia.

"Oh—" Lilia swallowed hard, averting her gaze as the waitress came over.

"Hello, Mr. Reid. Welcome back. Seafood fettuccini?" the waitress asked.

"For two please." Lilia spoke up with a smile.

Warner looked at Lilia and smiled. "You didn't want to try something new?"

"When you find something you like…" She began as Warner smirked at her.

"Okay—arraignment. Tell me what happened." Lilia felt too comfortable with their banter and wanted to get back to work topics.

"I still couldn't convince him to change his plea. We went before the judge, charges were read, he plead not guilty, the trial date was settled and bail was set at $250,000,." He said curtly. "When you're back, we're going to go through every inch of this case. There has to be something we're missing. Something he's not telling us. He won't give me an alibi for where he was during each attack. We have no defence. We have to find some reasonable doubt." Once Warner was finished with his statement, the food arrived so Lilia reserved what she wanted to say until after the waitress left.

"I agree with you, Warner. There has to be something we haven't uncovered. Yet. But we'll find it," Lilia stated. "I think that Melinda had some files at home." Lilia continued, "I often saw her leave the office with them. Maybe there's something there. Do you think we could commission the police to release any Hale & Cross files found on her property?"

"Good thinking. If they don't release them, I'll ask Chris and Shawn if they can get a subpoena to access any documents. I'll handle it."

Just then, Warner's phone rang, and he answered it.

Lilia tried to be polite and not listen to his side of the conversation while she finished her meal.

Warner hung up and spoke: "Wilkins just posted bail."

"Did you know he had access to that kind of money?"

"It was with a bondsman." Warner was interrupted by Lilia's phone.

"Looks like we're both popular today," Lilia said as she took her phone out of her purse.

"Hello?" Lilia paused as she listened to what the caller was saying. "The police," she mouthed to Warner. He nodded his understanding.

"Tomorrow at noon is just fine." Lilia listened again, "Okay, thank you. See you tomorrow." She hung up the phone.

"Do you want me to come?"

"I think I'll be fine. It's the police. They won't do anything to me." Lilia smiled.

"I just wanted to support you if you needed it. "

"Thanks again."

"Ready?"

"Yes I am."

"Are you still coming back to the office to speak with Chris and Shawn?" Warner asked.

"Yes, I will. But I'm going to go home first to change. Wear business attire." Lilia laughed as she explained.

"You know you look fine, right?"

Lilia just smiled at Warner as she got into his car. They both sat in contented silence with their own thoughts on the way back to the library.

"Thanks for lunch," Lilia said as she got out of the car.

"See you at the office." Warner said and then waited for her to start her car.

Lilia waved at Warner as she pulled out of the library parking lot and headed in the direction of her condo to change.

Arriving at the firm, Lilia headed in the direction of Chris and Shawn's offices when Warner walked up to her. "Hey," he said.

"Hi. Are Chris and Shawn in their offices?" Lilia asked him.

"Yes. I was just heading in there to ask about the subpoena if the police aren't helpful. I've just put a call in to the detective in charge and I'm waiting for him to call me back."

"That's great." Lilia said.

"I can wait, if you want a moment with them." Warner said.

"No, it's okay. I want to hear what they say about the subpoena, so it's great timing on my part, I guess."

"Yes, it is," Warner said as they walked side by side towards their offices, asking Chris's executive assistant to let him know they were there.

Chris opened his door as Warner and Lilia walked towards it. "Lilia, it's good to see you, though I wish the circumstances were different." Warner paused allowing Lilia to enter Chris's office ahead of him, as Chris walked behind his desk and picked up his phone. "I'll ask Shawn to come in." As Chris phoned Shawn's office, Warner and Lilia took seats in the armchairs in his office.

Chris sat down as Shawn entered the office. "Warner. Lilia." Shawn greeted them both, with Warner and Lilia standing to greet him.

"Shawn. Chris. How are you both doing?" Lilia asked.

"It's been difficult. We are confused and upset of course. Trying to help the staff grieve, and increase morale, while trying to calm the fear as there's gossip about Melinda being targeted. We are having a grief counsellor come in for the next few days to speak to staff who need it." Shawn stated as he sat on the edge of Chris's desk.

"That's good, for the staff to be able to speak to a professional. I'm sure the detectives asking to speak to everyone doesn't help if there's gossip." Lilia continued, "They contacted me, and asked if we worked on cases together. They seemed to insinuate that her death could be related to one she was working on."

"Was there anything going on that made you suspect anything untoward?" Chris asked.

"Not anything that I can think of. She did work a lot at home, however. I was talking to Warner about it. Perhaps she kept something there?" Lilia asked.

"I placed a call in to the detective. I'm hoping they will give us all Hale & Cross property without bothering with the subpoena. Based on Lawyer/client privilege…" Warner added.

"Great thinking. That's definitely the way to go. Fill us in when you find out. If we have to get a subpoena, I'll call Judge Francis." Chris said. "Let's keep this between us four. No need for anyone else in the office to be involved or give them more to gossip about."

"Agreed." Warner said and stood to leave. "Lilia, I'll speak with you later. I have a client to track down. Chris, Shawn." Warner nodded at them and left.

"Good luck. Bye, Warner." Lilia said as Warner left Chris's office.

"How are you doing, Lilia?" Chris said.

"I'm okay. Still a little stunned. I feel bad that I knew her for two years, yet I didn't know her at all. Does she have any family? Friends?' Lilia asked.

"She had no family that we know of. There's no one listed in her employee file. The police are checking. If not, we are going to organize a memorial and a funeral, when her body is released." Shawn said.

"I can help with anything that's needed." Lilia offered.

"Thanks, however, you will have enough to do after you pass the Bar." Chris said.

"I appreciate the confidence you have in me." Lilia smiled.

"It's deserved. We know you'll be successful." Chris said.

"Thank you again." Lilia stood, "Thank you for seeing me."

"Of course. Thank you for coming." Chris said as he stood.

"See you soon, Lilia." Shawn stood and followed her to the door.

Lilia left the office and was happy that no one was hanging around the common area—she really didn't feel like talking to anyone. She got into her car and decided to head home to do the rest of her studying so she could have an early night.

The next day, Lilia rose early so she would have time to study before the police came to question her. She got so involved that she didn't even realize the time until she heard her phone ringing, indicating that someone was in the lobby.

"The police!" Lilia got up quickly and answered the phone.

"Hello?" she answered.

"Hello, Lilia Bennett?" a male voice asked.

"Yes. Who is this speaking?"

"Miss Bennett, this is Detective Briggs. I called you yesterday about coming to speak with you. Can Detective Conner and I come up?"

"Yes. I'll buzz you in," Lilia stated.

Lilia quickly tidied the condo as she heard the knock on the door. The Detectives had arrived. Opening the door, she let them in.

"Thank you for agreeing to meet with us. I am Detective Briggs, and this is Detective Conner," the taller, broader of the two men spoke while he stuck his hand out to shake hers.

The lawyer in Lilia quietly assessed the two men while she shook both of their hands. Detective Briggs had dark brown hair which was speckled with grey and seemed to be the older, more experienced of the two Detectives. He wore a ring on his ring finger, which Lilia had noticed first as they both pulled out their badges to show her their identification. The younger Detective seemed to be less aggressive and followed Detective Briggs's lead.

"Please have a seat," Lilia indicated for them to have a seat on her sofa.

"Thank you," Detective Conner said, clearing his throat, and sitting down.

"Can I get you anything to drink?"

"No, that's quite alright, Miss Bennett. We won't be long. Some of your colleagues at Hale & Cross told us that you are currently studying for the Bar exam. We don't want to take up too much of your time."

"Oh, that's quite alright. I feel like I've been studying forever," Lilia said as she sat down in the armchair across from them.

Detective Briggs reached into his pocket and took out a notebook and a pencil. "Miss Bennett…"

"Please, Lilia," Lilia stated.

The Detective gave a slight smile, "Lilia," he looked down at his notebook as he flipped to the correct page,

"How long would you say you knew the deceased, Melinda Kent?"

"Um… I applied and got the job as Melinda's law clerk at Hale & Cross about two years ago."

"How would you describe your relationship with Melinda?" Detective Briggs asked.

"She was my boss. I tried to do my job effectively for her. I wouldn't say that I knew her on a personal level." Lilia said.

"In speaking with your colleagues, Melinda was fired due to an altercation the two of you had. Would you say that that was correct?"

"Unfortunately, Melinda and I had several disagreements—if you can call them that. She wasn't particularly nice or close to anyone in the office that I know of. I was her law clerk, and she was my mentor. I worked the closest with her, so when I didn't meet her expectations, she let me know it. In private and in public." Lilia paused continuing, "I'm sure you also heard that I was offered her job?"

"As a matter of fact, we did hear that," Detective Conner stated, "do you want to add any information to what we already know?"

"I actually have to pass the Bar to be formally offered her position, but Mr. Hale and Mr. Cross did offer it to me. I worked hard for Ms. Kent. Very hard. Mr. Hale and Mr. Cross saw that. I have not been given anything in life that I didn't work for." Lilia took a deep breath as she tried to calm down from her anger at what else Kathy and the other gossips may have said to the detectives.

"Melinda was not kind to me. Less than two weeks ago, my resignation letter was written and on Ms. Kent's desk. I was quitting, taking the Bar exam, and getting a fresh start. That was my plan. I can show you the letter if you want. I didn't know they were going to fire her."

Lilia started to feel emotional at this point and tried to clear her throat, "When I found out, I felt sorry for her. She used to be a good lawyer. A powerhouse. I respected her back then. She had gotten meaner over this last year. She wasn't the lawyer she was," Lilia shook her head, "But what could I do? I was her law clerk, what partner was going to listen to me? So, I did what I needed to. I researched every case so she had what she needed and took her anger afterwards."

Lilia continued, "I actually suspected that she was losing cases so that she would win on appeal and make more money for the company. But a lot of clients didn't appeal so I knew she was losing her edge. That's when I decided to leave. I couldn't learn any more from her."

"Thank you for being so honest, Lilia," Detective Briggs said, "Now, just a couple of more questions and then we'll get out of your way. Is there anyone you can think of, disgruntled clients, other colleagues that might want to harm her?"

"I'm sorry. I really don't know. Even though she was mean, she didn't deserve t-to… die." Lilia choked on the word, barely feeling the tears falling down her cheeks, "What could she have done? Who would have done that to her?"

"We are doing our best to find out, Lilia," Detective Conner stated. "Was there anyone who might have stood out to you? Someone who may have displayed anger directed towards Ms. Kent? Maybe a client? A colleague?"

"Not that I can think of. But I wasn't in court for many of her later proceedings. She stopped letting me sit in."

"What do you think happened at that time? When she stopped allowing you to sit in? Was there a particular case she was working on?" Detective Briggs continued to question.

"I don't really remember at what point, which case she stopped… I remember that she went from saying mean things to me in private to saying them in public. She would say whatever she wanted in front of everyone."

"Now, Lilia, where were you on Saturday, between two and six p.m.?" Detective Briggs asked her.

"Am I a suspect?" Lilia asked in shock.

"Everyone that knew her is a suspect until they aren't. Again, Lilia, where were you on Saturday, between two and six p.m.?" Detective Briggs looked her straight in her eyes waiting for her answer.

"I was at the library. Definitely the Law Library. I've hardly been anywhere else for the last couple of days," Lilia said matter-of-factly. "I was there all day Friday and Saturday. It closed at six p.m. and I got home after six thirty p.m."

"How do you know the time you got home so distinctly?"

"I remember because I was so hungry when I got home. I hadn't cooked, so I ordered a pizza. The driver was really late—I kept checking the time."

"Do you have the receipt for the pizza, Miss Bennett? To corroborate the date and time?" Detective Briggs asked.

"No, I don't unfortunately. Because it was late, I got the pizza for free. I can contact them." Lilia asked.

"We will contact them. Which company did you use?"

"Vestuvio's Pizzeria. It's a place just down the street."

"Okay. Thank you for your time, Lilia. That's all of the questions we have for now." Detective Briggs stated as he flipped his notebook closed. Both he and Detective Conner rose to their feet and began walking to the door.

"Thank you," Lilia shook their hands, "Detective Briggs. Detective Conner."

As Lilia closed and locked the door after the detectives, she realized that as personally offended as she was that they could suspect her of murder, the practical side of her knew that they were right. Everyone was a suspect until they weren't. She also knew that they would get the security video tape from the library to confirm she was there, and contact Vestuvio's Pizzeria, just as they would be confirming everyone's alibi until they uncovered who did it. Who murdered Melinda.

Lilia began preparing her dinner and thought more about the detectives' questions. *When had Melinda stopped letting me sit in? Was it a particular case?* Lilia thought back to some of the more difficult interactions with Melinda. Her excuses for not letting Lilia sit in the courtroom were different every time and sometimes seemingly random.

Like the time when Melinda claimed Lilia's blue suit jacket was too distracting. It confused her as much now as it did then.

After Lilia finished eating her dinner, she knew that she had to stop thinking of Melinda and think about the Bar. The next two days of exams and essay writing would be exhausting. Lilia had studied cases and litigation in all the areas of public law, criminal procedure, family and civil law, and the ethical and professional responsibilities of litigators. She felt ready and was determined to get a good night's sleep so that she'd be prepared for tomorrow.

Just as she finished cleaning up to get ready for bed, Lilia's phone rang.

"Hello," she answered.

"Hi, Lilia," Warner's voice answered her back, "How was your day? Did the detectives come by?"

"Yes, they did."

"Are you okay?"

"I'm fine. At the time I had a range of emotions, anger, sadness, shock… I understand that everyone is a suspect, however it's still hard to practically be accused of murder."

"They asked you where you were when she died?"

"Yes, they did."

"You understand that they had to ask? They wouldn't have been doing their job if they didn't. They asked me as well. The way I understand it, they asked everyone in the office where they were the day Melinda was murdered."

"I expected to hear that. Did you get a response from the detectives about releasing any case files found in her home?"

"They agreed to release any property of Hale, Cross & Associates directly to us once they have been processed and logged in as evidence."

"What about attorney-client privilege? Does that not apply?"

"Yes, it does, even when the attorney dies, but because the files were on her property, they still need to be logged in. Shawn and Chris are working on it though. I have a meeting with Wilkins tomorrow. I found him."

"Great," Lilia said emotionlessly.

"You don't sound excited."

"I'm not. Just the mention of his name gives me the heebie jeebies." Lilia shivered.

"He's definitely seedy. Are you ready for the exam?"

"As I'll ever be, I guess."

"Good luck. I'm sure you don't need any though. You know it. Be confident in that."

"Thank you, Warner. I appreciate your call."

"No problem. My only advice is to get some rest."

"I will. I'm not studying any more. I know what I know. Goodnight, Warner."

"Goodnight, Lilia." Warner disconnected the phone.

As emotional a day as it was, Lilia went to bed that night with a slight smile on her face.

# CHAPTER 5

The next two days were a blur as Lilia knew that they would be. There were so many candidates called to take the Bar exam, putting their years of study, articling, and practice into writing the exam. Lilia had done the same. After three years of law school, she completed the requirement of Articling for the required ten months, and then working as a clerk with Hale, Cross & Associates for the experience and mentorship. The Bar exam was only offered three times a year and Lilia hoped this would be the only time she took it. She couldn't afford to fail.

Thursday was draining and Lilia barely remembered sleeping that night before getting up the next morning for day two. Friday was more of the same, though there were a significant number of candidates missing from day one. They must have chosen not to return; however, for Lilia, the day ended with her feeling confident that she had passed. Now it was time to wait. Getting the news, pass or fail, could take as little as four weeks to as long as a couple of months. Hopefully she would find out sooner rather than later. Until then she would continue her role as a clerk at Hale & Cross and continue to learn from them.

Once she got home on Friday evening, all she wanted to do was sleep. She was too mentally exhausted to even think about eating though she was hungry. She pulled into the underground garage at her condominium and went up the elevator, automatically stopping in the lobby to check her mail.

*I just checked my mail yesterday.* Lilia thought just as she discovered what had been pulling her off the elevator. Staring at her from the lobby's glassed-in enclosure with the phone to be buzzed up in one hand and a bag of take-out in the other, was Warner. Upon seeing her, he slowly put down the phone as she made her way over to him to open the locked door.

"What are you doing here?" Lilia asked as she let him into the lobby.

"I brought you food," Warner said, "I remember how exhausted I was when I did the exam." Warner handed the food over to her and continued speaking, "I brought you dinner, fettuccini, of course, and breakfast, pancakes and eggs. If you're really too tired to eat dinner now you can have breakfast in the morning."

"Wow. Thank you," Lilia said looking at the food he had handed over, "I don't know what to say. You're so thoughtful…" Lilia looked at the bag of food not daring to make eye contact, "Are you going to come up and eat with me?"

"No. I only came to bring you food. I can see you're exhausted." He said with a smile.

Lilia met Warner's gaze and smiled back at him. "I can't tell you how much I appreciate this. As you know, I'm not used to anyone doing things like this for me."

"I know. And you're getting used to it right?" Warner said as he reached out to touch her chin gently.

"I am. Thank you." Lilia said again quietly, as Warner turned to walk away, "Goodnight. Drive safely."

"Goodnight, Lilia," Warner turned to look at her as he walked through the door.

Lilia made her way to her condo, her legs automatically taking her there as she moved in a dream-like state thinking of Warner and how good, unpredictable, and unassuming he was.

Once Lilia was settled on her couch with her plate of fettuccine, she realized that she actually felt relaxed— which she hadn't felt in years. Years of hard work, embarrassment, lack of sleep, sacrifice, all culminated in this moment. It was over. And now all that was left to do was wait. Hopefully she'd be practicing law as an associate before she knew it.

The weekend passed by quickly with Lilia feeling varied levels of excitement, feeling both excited and a little apprehensive.

She shook her head, starting to feel guilty. Guilty, that she felt happy going to work and the reason was because Melinda was not there. Melinda was dead. She wondered whether the detectives had any suspects yet. She hadn't heard from them again after they interviewed her, and she wondered if Warner knew. She would definitely ask when she saw him at the office.

She got in the office on Monday morning very early as she wanted to be organized and ready for anything Warner and any of the other associates needed, especially the Wilkins case. She knew that Warner had found him, but she hadn't had an update since, as she had been so focused on studying.

When she walked into her office, there were several files on her desk that were not there when she left. She smiled and sat at her desk opening the first file to see what the case was. What only seemed like moments later, Lilia heard a knock on the door, and looked up. Warner stood there.

"Lunch?" he asked.

"Lunch? It's only—" Lilia questioned as she turned her arm to look at her watch, "Oh, where did the time go?"

Warner chuckled, as Lilia asked, "Did you just come in the office?"

"I poked my head in earlier. You had your nose in whatever file you were working on, and I didn't want to break your concentration."

"When I came in there was so much to do, I decided to get to it."

"Do you want to go for lunch? Are you ready?"

"I've still got so much to catch up on; I think I'll eat at my desk today." Lilia responded. She was nervous to spend time with him.

"Are you sure? I was thinking of trying a new restaurant, and I was going to fill you in on the Wilkins case."

Lilia fought with herself. She wanted to spend time with him, however the more time she spent with him, the more time she wanted to spend. "Why don't you fill me in when you get back. I'll have gotten through most of this. At least enough for Grace and Carl to go forward with." Lilia mentioned the two other associates who also had some of Melinda's open cases.

"Okay. I'll see what you're working on when I get back." Warner walked out of her office and Lilia tried to put him out of her mind while she got her sandwich out of her bag and got back to work.

When Warner came back, Lilia was ready. When he didn't immediately come into her office after lunch, she went to find him. She took some files off her desk, intending to deliver them to the other associates. When she passed his office, she didn't see him inside, so she continued walking to Grace Hall's office, to find her sitting at her desk.

Lilia knocked on Grace's door, "Grace," Lilia started, "I have an update on the Parker case. I've completed the research on the new evidence and provided other cases citing precedence."

"Didn't you just come back today Lilia?" Grace asked.

"Yes. I came in early to get started. I'm very familiar with the case, so I wanted to dig right into it."

Grace continued to stare at her. Then shook her head slowly, "How did you do?"

"The exam?" Lilia responded, "It was tough and exhausting," she said, "the hardest part is waiting for the results."

Grace looked down, opening one of the files Lilia had handed her, "I'm sure you nailed it. Thanks." Grace then began turning the pages that Lila provided already getting immersed in the file. Grace had a very serious demeanor and had been with the firm for several years. Lilia had a lot of respect for her and had often wished that she had been hired as her law clerk.

Lilia turned and continued down the hallway when she heard Warner's voice coming from Chris Hales' office. Her feet led her towards Warner's voice automatically, past Chris' empty assistants desk, to stop at the open door. Warner had been sitting with his back to the door facing Chris, and when Chris saw her, he rose to his feet.

"Lilia," he announced, "welcome back, I trust everything went successfully with your exams?"

Warner rose as Lilia answered, "I hope so, but I expect to find out for sure within a month or so."

"I will leave you to your conversation." Warner said stiffly.

"Warner," Lilia stopped him before he left the office, "I wanted to meet with you regarding the Wilkins case."

"I'll get the file together and put it on your desk to look over while you speak with Chris. I don't have anything for you to research at the moment."

"Alright." Warner walked out of Chris's office and Lilia stared after him.

"Lilia?" Chris called for Lilia's attention, "As soon as you find out, Shawn or I are your first phone call. Warner, Grace, and Carl have a heavy load. I know they can handle it, but we can't take on any new cases."

"Of course," Lilia said.

"You're very good. You know exactly the way a case is turning and what to research. Shawn and I are confident you will pass, so we're willing to wait. We want to have you as an associate here at Hale & Cross."

"Thank you, Chris." Lilia gave a slight smile to Chris.

"Did you need something else, Lilia?" Chris asked her.

"Yes, I had wanted to ask if you had heard anything new from the detectives regarding Melinda and the case files?"

"We got the records from her house released thanks to Warner. He was able to get them to release them."

"That's great," Lilia said.

Chris went behind his desk to sit down, "Warner is very good at what he does. While you are working this Wilkins case with him, learn as much as you can, Lilia."

"I plan to. Thank you for your time, Chris," Lilia said, again turning towards his office door.

"My door is open to you any time, Lilia."

"Thank you, Chris." Lilia said leaving.

Lilia returned to her office, feeling dejected that Warner had put the Wilkins file on her desk, rather than spend time with her talking about it.

When she got to her desk the file was not there, so she used it as an excuse to find Warner.

She walked slowly to Warner's office, preparing herself to speak to him. When she got to his office door, she saw him sitting at his desk, so she just watched him for a moment while he was immersed in a file.

"Are you going to stand there or are you coming in?" his question startled her, and she took a step backwards. "Where are you going now?" he said, not missing a move she made, "didn't you come here to see me?"

"I came here for the Wilkins file," she paused. "You said you would put it on my desk, but you didn't."

"Is that what you want Lilia?" Warner tilted his head looking directly into her eyes. She felt as though he were looking straight through to her truth.

"I want…" Lilia felt hot and tried to regain her composure. "Yes, I came for the file."

"Okay, Lilia," Warner said. "Here it is," he said, handing it to her.

"When we met—I tried again to reason with him to change his plea. He refused. I reminded him about all the evidence against him. The hairs found at the scene match his hairs. I've been trying to find a genetic specialist that will testify that there's a possibility they aren't, but I can't find one. His fingerprints and DNA are at all of the crime scenes." Warner rubbed his hand over his face in exasperation.

"I met with the District Attorney, off the record, and they are comparing him to a young Bundy. Yes, Ted Bundy who strangled his victims while he raped them until they died. I've been trying to find any evidence at all to give some doubt. I can't. Maybe if you have a look, you'll find something. The DA's office has released all of their evidence to us, and I can't even find any mishandling of the case. Nothing."

"I'm sure you've done all you can. I'll definitely take a look." Warner passed the file over to her.

She walked over to his desk to take the file. "I'll let you know if I find anything we can use." Walking back to his door, Lilia asked, "Did he say why he won't take a plea?"

"He only said that Melinda didn't have a problem with his plea. She had promised to get him off and I need to do the same. He's psychotic. The way he looked at me…" Warner ran his hands over his short dark hair. Lilia watched his strong hands rub his head, and she quickly got lost in her thoughts. She fought the desire to walk over to him and touch him, comfort him by rubbing his shoulders… she shook her head bringing herself back, before she got too lost in more thoughts of him.

When Lilia roused herself, she noticed he was now watching her, "When you know what you need from me, Lilia, you only have to ask for it." Warner stated.

"I don't need anything," Lilia stammered and walked out of his office before she got flustered again.

Lilia went back to her office to review the file looking for anything that Warner could have missed, but she knew she wouldn't find anything. Warner was far too thorough for that. Lilia worked on the file for the rest of the day, not noticing that the time was passing and that others were leaving.

Before she knew it, she heard a knock on her door.

"Are you ready to go? I'll walk you to your car," Warner stated.

"Yes, thank you."

"I'll get my things and meet you at the front." Warner said and walked back to his office.

As they walked out of their building and to their cars in silence, both were lost in their own thoughts. When they got to Lilia's car, Lilia unlocked her car and as she went to open it, Warner stepped in front of her, blocking her way.

"Don't keep me at arm's length, Lilia. You can trust me."

Lilia opened her mouth to say something, anything to deny how she was feeling, "I don't know what you mean. Goodnight, Warner." Lilia reached past him to open her door.

"Night." Warner said quietly and turned to walk to his own car.

Warner waited until she started her car and followed her out of the parking lot. Looking out her rear-view mirror, Lilia was a little worried he would follow her home. Feeling very weak at this moment she didn't know that she would be able to deny her feelings and send him away. Lilia was relieved to see his car soon turn from behind hers in the direction of his own house. Lilia sighed, feeling a cross between relief and longing, a small piece of her wishing he had followed her home. She went home, by herself as she had for so many years. This was the first night that she had wished it weren't so. She would have liked having someone to come home to.

# CHAPTER 6

The next week passed quickly as Lilia stuck to a specific routine, which was designed to avoid Warner, only interacting with him when she had to discuss the Wilkins case or if she bumped into him in the office by accident. She left the office at night when her other colleagues left, walking with them to the parking lot. Any unfinished work would follow her home and she would complete the rest of it there.

She didn't want to chance being the last ones in the office at night anymore. She was not the type to have an office fling, and she didn't think he was the type either. She didn't participate in office gossip, so she hadn't heard about him having office romances, but she would definitely be surprised to hear that none of the clerks were attracted to him.

Lilia was so focused on trying to avoid Warner, she only began to notice that Warner wasn't around at the end of the week. She passed by Grace's office, to bring her one of the case files and decided to ask where he was.

"Here are the files, Grace," Lilia started.

"Thanks, Lilia," Grace replied, reaching her hand out to take it, "Are you sure you want to be an Associate? You're so good at fact checking, finding just the right cases that set precedence. And so quickly." She said in wonder, "I gave you these files yesterday."

"I try to keep up on the direction of all the cases and the evidence that the DA has so that when you go to trial, you already have something to go on."

Grace stared at Lilia and just shook her head slowly.

"Have you seen Warner?" Lilia asked, "I haven't seen him, and I wanted to discuss some things about the Wilkins case."

"You didn't hear?"

Lilia shook her head, "Hear what?"

"One of the witnesses in the Wilkins case was found dead in a hotel room. There was a suicide note, apparently."

"What?!"

"Yeah. Warner has been gone, trying to find out more information."

"That poor woman." Lilia said thoughtfully.

"One witness gone certainly helps your case." Grace said heartlessly.

Lilia stared at her trying to figure out if she was serious.

"Lilia, we have a job to do, her death just made it a little easier. I heard that there is so much evidence against this guy, the case isn't even winnable. He won't even take a plea deal."

"A woman died, Grace. How can you be so cold?"

"Melinda died Lilia. We are surrounded by death. Most of our clients are accused murderers. You're a criminal defence lawyer. You need to get used to it," Grace picked up one of the files on her desk and flipped it open again, effectively dismissing Lilia.

Lilia walked to her office, thinking of what Grace said. She didn't want to believe this to be true. She sat at her desk trying to work, and when she finally decided that she wouldn't get any work done until she spoke to Warner, she picked up her cell phone to call him.

"Warner Reid," Warner answered the phone with a strong voice.

"Warner, it's Lilia."

"What do you need, Lilia?" Warner responded.

"Grace just told me one of the witnesses was found dead and that you left to get more information."

"Yes, that's true."

"Why didn't you tell me?" she asked.

"You were busy trying to avoid me. I figured you would find out eventually."

Lilia paused, "I wasn't," Lilia lied quietly.

"Don't lie to me right now, Lilia. I'm dealing with enough here right now."

"You're right. I know, and… I'm sorry," she replied quietly. "What happened?" Lilia asked.

"I've only been able to find out that she was found in a hotel room, and right now evidence points to suicide as they found a letter. She had been there for at least a few hours. She had taken the room and left a credit card with the manager to be charged. When the payment didn't clear, the manager went to her room. She didn't answer, so he called the police to have her removed. She was dead."

"Oh my… I don't know what to say," Lilia was saddened.

"What did you hear and from who?"

"I asked Grace where you were, and she told me."

"Did she mention that our case would be easier to win?"

"Yes, she did."

"She said the same to me. What do you think?" he questioned.

"I think that's a cold response. I never want to be the type of lawyer that thinks of someone's death as a plus in a case I'm working on—that it could mean a win. What do you think?"

"I couldn't agree with you more, which is why I'm here. To get the truth."

"And where are you?"

"A little town called Brantford, just outside of the city. She must have driven or was driven out here. I'm trying to find out. I expect another day or two before they release any information."

"Why will it take that long? Can't you just ask?"

"I'm Warner Reid, Attorney for the Defendant, whom she was about to testify against. I'm going to have to subpoena them for any information. I'd rather get it firsthand."

"I understand that. Okay. Get back safe. Let me know if you need anything."

"See you soon, Lilia."

"Bye, Warner," Lilia answered.

As soon as Lilia hung up the phone, she began thinking about who she could contact to get information from in Brantford. She logged onto her computer and began looking up reporters, hotel employees, detectives, autopsy lab personnel in the area. And then began calling every single one, with the purpose of finding out what they knew and how they found out. She pretended to be who she needed to be to get the information she needed.

By pretending to be a sister, she soon found out which victim it was: Lucille Diaz, "Lucy" to close friends and family. She didn't even have a sister, but the hotel employees that she contacted didn't know that. Now that she had a name, she began making other calls, speaking with everyone from the cleaners to the clerks, forensic technicians, and, finally, the medical examiner. With every call she got more information, and used that information to make the next phone call.

By the end of the day, less than six hours later, she had uncovered many of the details she was sure Warner was trying to find out.

Lilia's next call was to Warner.

"Warner Reid."

"Warner, it's Lilia again."

"You spend the beginning of the week avoiding me and now you can't resist calling me? Twice in one day?" Warner teased.

Lilia shook her head with a smile, "Have you gotten any new information?"

"No. I'm still waiting. I've been trying to find out which witness it was."

"It was Lucille Diaz."

"How do you know? How did you find out?"

"I spoke with who I needed to speak to. I found out that even though there was a suicide note, they have evidence of foul play. The empty pill bottle, the prescription medication—that was not in her name, by the way—was sitting beside the bed. Suspiciously absent is the glass of water. Also, in the lab, once she has been there for a few days, bruising started to appear around her mouth. The evidence points towards someone covering her mouth, forcing her to swallow the pills."

Lilia paused and Warner took that moment to take an opportunity to speak, "Who are you? I've been here for two days and I couldn't get a name. You have—what, five hours—and you have all the answers." Warner paused, "How did you get this information? You know what, don't tell me. I'm on my way home. Next time I need something, I'll ask you first."

"Bye, Warner. See you soon."

"Do you even know where Brantford is?" Warner asked facetiously, "Bye, Lilia."

Lilia hung up the phone, smiling, and hoping that Brantford wasn't too far away.

Lilia packed up the files that she was going to be working on over the weekend and left the office with several other staff, walking with them to the parking lot.

Once home, Lilia decided that she would rest with a glass of wine and her thoughts for the remainder of the evening. First Melinda Kent, now Lucille Diaz. Two women dead, one definitely murdered and the other under suspicious circumstances. Both connected in different ways to Luke Wilkins. Lilia wondered what Lucille had been going through. Why would she have committed suicide when she had the opportunity to stand against her attacker? And she was standing beside three other women who were willing to testify as well. It didn't make sense. It made more sense that someone wanted people to think she had committed suicide. And Melinda… Lilia had heard nothing more. She wondered if the detectives were getting closer to the answers.

Lilia had been so lost in her thoughts of death and sadness, she hadn't even noticed that she'd poured the last of the bottle of wine. Once her glass was finished, she decided that she would get ready for bed and think of other things. Her thoughts went to the other topic she didn't want to think of… Warner. She wanted to know if he was back home safe yet, but her pride wouldn't let her call. She pushed thoughts of him out of her mind and attempted to fall asleep.

Over the weekend she filled her hours with puttering about her condo and working. Trying not to think of the painful topics that had been on her mind all night. Instead, she thought of all of the things she had shut out of her life over the years, so focused on getting to where she was right now. She had sacrificed relationships and friendships. Once her parents passed away, she not only shut friends out of her life, she made every effort not to allow anyone in. Afraid that if she made connections with people, fell in love, that they would be taken away from her, just as her parents had. Lilia knew that building the wall around herself had been for self-preservation all those years ago. Now the wall only made her alone. And she didn't know how or where to start breaking it down, and if she even wanted to. Could she risk it?

The buzzing of her phone snatched her out of her thoughts, so she answered it.

"Lilia, it's me, Warner," he said.

"Hi, Warner. Are you back in town?" Lila questioned him.

"Not only am I back, but I'm in your neighbourhood and I thought I'd pop by."

"I don't know if that's a good idea, Warner. We should probably just see each other in the office."

"Don't worry, Lilia. I know where I stand with you. You've made it clear this week. I want to speak with you about what you told me about Lucille Diaz. I also have some more news to tell you."

"Whenever you have news, it's never good. You do realize that, don't you?"

"I'm sorry but this isn't good either."

"Come on over then."

Warner arrived quickly and pressed the buzzer letting him in through the lobby. She looked around the living room, confirming that it was tidy. When she heard the knock on her door, she let him in.

"Thanks. How are you doing?"

"I'm good. How are you? How was the trip?"

"Trip? It was a two-hour drive. I knew you didn't know where Brantford was." He smiled.

She smiled slightly, "I don't."

She walked with him into her living room and motioned for him to have a seat.

"Do you want anything to drink?" Lilia asked him.

"No, I'm fine thanks. Come sit down."

"And telling me to sit down. This must be bad."

"How did you get the information about Lucille Diaz?"

"I have my ways." Lilia said coyly.

"Lilia," Warner warned her seriously.

"I lied. I called anyone and everyone that could have heard or seen anything. The manager, the owner to the maid at the hotel. The forensic technician, the operator, the medical officer. They all individually had a piece of the puzzle. I used each piece to get me to the next piece." Lilia then smiled, "Alright. Now what did you have to tell me?"

"Another witness was found dead."

"What?! Who? How? From the Wilkins case?" She asked.

"Yes. Callie Simmons was found dead in her home. The evidence points to suicide as well. Coincidence?"

"What is going on? What are the chances that they both committed suicide?" Lilia rose to her feet and began pacing the living room.

"It's too much of a coincidence. Callie also died from an overdose. This time it could actually be a suicide though as the pills were actually hers. She had a prescription, and she ingested the whole thing. Bottle of water beside her." Warner shook his head, "So much death and pain connected to this case."

"How did you get so much information this time?" Lilia asked.

"Because it seemed like a cut and dry suicide, the detectives weren't trying to hide anything. With Lucille, they don't want to release to much information. So, the fact that you found out so much so early, really helped not to waste time."

"What do we do?" Lilia asked.

"What do you mean? There's nothing we can do except to try the case and give Wilkins the best defence possible, no matter what. There is definitely something going on. First, Melinda is murdered. Then, Diaz is found dead, and Simmons commits suicide?" Warner continued, "I wish there was something we could do, but we are not the detectives, investigators, or forensic scientists. We took an oath to give him the best defence."

"I understand that, Warner. I know that we have a duty to defend him. It just seems so wrong that so many women tied to him, to this case, have died."

"We don't know the circumstances of each situation. We both know that Melinda wasn't averse to making enemies, so anyone could be responsible for her death, which I don't like saying no matter how true it is."

"Have you heard anything from the DA's office yet?"

"Not yet, but I wouldn't be surprised if the paperwork for a Stay of Proceedings hasn't already been filed and isn't already on the Judge's desk." Warner responded.

"They would need to motion for a Stay. Two of their four witnesses are deceased. They definitely need time to regroup and solidify the two witnesses they have. They should also request for his bail to be revoked and Wilkins to be in custody."

"Depending on whether the Stay is granted or not, he was only out on bail for two weeks so he should be in custody again by Wednesday. The original trial date is Thursday, so we'll see what happens."

"Alright. That's good. Before another witness ends up dead."

"Don't say that—we don't know that he had anything to do with it."

"It's quite a coincidence then isn't it?" Lilia said sarcastically, "Quite convenient for him that two witnesses testifying against him are dead."

"There is still DNA evidence against him. I have a DNA analysis expert that's willing to testify that the DNA belonging to all humans is 99.9% identical and the remaining 0.1% is different between individuals, which represents three million differences. He will testify that that 0.1% could belong to 26% of the population here in King City."

"I can't believe you found an analyst to testify to that." Lilia said.

"I have resources just like you," Warner joked, then turned serious, "We have a responsibility to give him the best defence we can to create doubt. The burden of proof is the responsibility of the DA's office."

"It would be so much easier if he'd pleaded guilty and taken the deal." Lilia finally sat down on her couch.

"I agree. But we can't make him."

"I guess at this point we wait to find out if the DA has requested a Stay."

"Yes—we should hear tomorrow. I'll contact Wilkins and let him know that it would look very good for him to remand himself into custody early. That way if anything else happens he'll have an airtight alibi. I'll also ask him where he's been during his release. We'd better find him a credible alibi during the time frame of the two incidents."

"Is there anything specific you want me to do?" Lilia asked.

"Since you have such amazing investigative skills," Warner said smiling playfully at her, "Can you see if you can find out where he's been since he stepped foot out of jail? See if you can get any proof like security cameras from stores, street surveillance videos, friends… witnesses, receipts that would place him in certain areas at specific days and times. Let's see if he tells us the truth, while not killing our case in the process."

Lilia noticeably shivered when Warner said the word "killing." He grimaced and apologized, placing his hand on her knee. Lilia looked up making eye contact with him as she felt the skin under his hand begin to tingle. He let his hand slowly slide off her knee, prolonging the contact for as long as possible while not breaking their locked gaze.

"I'd better get going, I've kept you long enough," Warner said, standing to his feet.

He put out his hand for her to take to help her up. "Walk me to the door?" He stated.

She took his hand and slowly rose to her feet walking with him towards the door, their fingers still slightly entwined.

She slowly pulled her hand away once they reached the door, and as Warner raised his hand to the doorknob, Lilia rubbed her hand against the side of her thigh—trying to get the tingling feeling to disappear.

"I'll start working on tracking Wilkins's alibi down tomorrow." She said bringing their conversation back to business.

"That would be great." Warner said opening the door, "Have a good night, Lilia." Warner said, making eye contact with her as he opened the door.

"Night."

As the door closed behind him, Lilia locked up and leaned against it, closing her eyes to try to divest herself of thoughts of Warner in her head.

Shaking her head, Lilia decided that she should get to bed as she would get to work early to begin solidifying Wilkins's alibi.

As she got ready for bed, she turned her thoughts to Wilkins as she wondered if Warner would be able to convince him to turn himself in and if she would find evidence absolving him of having anything to do with the deaths of Callie Simmons and Lucille Diaz.

Doubting she would, Lilia tried to turn her mind off to get some much-needed sleep.

# CHAPTER 7

The next day, Lilia got to the office early to start working on tracking down Wilkins's every move since he was released on bail from prison. She first tried to get in touch with Wilkins's bail bondsman, Sean Hindson, as Wilkins was to check in with him. When she was unable to reach him at the Bonds Office, she tried his home and cell phone numbers with no answer. She then looked up the address Wilkins had on file, where he was living upon his release, to see if there were businesses on, surrounding, and near his street to access their security cameras. She called all of the businesses to find out which ones had security cameras, and which were facing the street. Then made arrangements with each owner to see if she could access the video to view them on the days in question.

After working diligently on this and threatening a few owners with litigation if they refused to release evidence, she accessed as many videos as she could and requested a couple of Hale & Cross's investigators to go view each one.

Lilia worked tirelessly all day. Not only trying to trace Wilkins's whereabouts but to also find out where Sean Hindson was. She had heard back from his assistant who had said that the office hadn't heard from him. He had contacted them a week ago stating he needed a few days for a personal matter, and they hadn't heard from him since. Lilia suggested they contact the police to do a welfare check at his property just to ensure that everything was alright. Hindson's assistant said that she would, and Lilia made a note to contact her again tomorrow to see what came out of it.

While Lilia continued to work, she had just put the phone down to look up and see Warner leaning against her office door jam.

"So that's how you get all of that information. You bully them into it."

"Some people need to be threatened with a lawsuit. They don't need to know that I can't technically sue them." Lilia laughed. "Anyways, I've only had to do that with a few. People are usually very helpful when you tell them you are trying to track down a missing young woman who was last seen in their area." Lilia said slyly.

"It seems as though you have made better progress than me. Wilkins has refused to turn himself in early and told me a few choice words when I asked him where he was on the days Diaz and Simmons were found dead. He reminded me that we are to defend him and that he knows he will be walking free after the trial—whether the witnesses are alive or not." Warner shook his head.

"Oh dear. I've definitely had better luck than you. John and his team," Lilia mentioned the investigator's name that was looking at the video cameras, "have already been able to track his comings and goings on the first three days of his release with the cameras we've accessed so far. And he still has more to go through."

"Do you know what time it is?" Warner asked her, knowing she didn't, as she looked at him questioningly. "What did you eat for lunch?"

Lilia tried to remember what she'd nibbled on, "I've been eating fruit… I think I ate my sandwich," Lilia looked in her bag. "I guess I didn't," she said, pulling it out of her bag.

"Well, don't eat it now. Let's go get an early dinner. It's after four p.m. and I can't believe you haven't had a proper meal all day."

"I still have work to do Warner."

"Come on. We'll come back to the office after. I still have stuff to go through too. We can pull an all-nighter— AFTER we get some good food."

"That does sound good," Lilia admitted as she got to her feet.

"Then let's go. There's a new Mexican restaurant I want to try. Is that okay with you?"

"For sure," Lilia said.

By the time they got to the restaurant Lilia was thankful that Warner had convinced her to stop working and eat; she was hungry.

While they were seated, eating in comfortable silence, Lilia tried to take subtle looks at Warner, hoping he wouldn't notice. When she glanced up once more, her eyes met his, and she could read in his eyes that he knew that she had been watching him.

"So, Sean Hindson, Wilkins's bondsman is missing," Lilia stated, deciding to lead them back to business, "I asked his assistant to call the police to do a welfare check at his home. Hopefully he's okay, it seems as though everyone connected to Wilkins is…" Lilia didn't complete her sentence.

"I'm sure he is fine." Warner said.

"I will call tomorrow to confirm," Lilia said, being interrupted by Warner's ringing cell phone.

"Excuse me," Warner said, holding up his hand, with his phone in the other.

"Reid," He answered.

Lilia tried not to eavesdrop on his end of the conversation, however when she saw his facial expression change into a cringe, and heard him question, "Graham?"

She knew a "Graham." Linda Graham, one of Wilkins's victims that was to testify against him. Sadly, she knew what this call was about.

She waited patiently for him to end his call, quietly placing his phone back into his suit jacket pocket before he said anything.

"Linda Graham is dead," he stated matter-of-factly, finally making eye contact with her, his eyes dejected. "Her body was found this morning in her home. She had been dead for a few days."

Lilia had no words. She looked into his eyes and knew hers reflected the same sorrow.

"Suicide?" Lilia asked.

"'Suspicious circumstances' is what was said," Warner answered.

"So not the same? No prescription pills found beside her?"

"No, they suspect foul play," he said flatly, breaking eye contact with her.

"So only Cindy Carelli is still alive? I hope they give her protection."

"It's the detective and the prosecutions job to protect their witnesses, Lilia. You know that."

"I know that, Warner. But these women… they've been attacked and were strong enough to fight. Only to be attacked again. Left unprotected. Victimized again. How is this okay?"

"Let's go." Warner called for the bill. Both having lost their appetite, their food was left unfinished.

Within a few minutes, they were in Warner's car headed back to the office.

"Are you going to stay and work?" Warner asked.

"I think I want to go home," Lilia said. "This is too much. I can't be here," she explained.

"I agree. Let's get our things and I'll walk you to your car."

They headed up to the office, quickly packed their belongings, and made their way quietly back down to the parking lot.

Warner walked her to her car holding the door as she climbed in. Both silent and lost in their own thoughts.

"Goodnight." Lilia said quietly.

"Goodnight." Warner closed her door and walked to his own car, climbing in.

Out of her rear-view mirror she watched Warner's car follow hers out of the parking lot. And, not for the first time, was disappointed to see his car turn off towards his home, not following her car down the street. Tonight was a night that she didn't want to be alone.

# CHAPTER 8

First thing in the morning, after getting to the office, Lilia contacted Sean Hindson's assistant to see if there was any word on the missing bail bondsman.

"The police conducted a welfare check, but there was no sign of him," Hindson's assistant continued, "He was supposed to be taking a few personal days, so I'm trying to get in touch with his family and friends to see if they've heard from him. If he doesn't turn up, I'll file a missing person report."

Lilia thanked her and shared her own contact information and requested for Sean Hindson to contact her as soon as he returned.

Regretfully, Lilia didn't think that she would be hearing from Sean Hindson, and she made a note in her calendar to contact the office again in a couple of days for an update.

After a few hours of working steadily, Lilia checked the time. It was well after two and Warner had not come to check on her for lunch. After processing that, Lilia started to chastise herself about why it affected her so much, and sternly told herself that it shouldn't.

She aggressively handled her lunch bag, pulling out her sandwich and fruit, and told herself to get back to work. After finishing her lunch, her curiosity got the better of her, and she decided to stretch her legs and take a walk past Warner's office to see if he was indeed there. Seeing only Mary, his assistant, Lilia asked her when Warner would be in as she had an update on the Wilkins case.

"He left for a meeting with the defendant in the James case. They are expecting a verdict today."

"Oh right, yes, of course."

"Do you want me to tell him to meet you at your office when he returns?" Mary replied.

"No, it's okay. If I see him before I leave, I'll catch him up. Thank you, Mary."

Lilia turned and walked back to her office. She had been so absorbed in the Wilkins case for the last couple of days that she hadn't designated any time on researching any of the other associates' cases. Lilia decided to stop by Grace and Carl's offices to see if they were in and if they needed anything.

She found out that Grace was in court litigating the Parker case that Lilia had helped to research, and although Carl was in the office, he didn't need any assistance.

"I heard your hands were full with the Wilkins case. I've been trying to give more research to some of the other clerks," Carl said.

"I got John and his team to review a lot of the videos I was looking at to piece together the defendant's whereabouts, and now Warner's in court, so I just thought I'd check in to see if you needed any support."

"No, I'm all good. Good luck with that case. That Wilkins is a real piece of work. I heard about him from Melinda."

"What did she say about him?" Lilia questioned.

"Just that he was getting tough on her to get him off scot free. Can you believe it? With all of the evidence against him, he was expecting her to perform a miracle. I don't know any lawyer that would be able to get him off. And I know some great ones." Carl explained.

"It's definitely a hard case. Warner is going to have a difficult time finding enough reasonable doubt, that's for sure."

Just then the phone on Carl's desk rang, and he held up his hand as he picked up the receiver.

Lilia shook her head, backing out of the office, making her way back to hers.

Once she got there, she contacted John to see how far they had gotten with the videos and was on her way out again when John asked her to come to the investigation offices to talk about what the team found.

"Hi, John! What did you get?" Lilia questioned excitedly.

"Lilia." John rose from his desk and walked over to shake her hand.

"We've put together some of his whereabouts. He goes off the map for several days. He disappears and pops back up a few days later. We tried to pick him up at different businesses and residences. Either we couldn't locate him or there were no cameras."

John walked over to his desk and picked up a file. "Here are some still photos and details with the dates, times, and locations he was IDed." He handed the file over to Lilia.

Lilia opened the file to review the locations and dates listed.

"Could you see if you can locate him at any of the crime scenes? Where Diaz, Simmons, and Graham were found?"

"Where he shouldn't be?" John questioned.

"Yes," Lilia answered.

"Is this wise?" John questioned again.

"What if we can prove he wasn't there? And someone else was? If someone who happens to look like him was there, we need to provide reasonable doubt that it wasn't him. Height comparisons, shoe size, hair colouring, body type…" Lilia allowed her sentence to trail off. "Whatever we need to do," she added thoughtfully.

Lilia reminded herself that she was a part of Luke Wilkins's defence team. She knew that if John and his team accessed the security footage of businesses and residences from around the areas where Callie Simmons, Lucy Diaz, and Linda Graham's bodies were all discovered, he would be identified. And it would be Warner's job to prove it wasn't him to the jury. To create reasonable doubt regardless of his guilt.

"Get me the locations. I'll get on it." John interrupted her thoughts.

"Thank you, John. I'll email you the info as soon as I get back to my office." Lilia held up the file in her hands, "Can I keep this?"

"Yes." John stated with a smile. "It's a copy."

Lilia smiled, "You knew I'd ask you for the new locations."

"Of course. You're always thorough. I like it." John declared turning back to walk behind his desk.

"Thanks, John," Lilia laughed softly, shaking her head as she turned towards the door to head back to her floor. "I'll get that info to you as soon as I get upstairs."

"The sooner the better, before another associate sends a clerk down here."

"Done," Lilia stated as she rushed out of the office.

Lilia took the elevator back to her floor, with her head in the file perusing the photos and information John had given her. When the elevator stopped, she walked off without looking up, walking instantly into what she thought was the wall.

"Ooof!" she groaned.

"Hey, are you okay?" Warner asked.

Looking up, she noticed the extremely hard wall had a very handsome face.

"I'm so sorry, I was so engrossed in this file, I wasn't paying attention."

"I know," Warner chuckled, "are you okay?"

"Oh yes, I'm fine. Are you okay?" She asked.

"You're five foot three inches, and maybe a hundred and thirty pounds… I think I'll be fine."

"Anyways," he continued, "what has you so captivated?"

"I just got information from John with Wilkins's supposed alibi, which isn't an alibi. I'm just headed to my office to send him some more information, which I need to get a move on before they're given anything else. I can give you an update on everything I have in an hour or so if you're available?"

"I'm just heading back out. I came in to pick up some files. The James verdict just came in, so I'm headed back there."

"If you come back to the office early, see if I'm here. I have a few updates."

"I probably won't be back," said Warner checking the time on his watch, "Make sure Jeff sees you out."

"I'll leave with the others at the end of the day." Lilia smiled, "And good luck with the verdict."

"Thanks. I expect it to come back in our favour. He didn't do it and we proved it."

"Okay, I'll see you tomorrow. I have to get that information to John."

"See you tomorrow."

Warner pushed the button for the elevator, as Lilia turned and made her way to her office.

Approximately an hour later, Lilia pressed send on her email to John, satisfied that she had given him as much information as she could for his investigation team to start working on. She ensured that she gave him a four-day window for each of the victims as the police had not released the day and time of death, and the locations that their bodies were found.

Once she received John's confirmation that he had received the email, she checked the time and decided to prepare to go home for the day as she noticed other colleagues leaving as well.

As Lilia walked just behind some of the other law clerks to the parking lot, she felt an eery feeling of being watched. She looked around, seeing them getting into their cars, but as she walked further, she couldn't get rid of the feeling. She looked around once again, her eyes finding Jeff, the security guard, standing off to the side of the parking lot.

"Jeff!" she said with relief, "Have a great night tonight. I hope it's quiet." She was relieved to know that it was Jeff that her senses had been aware of.

"Goodnight, Miss Bennett. Have a good evening." Jeff said staring after her.

Lilia continued to her car. *I wonder if Jeff is okay?* Lilia thought as his response was not as friendly as normal. Her thoughts went elsewhere as she realized that she was going home early for once and didn't have any work to do. These nights were few and far between, so she would enjoy it by doing something she didn't normally get to do. She would read.

She had one on her reading list about forensic psychology by famous profiler Frank Durst. And once Lilia was home, she sat down with Frank and a glass of wine.

# CHAPTER 9

Upon arriving at the office, the next morning, Lilia put her belongings away, took the files out of her briefcase, and then went to see if Warner had already arrived. She wanted to update him on John and the investigators' findings, as she knew he would be having a meeting with Luke Wilkins the following day.

She, of course, found him working diligently with his head buried in files, so she knocked on the open door to get his attention.

"Lilia," Warner raised his head acknowledging her and then standing, "Good morning, how are you? Come in."

"Good morning, Warner. I'm well, thanks. How are you?"

"I'm well, thank you." Warner replied taking a seat after Lilia sat in the chair in front of his desk.

"Did the James verdict come in yesterday?"

"Not guilty. Just as I expected." Warner smiled, "The James family was certainly happy to have Paul released to them." Warner said thoughtfully.

"That's great. Congratulations." Lilia smiled.

"I've been going over the Wilkins file to prepare for our meeting tomorrow. The police contacted me and want to question him about the witnesses' deaths. Did you get any information from John's team?"

"That's exactly what I came to update you on." Lilia replied, holding out the file containing John's investigation notes and pictures. Warner took the file and began to review it.

"So, based on this information, he is not tracked on camera anywhere around his neighbourhood on the days the victims are murdered, so we aren't able to verify his whereabouts."

Warner tossed the pages back down, and sighed in frustration, rubbing both hands over his face and head.

"I don't have to ask if John is sure. His team is diligent, so I know they looked at everything."

Lilia continued, "Last night I gave John the locations and dates, within a four-day window, for each of the victims to see if he turns up on any security camera footage in any of those communities."

Warner stared at Lilia thoughtfully as she stated, "If they locate him, we can work on discrediting the tapes, based on height, colouring, clothes, shoe size, anything, especially if we find out that the police have obtained any security videos already. If we can place him anywhere else the day of or day before, we can use that as an alibi as well."

"Great insight, Lilia." Warner said, "As we uncover more information to prove our client not guilty, the more we find him being guilty of. This is too much. What do we do with this?" He said shaking his head. "I have a meeting with Wilkins tomorrow. He was placed back in custody today. Do you think John will have the information by then? I can show it to Wilkins and try to talk him into taking a plea bargain."

"I don't know. I'll follow up with him today and see. What time is your meeting?"

"Two p.m.," Warner replied.

"If he doesn't have enough to go on by end of day today, I'll get whatever he does have to you by then, if it will be helpful in convincing him."

"Great." Warner said and then continued, "Good thinking on that, Lila. If we find nothing that can help us, and Wilkins won't change his plea, at least we have some information. Hopefully we can have time to figure out some kind of defence. Thank you. You are going to be a great Lawyer, Lilia."

Lilia smiled appreciatively, "Thank you, Warner."

"I have one more update on Sean Hindson, Wilkins's bail bondsman. He's still missing unfortunately. I don't have a good feeling. His assistant is trying to track him down through family. I'm going to follow up with her tomorrow to find out if there has been any update."

"I hope they find him alive and well. Let me know as soon as you find out please."

"Of course, I will." Lilia responded raising to his feet.

"Do you want to go to lunch today? I could use some seafood fettuccine."

Lilia didn't want to want to go. She wanted a break from him, she didn't want to spend more time with him.

"Sure." She said nodding. "One o'clock?" she asked.

"I'll meet you at the elevators." Warner said smiling.

"Okay."

Lilia immediately turned and walked quickly back to her office, checking her email and messages to see if any of the other associates had left information for her. Once done, she picked up her phone to call John on his cell phone. As she gave him work yesterday, she knew today would not find him in the office, but on foot tracking down information.

After John answered, Lilia greeted him, to which John responded, "When do you need it by?"

Lilia smiled answering, "Anything you have, if there's anything, by end of day today?"

"We already have footage to review. Give us the day and we'll see what we can get you. What's the latest?"

"One tomorrow?" Lilia answered.

"Okay." John abruptly hung up.

*He certainly doesn't mince words*, Lilia thought as she replaced her phone, beginning to work on the information requested by some of the other associates for the cases they had that Melinda had been working on.

It felt like no sooner than she had opened her first file, she heard a knock on her door. She looked up to see Warner leaning against her door jam.

"Is everything okay?" She asked.

"It will be by one thirty if you can manage to leave your desk in the next five minutes."

Lilia looked down at the time on her laptop: one ten p.m.

"Oh no! I'm so sorry, Warner."

"I know you got engrossed in your work as always. I don't know about you, but my hunger will not allow me to continue to work until it's satisfied. So grab what you need and let's go." He said smiling at her.

Lilia smiled at him as she gathered her belongings and walked with him to the elevator.

They drove to the restaurant in comfortable silence. Upon parking, Lilia relayed her talk with John to Warner.

Once they were seated, and were waiting for their fettuccini lunches to be served, Lilia asked Warner, "Have you had any updates about Melinda? Have the police provided any information at all?"

"No, I haven't heard anything. We can check with Chris or Shawn but I'm sure if they heard anything, they would have told us."

"I'm sure the detectives are still checking everyone's alibis. There's a lot of people to clear. Her colleagues, clients, neighbours, family... if there is any." Warner continued.

"I wonder if they have any suspects yet." Lilia wondered.

"Most of her clients are probably suspects right now. She had mostly clients accused of violent crimes. Probably people from the office are still suspects, unless their alibis were corroborated."

Warner stopped speaking as the waitress brought their food over to them. They paused while taking a few bites of their lunch.

"Where were you?… When she was murdered," Warner asked, "If you don't mind me asking."

"I don't mind. I was home, on my own. But I did have a pizza delivered that night. They should be able to corroborate. And you? Where were you? If you don't mind me asking."

"I was at my sister's house all day and into the night. It was my niece, Mia's birthday. They had a party for her, and I stayed late helping clean up." Warner paused. "Sometimes I walk into the office and I still can't believe it. I expect to see her there."

"Me neither. I still feel awkward walking into that office, sitting in that chair."

They both resumed their comfortable silence, absorbed by their own troubled thoughts, and returned to eating their lunch.

Once their hunger was satisfied, they returned to Warner's car and drove back to the firm.

While in the car, Lilia's phone rang—it was John.

"Hi, John, do you have something for me? I'm actually with Warner now."

"I think you should come to my office. I found something." John stated simply.

"Okay, we should be there in twenty minutes." Lilia stated.

"We have to go to John's office." Lilia repeated to Warner. "He found something."

"Okay. Did he say what it is?"

"No, but it must be big. He wouldn't tell me over the phone."

They got back to the office building and immediately took the elevator to John's office. Lilia knocked on the door.

"Come in," John said from inside.

Warner opened the door and let Lilia proceed him into the office.

"John, thanks for calling me."

"Lilia, Warner." John acknowledged both of them rising to his feet to shake their hands.

"John." Warner shook his hand.

"Have a seat." John gestured to the chairs in front of his desk.

Taking their seats, Lilia asked, "What did you find, John?"

"Well, on the days and locations that you indicated, my team was able to identify someone in several of the footage that we accessed that fits the description of Luke Wilkins."

"Oh boy." Lilia sighed.

"But we found someone else too."

"Someone else?" Warner questioned.

"Yes. There's another person who is in the same footage, same day, same time frame as your client. We then went back and reviewed all of the footage for the new individual. We found this person in different footage, in different locations around the town; however, we didn't see Wilkins." John stated handing over the still shots to Lilia and Warner.

The still shots were of Wilkins standing, with his head turned towards the unidentified person. As the person was had their back to the camera, it wasn't obvious whether they were male or female. Though their stature— a few inches taller than Wilkins—made them appear to be male. They had short hair sticking out from under a baseball cap. Lilia thought to herself that there was something vaguely familiar about the person, but she shooed the thought out of her head.

In the other photos, Lilia saw the same person standing on their own with their head slightly turned to the side, so only a little more of the face could be viewed. However, due to the angle of the camera, not much more of the person's face could be identified.

Lilia turned to Warner, "So maybe Wilkins wasn't alone… There could have been someone else working with him."

Warner looked at Lilia silently. "Or he could have been meeting up with a friend. It was a coincidence that he was in the same town."

"I wanted to get you the information as soon as possible. My team worked through the night once we discovered that second person with Wilkins. Here is the video footage and the rest of the photos." John handed over the evidence, "We'll see if we can identify him."

Lilia and Warner got up and walked to John's office door.

"Thank you, John. Thank your team. We needed this evidence to push Wilkins into taking a plea bargain." Warner said.

"Do you know if the police acquired the video footage yet?" Lilia asked John.

"Not to my knowledge. We were the first to inquire most places."

"Thanks again, John."

Lilia and Warner left John's office and walked to the elevators in silence, armed with new evidence.

"I wonder who that guy is?"

"Let John and his team work." Warner stated, "We now have evidence that someone else was there. Either we get Wilkins to take a plea, or we use this evidence to prove that someone else was there and could have committed the crimes. This person that John may just have discovered for us."

"Now I take this to Wilkins and see if he will identify the person." Warner continued.

"Do you think it will work?"

"I hope it will." Warner stated.

They got off of the elevator and headed to their separate offices, lost in their thoughts. Lilia again thinking about the photo of the person.

"Lilia?"

Lilia lifted her head from the files that were laying open on her desk, although she hadn't really been paying attention to anything, still lost in her thoughts.

"Shawn. Sorry. I was lost in the files I was reviewing."

"That's okay. I was just getting an update on the Wilkins case from Warner and he said that you had questions about Melinda."

"Yes. Have the detectives gotten back to you? Have they found any relatives?"

"I found out that she does have an aunt and a cousin. They weren't close and are allowing us to organize the memorial and funeral."

"Really? Will they at least attend?"

"I don't know. We'll give them all of the information once it's arranged, of course."

"Thank you, Shawn. I appreciate you letting me know."

"Warner told me that you and John have been doing a lot of leg work on the Wilkins case, and that your intuition on what to investigate has been significant. Thanks to you, he may be able to establish reasonable doubt or get Wilkins to take a plea bargain. Good work, Lilia."

Lilia smiled under Shawn Cross's praise. "Thank you, Shawn. Your recognition means a lot."

"Hearing this from Warner makes me think about how essential you've been to this firm, and how close you were to losing you."

"I'm glad I didn't. I'm grateful to have learned everything I have from all of the associates at this firm. Including Melinda." Lilia stated.

"Melinda was a good lawyer. Had we known she wasn't a good mentor we would have done something about it."

"It's fine now, what's done is done. However, I do appreciate your remarks."

"Oh, and make sure you go with Warner tomorrow to meet with Wilkins. He said he would be open to listening to all of the options presented if you were at the meeting."

"Are you kidding me?" Lilia looked at him shocked.

"I know he's been a…" Shawn paused as if searching for a word, "… difficult client. But this could make the difference in closing this case, getting him to take the plea and not going to trial."

"Difficult is not the word I would use to describe him."

"Agreed. Warner used some harsher words. However, he's our client and we need to represent him." Shawn pressed.

"I understand, Shawn. I'll go with Warner."

"Good. Now, pack up and go home. You've put in enough hours. You deserve an early night."

"I'll take you up on that. It's definitely going to be a long day tomorrow." Lilia said ruefully.

Lilia decided she would first contact Sean Hindson's assistant to get an update on his whereabouts before heading for home. It had been a very overwhelming week and would be an extremely stressful day tomorrow, needing to meet with Luke Wilkins. Lilia shuddered at the thought, while picking up her phone.

Lilia called the bondsman's assistant and upon hearing her name, the assistant said, "Unfortunately, we have not yet been able to locate Mr. Hindson."

"Did you check with his family members?"

"Yes, none of his family members were able to provide any information so we have notified the police and filed a missing person report."

"This is very unusual for him and we are all very worried," the assistant continued, "Why have you been calling for him?" She now questioned.

"I am calling from Hale, Cross & Associates. Sean Hindson bonded one of our clients and I have been trying to contact him to clear up some details."

"If you send me the information required via email, I will have his partner try to access the data for you. I'm not sure how much he can help as they both had their own clients and systems."

"It's okay. We can wait for the details. Thank you for your help. I'm sure Mr. Hindson will be discovered safe and sound."

"I hope so as well. Good day."

"Goodbye." Lilia answered.

*Another mystery involving someone unfortunate to have been around Luke Wilkins*, Lilia thought as she packed her bags to leave. First Melinda, then Lucille Diaz, Callie Simmons, Linda Graham, and now Sean Hindson was missing.

# CHAPTER 10

Lilia walked into the office the next morning, determined to find more information. She wanted to get John and his investigation team more details surrounding a possible new victim, Sean Hindson. She worked hurriedly all morning, putting together Hindson's personal information, including his address, to get John started on his search.

Once she had organized the details, she emailed John, including some photos she'd acquired of Hindson. She wrote John asking him to specifically look for either of the two men he'd previously identified in any of the video footage he had obtained.

No less than five minutes after sending the email, she had a response from John.

*On it*, his email stated, *Rush?*

*ASAP.* Lilia emailed him back. *Thank you.*

She had one hour before she had to join Warner to attend the meeting with Luke Wilkins, so she decided to grab a bite to eat as she didn't think that she would be able to hold anything down afterwards. She started to feel ill thinking about him, as she tried to choke down her sandwich.

When she finished eating, it was time to meet Warner, so she organized all she needed and went to his office.

"Ready?" Lilia asked.

"I'm coming now," Warner responded. "How are you doing? Are you ready for this?"

"I'm not ready. But I have to be, don't I? As Shawn said yesterday, he is our client, and we represent him, which means I have to be there."

"He's right. Although we can pick and choose who we represent as a firm, once we decide to represent them, it's our duty to do so with integrity."

Lilia remained silent as Warner filled his briefcase with files.

As they walked over to the elevator, Lilia began to inform Warner of the investigative tasks she recently placed on John's investigative team.

"Hopefully he'll have the information soon."

"Good thinking, Lilia. One thing about you, you're always thinking one step ahead."

Lilia smiled, "I'm hoping he'll be able to identify that second person in the footage. If he or Wilkins are any-where around any of their last known sightings, John and his team will find them. I'm sure of it."

As they got off of the elevator and made their way to Warner's car, Lilia noticed a man standing in the lobby, with his back to them talking on the phone. Just as she had a feeling of recognition, he turned and glanced quickly at her and Warner. He turned back around and ended his call. Lilia paused as she realized it was Jeff Sanders, the night security guard, and Lilia thought it was odd that he was there in the afternoon.

"Hi, Jeff. I thought you were on the night shift. What are you doing here?" Lilia walked towards him causing him to turn back around.

"Hi, Ms. Bennett. I must have gotten confused. I thought Lou asked me to switch shifts with him today. I got the dates wrong cause he's here. I'll just hang around and wait for my shift to start since I'm already here." He gestured to his phone, "I was just calling my wife to tell her my mistake. She was not happy." He chuckled slightly.

"You have a couple of hours to waste before your shift starts then," Warner stated matter-of-factly, placing his hand on Lilia's back and guiding her to the front entrance, "We need to go, or we'll be late."

"See you later, Jeff. I hope it's not too long of a day for you."

"Goodbye, Ms. Bennett. I'm sure it won't be."

"Do you stop and chat to everyone you encounter?" Warner asked Lilia as he opened the car door for her.

"Jeff's a nice guy." She responded climbing in the car.

"He does a good job patrolling the area. I see him in the parking lot more than I have the other nighttime security guards," she finished as Warner got behind the driver's seat.

"Do we have a game plan for our meeting with Wilkins?" Lilia asked changing to the subject at hand.

"You mean like you be bad cop and I'm the good cop?" Warner said smiling.

Lilia shook her head, smiling, "No, I mean, what are we going to discuss with him? The way the trial is going to run, what will be presented by us, the death of the witnesses, his alibi?" Lilia looked at Warner.

"Yes. All of it." Warner stated.

They both went silent lost in their own thoughts for the rest of the ride to the prison.

Once they arrived, they handed in their identification and then were escorted into the meeting room by an armed guard and instructed to sit at the table where another guard was stationed at the door.

"Wait here please." The guard stated and left closing the door behind him.

Lilia and Warner sat silently.

A few moments later, two guards brought Luke Wilkins into the meeting room. His hands were cuffed in front of him, and the guards flanked him on either side. As soon as he entered the room, Wilkins's eyes were transfixed on Lilia. He smirked at her, looking first directly into her eyes, and then letting his eyes move down slowly to her chest. Lilia felt extremely exposed as she then watched him lick his lips slowly.

The two guards lowered him into the chair across from them.

"I've been wanting to see you again, Lilia." Wilkins leered at Lilia, "Did you dress up for me?"

"Wilkins," Warner said sternly, "First, it's Ms. Bennett, and second, you are addressing me. Ms. Bennett is only here as a collaborator, assisting me with your case."

"I'll have her assist with sucking my—" Wilkins grinned.

"Wilkins!" Warner cut him off giving him a dangerous look, "As we've been reviewing your case and investigating there are a few things I want to go over with you."

Wilkins didn't take his eyes off Lilia as Warner continued.

"First, the DNA evidence. I have gotten a forensic scientist to testify that the DNA could belong to a number of people," Warner started.

Wilkins looked at Warner, "I don't need to know all this shit. Just do your job—what I'm paying your firm to do." Wilkins then turned his leer to Lilia, "Get me off." He smirked and said suggestively.

Lilia felt sick at having to stay there in his presence, but she continued to stare him down to let him think that what he said or did didn't affect her.

"Look, Wilkins, I told you to stop directing any comments to Ms. Bennett. Now, did you know that three of the witnesses tied to your case have died while you were out on bond? Can you let me know where you were for when the detectives ask? Because they will."

"I was home." Wilkins answered, not looking at Warner.

"I didn't tell you when."

"I was home the entire time I was out." Wilkins then stared at Warner.

Warner took the still photos out of his briefcase, placing them on the table, "Then this isn't you?"

"Nope," Wilkins stated not even glancing at the photo.

"Do you know who this is?" Warner asked pointing to the still of the unidentified man on the table.

"Are you a cop or my lawyer?" Wilkins demanded, glaring at Warner. "It seems to me, if those bitches are dead, my case is better, so why are you questioning me."

"I need to know where you were!" Warner slapped his hand down on the table. Lilia jumped, startled, while Wilkins just laughed.

One of the guards yelled at him, "HEY! Do you want this meeting over?!"

"Sorry," Warner apologized to the guard, then looked at Wilkins, "If you know who this guy is then maybe we have someone to direct the cops to. Someone else who was there, who could have done it. Our investigators are looking for more video footage."

Wilkins just stared at Warner and then looked back at Lilia. "I can help you. If you help me. Get. Me. Off." He said smirking. Lilia felt the bile rising up her throat.

"This meeting is over. I don't know why you wanted it."

"I wanted her." Wilkins said, smiling and licking his lips again.

"Get him out." Warner told the guards, "We're done here."

"See you soon, sweetheart," Wilkins said sickeningly, "I can't wait to taste you. You'll beg me." Wilkins laughed and Lilia shuddered as he was escorted out of the room.

"That was such a waste of time." Warner said.

"It was like he just wanted me to be displayed in front of him. There was no point at all. He didn't help provide anything for his case!" Lilia yelled, pushing away from the table and walking away, frustrated and disgusted.

"I'm sorry about that, Lilia. I wanted to choke him," he said harshly. Then he looked at her softly, "Speaking to you, looking at you like that. I wanted to do more."

"I know Warner. I'm sorry too. My being here was a distraction." Lilia stared into Warner's eyes and felt an electric pulse, pulling her towards him, and realized she needed to deflect quickly, "I'm sure you could have gotten more done with the case had I not been here. I'll make sure to tell Shawn when we get back."

"Yes, the case…" Warner's voice trailed off, and he looked down and started packing all his documents back into his briefcase.

"I'll also check in with John to see if he has anything yet." Lilia felt as though she had succeeded in bringing their thoughts back to the business at hand.

"Are you ready?" Lilia asked.

"Let's go."

Arriving back to the office, Warner dropped Lilia off outside of the front doors, stating that he had another meeting and wouldn't be returning to the office for the remainder of the day.

"Okay," Lilia stated, "I'll call you if John found anything concrete."

"You can let me know tomorrow when I'm back in the office. I'll be pretty busy."

"Oh, alright then," Lilia said. When Warner moved to get out of the car to come around to open her door. Lilia said quickly, "I'm okay, bye," and rushed to open the door and step out of the car.

"Bye," Warner said, and waited until she walked through the entrance before driving off.

Lilia exited the elevator on her floor and found Jeff Sanders waiting.

"Jeff! What are you doing up here? Looking for things to do to pass the time?"

"I just finished passing out treats. I brought danishes and donuts. Too bad you weren't here, or you would have gotten one too. I just finished giving them out to everyone and was headed back down." Jeff spoke quickly, moving past her onto the elevator. "See you, Ms. Bennett." The elevator closed behind him.

"Bye, Jeff." Lilia shook her head, walking towards her office, stopping at Grace's office.

"I heard I missed donuts."

"Oh yeah. That security guard brought them up. How strange. No one even realized it was him handing out donuts. Mary had to send out an email so people would know who was walking around the floor."

"Well, that was kind of Jeff." Lilia stressed his name.

"Is that his name? Well," Grace raised her hand effectively dismissing the conversation saying, "I don't think you missed out, I heard him asking where your office was so he could leave one for you too."

"Oh, he didn't mention that."

"Well, anyways, when you have a moment tomorrow can we meet? I have a case I'm working on and I need some help with which direction to take it in."

"Of course. What time tomorrow?" Lilia said pulling up her schedule on her phone. "I just have to meet with John, but I haven't scheduled him in yet."

"How about ten in the morning? Does that work?"

"Yes, that's fine for me." Lilia stated putting Grace's meeting in her phone, "Okay—I'm off to eat my donut!"

Lilia made her way to her office. Arriving there was no donut to be seen, and she suspected someone must have eaten it or Jeff didn't remember to leave her one.

When Lilia pulled out her office chair, she noticed that her briefcase was on it and not under her desk where she normally kept it. Maybe she'd left it on her chair by accident in her rush to eat before the meeting with Wilkins and Warner. Her head certainly wasn't in the right place, so Lilia dismissed her thoughtlessness to the stress she was feeling beforehand. She thought over the horribly degrading meeting with Wilkins and reminded herself to tell Shawn about it. Hopefully he would support her not attending any more in-person meetings with Wilkins, no matter what the client demanded.

Opening her briefcase, Lilia noticed that her files were not alphabetized. The stress of meeting with Wilkins had really done a number on her, that's for sure. She was so out of sorts; she hadn't followed any of her normal routines.

Lilia shook her head at herself, logging into her laptop to email John to ask when he thought he'd be finished so that they could meet. As she awaited John's response, she got to work on the other case files.

A few hours later, Lilia opened her email to see a response from John. It stated that he would be able to meet with her tomorrow after two p.m. She responded that she would be there, and then sent an email to Warner to see if he was available.

As she packed up her files to get ready to go home that evening, Lilia began thinking about the meeting with John. *Had he identified the person with Wilkins? Will Warner be there?* As she had been trying her best to avoid him, it now was evident that he was trying to avoid her. She didn't like how it felt. She decided that she would pass by his office in the morning to see if he was there and ask him to go out for lunch before the meeting. Hopefully he was available, as she was considering being completely honest with him. *I'll let him know how I've been feeling. That I'm confused and that I don't want to feel this way. That I want to have a professional relationship with him and that my feelings will not get in the way of that.*

Lost in her thoughts, Lilia made her way out of the office and into the parking garage, making her way towards her car. She suddenly had the same eerie feeling of being watched come over her, so she stopped and looked around. As she didn't immediately see anyone, she began walking at a faster pace to her vehicle, getting out her keys.

As she reached her car, she felt more than heard a presence behind her, and as she turned to confront who was there, she felt a hand grab her, and saw, out of her periphery, a shadow rise over her head. She tried to move out of the way but was struck so hard that her eyes blanked. She was being attacked.

She screamed at herself, *stay on your feet*!

In a fog and her eyes unfocused, she whirled around quickly and lifted her arm to hit her attacker in the face with her keys. As her hand reached her target, she heard him moan, but felt herself get struck in the side and then again in the face. She started to buckle over in pain but knew that she couldn't go down.

*Fight back!*

She mustered up her strength and lifted her body and arm again with as much energy as she could to hit him in the face with her keys again. As she made contact, she heard him grunt, but before she could raise her arms to protect herself, another blow came down. In a haze, Lilia heard a shout from further away.

"Hey!"

As Lilia heard the attacker run away, she crumpled to the ground, all the fight in her gone.

"Are you okay?!" She felt her unknown saviour come to her side. "Lilia? Is that you? Who was that? I'm calling an ambulance."

She could not respond to any of the questions, though she heard them all through a fog. She just wanted to close her eyes and sleep. She knew the pain would be gone if she could sleep.

# CHAPTER 11

Beep... Beep... Beep... Beep.

*What is that noise?* Lilia thought to herself as she tried to open her eyes. She didn't remember setting her alarm with that ring tone.

*Why does opening my eyes hurt so much?* Lilia thought. As her memories came back of being attacked, she moaned. *Is this all a bad dream?*

Suddenly she felt someone hold her hand, "Lilia? Open up your eyes. Come on."

"Warner?" Lilia mumbled. "What are you doing here?"

Lilia struggled to open and focus her eyes, "Wait... where am I? Why does my voice sound like that?"

As she became more lucid, Lilia realized she was not in her bedroom at her condo. Her voice sounded very thick and unclear.

"Do you remember what happened, Lilia? You were attacked." Warner stated in a controlled voice.

Lilia moved her eyes to Warner's. "I thought it was a bad dream."

"It's not a dream. You're at the hospital, Wilson Memorial Hospital. You were brought in unconscious yesterday evening. Do you remember now?"

"I'm starting to." Lilia closed her eyes, "Someone grabbed me and hit me."

Lilia heard Warner suck in his breath, as she opened her eyes to look at him, she saw the rage in his face. As she felt tears roll down her cheeks, she saw the rage change to sadness as he took her hand in both of his and caressed them with his thumb. She raised her other hand to wipe away her tears and felt a flash of pain as she touched her face.

"Be careful," Warner said, "You have facial injuries."

"Yeah. I felt that."

"I'll get the doctor. He can talk to you. The police are also here waiting to speak to you about the attack. I'll tell them all you're awake."

"Okay. Thank you for being here for me, Warner." Lilia said as he stood to walk to the door.

Warner paused at the door and turned to look at her. "I wouldn't be anywhere else. I'll be right back okay?"

Lilia smiled at him as he left the room.

No sooner than he left, the doctor and two police officers entered.

"Ms. Bennett, I'm so glad to see you awake. I'm Doctor Webber."

"Thank you, Doctor. What happened to me?"

"Well, Ms. Bennett, you were assaulted last evening and have incurred some trauma." Dr. Webber stated as he flipped through her chart. "You have sustained contusions on your ribs, and there is physical trauma to your face. There are also contusions on your forearms and hands—most are defensive wounds. You fought, Ms. Bennett. Your injuries could have been much worse." He continued, "Your body will need time to heal. We will keep you for one more night for observation, and you should be able to go home tomorrow. We currently have you on morphine intravenously so you shouldn't feel much pain. I'll prescribe you a pain killer to take at home. Do you have any questions before I turn you over to the detectives?"

"No, thank you, Doctor."

"Okay. I'll be back to check in on you later." The doctor left the room.

"Ms. Bennett. I am Detective Collins, and this is Detective Gregg. We understand that you had a very frightening evening yesterday. Can you tell us what you remember about it?"

"I was walking to my car after work. I was in the parking garage. I felt weird, like I was being watched, so I started walking faster to my car."

"Have you ever felt like that before? Like someone was watching you?" Detective Collins asked.

"Yes. I have. But there is a nighttime security guard—sometimes he's on rounds and he watches everyone go to their cars."

"Were you alone in the parking garage? Did you notice any of your colleagues walking to their cars at this time?" Detective Collins continued.

"No… I didn't see anyone else." Lilia closed her eyes. "I looked around, got my keys out, then I felt someone grab me and hit me in the head, and then I started to lose focus…" Lilia continued as she felt the tears come. "I tried to hit him in the face with my keys. I hit him twice, I think. I heard him groan." She stated.

"Did you get a look at him? Was there anything familiar about him? Did he say anything to you?"

"I didn't see his face. He didn't say anything, I only heard him groan. Oh!" Lilia opened her eyes wide. "I remember grabbing at his face when I hit him with my keys. Just in case I didn't… I wanted to get his DNA… can you ask the Doctors if they scraped my fingernails?"

Both Detectives looked at each other then at her in a questioning manner.

"Oh, I work in criminal law."

"Ah, okay. It's good you fought back. This could have ended differently if you didn't. We will speak to the doctor about any evidence collected under your fingernails and on your clothes."

"I just kept thinking to myself that I couldn't go down. He would have the advantage if I went down." Lilia paused, swallowed, then continued. "Someone saved me. They yelled out and he ran away. Who was that?"

"He said he was a colleague of yours. Carl Jeffries? Do you know him?"

"Yes, he's a lawyer at the firm. I'll have to thank him. If he hadn't come when he did…" Lilia's voice trailed off.

"Detective Gregg will speak to the doctor about collecting everything." Detective Gregg left the room, as Detective Collins continued. "And we have detectives in the parking garage looking for evidence. Do you have any more to add?"

"Actually… I don't know how relevant this is… But I think I should tell you just in case." Lilia stated. "A lawyer at my firm was murdered several weeks ago, at her apartment. The investigation is ongoing. I'm just trying to remember the investigating Detectives' names." Lilia closed her eyes again, as it hurt her to think.

"Thank you. That could be very relevant. Don't worry about the investigators' names—I'll find out. What was your colleague's name?" Detective Collins questioned.

"Melinda Kent." Lilia stated just as the other detective walked in with Doctor Webber and a nurse.

"Ms. Bennett, this is the nurse examiner. She collected the evidence off of your clothes yesterday and also collected any evidence on your keys. Due to your statement to the police today about scratching the attacker she is going to collect any evidence under your nails. Is that okay?"

"Yes, Doctor Webber, thank you." Lilia stated.

The nurse examiner began laying out the supplies needed and inspecting Lilia's fingernails.

"Is Warner Reid still here?" Lilia asked the doctor.

"Warner Reid?"

"The man that was here earlier? My friend."

"Oh yes. He is standing like a guard dog at your door. He hasn't left your side since he arrived and now won't leave your door. He'd be in here now if the detectives didn't exclude him."

"Would you please let him know he can come in when the detectives are finished?"

"I don't think I'll have to say anything at all."

When the nurse examiner had finished, the detectives told Lilia she would be hearing from them and left the room.

Within seconds of the detectives and doctor leaving, Warner was right back beside Lilia again, holding her hand.

"Thank you, Warner, for coming and being here with me. The doctor said you were here all night. How did you know I was here?" Lilia asked him.

"Carl called Shawn and Chris, after the ambulance came. Shawn called me. Carl rode with you in the ambulance, and I came straight here. Shawn helped Carl get his car while Chris stayed at the firm with the police. I'm hoping they already have the security footage, and this guy is caught before you're released."

"While I was waiting outside, I tried calling Shawn and Chris to see what was going on but neither answered. Did the detectives say anything to you?" Warner asked.

"No, they just wanted my statement, and they collected, what I hope, was evidence under my nails. I scratched him."

Warner closed his eyes and put his head down. "I'm sorry," Lilia said, "you don't want to hear all of that."

"No," Warner said harshly, "I hate that you were attacked. I wish I could do something. I want to find him and…" He lowered his voice, "I should have been there. Walking you to your car. If I wasn't running from you… I would have been," he said softly.

"Warner, this has nothing to do with you walking me to my car. There are lots of could-haves and should-haves. I started avoiding you first. I should have left with someone else so I could walk with them. I didn't. I also could have let security know to keep an eye out for me. I didn't. This was his doing and his alone. Maybe if it hadn't been me, it may have been someone else. At this point, we don't know if it was random or targeted."

"You're right. There are a lot of could-haves and should-haves, but it doesn't take away the fact that I should have protected you." Warner looked at her.

"Warner…" Lilia started.

"No more talk about it. I'm going to call Carl and see how he is, let him know you're okay. Did you want me to give him a message?"

"Yes, please, Warner. Please tell him I said thank you for being there, for saving me. If he wasn't there…"

Warner rubbed her hand "Shh, it's okay. I'm going to step outside and call him. Close your eyes and get some rest, okay?"

"That sounds like a wonderful idea." Lilia said as she settled back against the pillows.

Before Warner had even reached the door he heard her breathing change as she settled into a deep sleep.

When Lilia's eyes opened once again, she wasn't surprised to see Warner sitting in the chair beside her bed. His eyes were closed, so she kept quiet as she didn't want to wake him, sure it had been a long couple of days for him as well. She closed her eyes and soon fell asleep again not waking until she heard voices whispering.

Her eyes wandered around to room until she located Warner standing in a corner of the room speaking with Shawn Cross and Chris Hale.

"Do I get to be included in the conversation?" Lilia asked.

"Oh Lilia! You're awake." Chris stated.

"Sorry, we didn't mean to wake you. We were trying to be quiet. You need to rest." Shawn said.

"No, it's fine—I was actually awake earlier and just shut my eyes for a second. What's going on?" Lilia questioned.

"First off, Lilia," Shawn moved closer to Lilia's bedside, "Chris and I are so upset and sorry that this happened."

"Yes, Lilia, we hope that they will find this... piece of filth as quickly as possible." Chris said.

"Are you going to be released today?" Shawn asked.

"I hope so. I'd definitely like to go home." Lilia said.

Shawn, Chris, and Warner all looked at each other. "Well, Lilia," started Chris, "if you are going home, Shawn and I would like to arrange security for you until this is all sorted out."

"What are you talking about? Don't you think it was a random attack?" Lilia asked.

"Lilia," Warner said, "we don't know anything yet. But I think you should listen to Chris. I think you should think about security. It's for your safety."

"I don't know. I don't want some guy following me around." Lilia shook her head, forgetting about her facial injuries and rubbing her hand on her face. "Ohhh…" she moaned.

Warner sighed and moved to her side, "Be careful." He smiled gently.

"Can I see?"

"See what?"

"Do you have a mirror? I want to see."

"I don't." Warner stated, obviously being difficult.

"I'll just have a look in the washroom." Lilia pressed the nurse's call button, "If you gentlemen will excuse me."

"We'll just wait outside." Shawn said.

"Why don't you guys head out. I'll stay with Lilia."

"We don't want to see you in the office today, Warner. Let us know how she's doing later. We will talk to John about security." Chris said as they began to walk out.

"Thank you for coming to see me, Chris, Shawn."

"Of course, Lilia," Shawn said as he opened the door for the nurse.

With the nurse in the room, Warner said, "I'll give you privacy," and then joined Chris and Shawn in the hallway.

"Thank you, Chris," Warner said, "I really don't want to leave her right now."

"I can see that." Chris said, "When you both get back to work and everything is settled, make sure you visit HR."

Warner looked at Chris confused, "HR?"

"I have a feeling you'll be declaring a relationship soon enough. As her superior, it's important that you have it declared to HR." Chris stated matter-of-factly.

"We, uhhhh, aren't in a relationship." Warner stated.

"But it's obvious you want to be," Shawn chuckled, "you just have to wait for her to realize it. If you want my advice?" Shawn placed his hand on Warner's shoulder, "Don't push her. Especially after this. It's going to be hard for her to trust."

Warner looked slightly defeated and ran his hand over his neck and head, "Yeah, I get that."

"Don't give up though. She needs you now." Chris said.

"How did you guys know?"

"We can see how you two have been acting towards one another. The way you reacted when you heard about her attack," Shawn said.

"I've been married for twenty years now. I met my wife at the first firm I worked at. When I saw Lilia looking at you, it reminded me of how I would catch my wife looking at me when we first met." Chris continued, "Seven kids and a law firm later, she looks at me a lot differently now." Chris sighed and rubbed his hand over his face.

Shawn laughed, "Maybe if you attempted to make it home for dinner at least three times a week, she wouldn't look at you like that, my friend." Shawn slapped Chris on the back and said, "Let's go. I'm taking my wife to dinner tonight. Maybe you should do the same. Try a date once in a while," Shawn continued as they walked away.

Once the nurse left, Warner re-entered the room. Lilia looked up at him when he spoke, "Well?"

"How can you even look at me? I look a mess. I can't believe it."

"It's mostly bruising that will fade. It looks bad now, but it'll heal eventually. It looks better than yesterday."

"Liar." Lilia stated.

Warner smiled, "How was it getting up? Painful?"

"A bit. My ribs hurt mostly, so the nurse taught me how best to move around and get out of bed."

"Okay. Did the nurse say what time the doctor would be around?"

"She said in the next hour. When he does his rounds and sets me free, she'll unhook me and hand me whatever prescriptions he recommends."

"That sounds promising."

"That I'm going home today? Yes, it certainly does. You don't have to stay Warner." Lilia said, although she didn't want him to go.

"Do you want me to leave Lilia? I don't want to go."

Lilia closed her eyes and took a deep breath that caused her pain, yet she still allowed herself to admit, "No, Warner. I don't want you to go. Thank you for staying with me." But she refused to make eye contact with him when she said it.

"There's nowhere else I'd rather be." Warner stated, smiling. He walked over to her bedside and touched her hand lightly, which made her eyes jump wide open. He caught her eyes and smiled, "You're still beautiful, bruises and all."

"Now you can really stop lying, Warner," she shook her head and rolled her eyes.

Warner smiled, "Number one. I never lie. Number two." Warner held up his fingers, "I'm giving you three choices once you are released from here, if you don't choose one, I'm going to the doctor right now to tell him you have internal pains you've been complaining about, so he doesn't release you from the hospital."

Lilia opened her eyes wide in shock. "But that's lying, Warner! You just said you don't lie!"

"Only when necessary." He shrugged. "This situation breeds necessity as it's about your safety."

Lilia glared at him. "Well?" Warner asked, "Do you want to hear your three choices?"

"Fine. Let's hear it." Lilia grumbled.

Warner smiled, "One, you accept Chris and Shawn's offer for security. Two, you stay with me at my place, in your own room," he stated when he saw Lilia look at him in shock, "Three, I stay with you at your place. I don't know your place, so a room or the couch will suffice."

"I'll give you exactly twenty minutes to consider it. I'm going to go to the coffee shop for a coffee and a muffin, do you want anything?" Warner continued.

"A coffee please?"

"Absolutely. And when I come back, I'd like an answer please." Warner smiled and walked out of the door.

*He has some nerve!* Lilia thought to herself, gently punching her fist on her bed, remembering to be gentle this time. *Three choices?! What kind of choices were those?*

She didn't want some stranger following her around, standing outside of her door. Just the thought of it stressed her out. Nor could she live in the same space with Warner.

There was absolutely no way she could live with him! The thought of living with Warner was equally stressful. Her heartbeat began to speed up just thinking about it. It was hard enough to have an office down the hall. Because of her lifestyle, with no close family or friends, she didn't even have someone else to stay with. Lilia spent the remainder of her twenty minutes trying hard to think of another solution.

When Warner reappeared, he placed her coffee by her bed and said, "Be careful, it's still hot," before sitting down in a relaxed manner in the chair beside her bed. He began to sip his coffee and calmly eat his muffin.

If he wasn't going to begin the conversation, then she wouldn't either. "Was the line long?" She asked, attempting to change the subject.

"Why? Was I longer than twenty minutes?" He asked, casually looking at his watch. "I actually have five minutes to spare, so I'll give you that time to ask any questions you have to help you make your decision." He stated bringing her back to the task at hand.

"I don't want a strange man constantly watching me."

"I understand that." He said nodding his head.

"And I don't want to live with you."

"Then your choice is for me to live with you?"

"No. My place is way too small. It's a one bedroom with one washroom. You can't stay with me."

"Then your choice is to live at my place? I have a four-bedroom house. The guest room has its own full bathroom. You could have that room. I have a housekeeper that does the cleaning and laundry once a week and makes me breakfast and dinner every day. I also have video security cameras with nighttime security drive by, and if the alarm is triggered the police are immediately contacted and a squad car dispatched."

Lilia looked at Warner curiously and Warner answered the unasked question, "We take on a quite a few controversial cases. I've never been threatened but I don't want to wait to protect myself until I am," He explained, and Lilia nodded.

Lilia thought it over. His place certainly seemed the safest and with the housekeeper there she wouldn't feel like she was alone with him, and the other choices didn't seem like choices at all to her.

"Fine. I'll stay with you."

"Great. I didn't want to lie to the doctor." He smiled, "Once you're released, we can stop by your place and pick up some things you need. Shawn told me to tell you to take the week off or longer, whatever you need it."

"Where did all of my stuff go? My purse, laptop, and briefcase… ?"

"Carl took everything in the ambulance with him. When I met him here, he gave them to me. Was it your purse and briefcase, with your laptop?"

"Yes, I'm pretty sure that's all I had with me."

Warner nodded, just as the door opened, and Doctor Webber walked in with a nurse.

"Hi, Ms. Bennett, how are you feeling today?"

"I'm okay, Doctor, thank you."

"Great, great. Nurse Claire is here to take your vitals and if everything seems okay, we will release you. Sound good?"

"That sounds great."

"The nurse told me that you needed a bit of assistance, due to the severity of the contusions on your ribs, to get to the bathroom. Do you have someone to help you at home? You really don't want to injure yourself further."

Lilia immediately looked over at Warner like he'd planned it. "Yes, I've arranged to stay with a friend of mine."

"Good, good." Doctor Webber stated making notes on the clipboard, as the nurse stated her vitals to him. "So, everything looks good, Ms. Bennett. Your facial contusions will start to darken and look worse as they are healing. They will take about two weeks to heal, though you will start to feel better, and they will feel less painful to the touch. Your ribs will take longer, about four to six weeks. The CT scan we conducted last night confirmed that there wasn't internal damage to any organs. Other than that, you have no other serious injuries, so nothing that needs you to prolong your stay at our illustrious hotel." He smiled at his own joke, "Do you have any questions for me?"

"Is there anything I can do to help the bruising heal? Especially my ribs?"

"Your ribs you are going to ice for twenty minutes, two to three times a day. The facial contusions, the same. I want to make an appointment with you for two weeks from now, to check in on you. My office will contact you with a date and time."

The doctor continued, "The nurse will give you a prescription for pain killers, further instructions and to show you some breathing exercises that will also help with your healing." He continued talking and Lilia looked with surprise over at Warner, who was taking notes on everything that the doctor was saying.

"Thank you for everything, Doctor." Lilia said as the nurse removed the IV from her arm.

"Take care, Ms. Bennett. Follow the instructions. Take the pain killers. You cannot heal if your body is always in shock. Ask for help when you need it. Give my office a call if you have any questions or feel anything different after you leave."

"Thank you, Doctor Webber." Lilia said gratefully.

"Thank you, Doctor," Warner said.

"I'll see you in two weeks, Ms. Bennett. You can start getting ready if you want. The nurse will be back with the instructions and show you the breathing exercises." He stated walking out of the room with the nurse.

"Since they're releasing you, you're going to need some clothes. I can run down to the store and bring you back some more comfortable clothing?" Warner asked after the doctor left.

"I would really appreciate that, Warner."

"I'll be right back." He said making his way to the door. "I'll get you a sweatshirt and jogging pants and some running shoes. What shoe size? Seven?"

"Yes, seven. Thank you, Warner."

Warner left quickly, and Lilia tried her best to slowly sit up in the bed, moving her legs slowly to the side to sit up just as the nurse walked in.

"You got up on your own! That's so good. You're on the road to mend already," the nurse said cheerfully. "I have everything here for you. Doctor Webber's instructions, as well as your prescription for Oxycodone. You are to take it every four to six hours for four days, then every eight to twelve hours for the next four days. After that, you can see how you are feeling."

"Thank you," Lilia said taking all of the paperwork and putting it on the table beside her.

"Are you ready to do the breathing exercises now?"

"For sure."

As the nurse showed her the exercises she was to do, she began to question Lilia.

"The gentleman that was here earlier, is that your brother?"

Lilia rolled her eyes. *Here we go.* She thought. "Nope, he's not my brother." Not giving any more information.

"Oh. Well, your cousin is very nice to spend so much time with you." She said not taking the hint.

"Not my cousin either. But yes, he's very nice. It'll be very sweet living with him and having him take care of me." Lilia warned the nurse away.

"It will be very nice taking care of you." Warner said, surprising them both from the door.

"You're back! That was quick." Lilia said.

"Yes, darling, the store is just down the street." Warner played along, coming over to the bed to plant a kiss on her head. He placed the bag down on the bed. "Are you all finished here? Is there anything I need to be aware of when I'm taking care of her? When helping her change her clothes and such?" Warner said suggestively.

"Ummm. No, I mean yes, we are all done and no there is nothing more that Ms. Bennett isn't capable of letting you know herself. Take care, Ms. Bennett, you can leave at any time. Here are your release documents." The nurse said quickly, adding the paper to Lilia's pile and turning to walk out of the door.

"Let me show you what I got you." Warner said turning to the bag, proceeding to take the clothes out of it.

"Warner. You didn't have to do all of that."

"Do all of what? You were giving her a warning to stay away from your man. I was just helping you along."

"Ugh. Warner. You are not my man. "

"Not yet anyways." Warner said with a smile. "Now look at these. Are they okay?" He asked holding up a pair of pants and sweatshirt. "Here are the shoes."

"They're great. Thanks for doing that. How much do I owe you?"

Warner gave her a dirty look and passed the clothing to her. "Get dressed, and let's get out of here. Let me know if you need any help." He said, turning away from her. "I'll just be outside of the door."

Lilia painfully put on each piece of clothing. It took her a long time however, she was determined to do it by herself. She bit her lip, determined not to cry out. She was grateful that he brought shoes she could slip her feet into, as they were the easiest to put on.

"Warner! I'm ready." Lilia called out loud enough that he would hear her.

Warner walked back into the room saying, "That took a while. Why didn't you ask me for help?"

"I need to do it myself; I can't ask you for help when you're at work, can I?"

Warner just glanced at her and shook his head slightly annoyed at her candidness.

"Do you have everything you need?" He asked as she picked up all of her paperwork.

"Yes. I do. Do you mind if we stop at the pharmacy to get my prescription filled as well?"

"I can go for you once you are settled in. I don't think you should be out for too long. You need to rest. We still have to stop at your place for your things. If you tell me what you need, I can go for you instead if you want."

"No, I'll do it." Lilia was determined to keep at least some privacy, knowing she was going to be giving up so much by staying with him for at least one to two weeks.

"Alright. Let's go if you're ready."

"Let's go."

Warner opened the door and waved someone into the room, "She's ready now. Thank you."

Lilia watched as an orderly walked into the room pushing a wheelchair. "I don't need that." Lilia stated, even as she felt relief at not having to walk all the way to the car.

Warner gave her a stern look, even as the orderly helped her sit in the wheelchair. Shaking his head Warner walked beside them to the foyer, asking the orderly to wait with her while he brought his car to the front.

Once Warner arrived with the car, Lilia was grateful for the four hands of extra support as Warner and the orderly helped Lilia painfully get settled into the passenger seat.

"Are you okay?" Warner asked.

"Yes, thanks Warner." Lilia turned to the orderly, "Thank you for your help."

"See, maybe you should just give me a list of what you need from your place."

"No way am I letting you go through my underwear drawer." Lilia said matter-of-factly.

Warner burst out with a hearty laugh, while settling himself into the driver seat. "You are willing to go through that agony, just so I don't see your underwear?!"

Lilia cringed in her seat, which Warner noticed and smiled. "No response?"

"How am I going to live with you?"

"It's going to be fun. I'm sure of it." Warner said, resting his hand on her knee. He removed it quickly to put the car in gear, before she could remove it for him. "Let's get this party started," he said, and drove quickly out of the hospital parking lot.

# CHAPTER 12

"Well?" Warner asked as they pulled up to her condominium. "Have you made a decision? Are you going to give me your list of everything you need from your condo or are you going to put yourself through extreme agony so I don't see your underwear?"

Lilia huffed, "I'll tell you what I need. I don't have my keys, but the security guard should let you in if you want to bring him to me to give him permission. I'll start writing everything down."

Warner got out of the car and went to speak with the concierge while Lilia wrote down what she needed and where Warner would be able to find it, starting with a small piece of luggage that he could put everything in. By the time Warner returned, she had completed the list. Lilia explained to the concierge that she'd had an accident and that she would be staying with a friend to care for her. He agreed to let Warner into her unit to collect her belongings, so Lilia handed Warner the list, along with a stern look, which warned him not to snoop.

In no time at all they had returned, suitcase in hand. Warner put her suitcase in the backseat and got into the car, saying, "I think I got everything."

Lilia rolled down her window to wave goodbye to the concierge, mouthing *thank you*, as Warner pulled out of the condominium and out into traffic.

The majority of the drive was spent in a tense silence, until Warner asked, "Are you in any pain?"

"No, I'm okay for now, thanks. The nurse said that I should be okay for at least four hours before needing a pain killer."

"Okay. Once you're settled in your room, I'll go get your prescription filled at the pharmacy. Which one do you use?" Lilia told him.

Upon arriving at a gated house, Warner pulled up to a keypad, rolled down the window, and pressed in a code. They drove through the now open gates and pulled up in front of his house. Once he'd parked, Warner came around to her side to help her out of the car. He was extremely gentle and, when she managed to get out of the car, she was able to take a look at his house.

"Your house is beautiful, Warner," she said as Warner took her suitcase out of the back seat.

"Thank you. I bought it a few years ago and then renovated it to my needs. I hope you feel comfortable here." He stated taking her suitcase inside. "Wait there, I'll come back to help you up the stairs."

Lilia stood there, taking in the beautiful landscaping of the house. She thought he must have a gardener, as his grounds were very well kept.

"Are you ready to see inside?" Warner surprised her by coming back so soon.

"Yes," Lilia smiled at him, "I'm ready. Thank you, Warner."

Warner placed his hand around her waist resting on her hip and the other on her arm, ready to brace her and giving her support as she took each painful step.

"Once we get inside there's only one more flight to go. Then you can stay up there until you are able to do the stairs with no pain."

After what seemed to take forever to Lilia, they finally made it into the guest room, and Warner helped her to sit in a chair in the corner of the room. Once Lilia caught her breath, she took in the beauty of the room. From the big luxurious bed to the comfortable sitting area she was currently in.

"I hope you like your room. The washroom is through this door. Do you want help before I leave for your prescription? I'll get us some dinner as well. I didn't tell Susan we would be here tonight—I had given her time off since I was at the hospital with you. She'll be back tomorrow." Warner rambled on as he placed her suitcase on a bench and opened it.

"I assume you'll want to put everything away yourself, but please don't do too much until I return. I don't want you to hurt yourself, or over do it." Warner stood at the door. "Do you need anything before I go? Anything to drink?"

"Thank you, Warner. I'll be fine until you come back." As Warner turned to walk out Lilia said, "And thank you for letting me stay here. The room is beautiful."

"Don't mention it." He responded. "I'll be back as soon as I can," he said as he left.

Lilia stood, walked slowly to her suitcase, and began putting her things away, working slowly and steadily, careful not to hurt herself. She really wanted to take a shower but didn't trust herself to make it in and out on her own. She certainly wasn't going to allow Warner to help her, so she'd just have to figure it out.

She went into the washroom and closed the door behind her. She slowly got undressed and walked over to the shower and began to run the water. She wasn't quite sure how she was going to do this on her own but decided to do her best with a sponge bath. It would have to do until she was able to ask Susan if she would help her.

After cleaning herself as best as she could, she was brave enough to look in the mirror. She winced as she saw all of the black, blue, and purple discolouration all over her face and chest. She wrapped the towel around her body and went back into the main room. She gasped in surprise to see Warner standing there. "Oh, Warner."

"Lilia," Warner looked at her in her towel and both of them halted.

"Ummmm…" Lilia held the towel tighter around her.

"Did you take a shower? Why didn't you wait for help? You could have hurt yourself."

"I was okay, Warner."

"I came to bring you your prescriptions and dinner. Here." Warner gestured to the table where he'd put everything. "I'll leave you to dress. Just yell for me if you need anything." Warner walked out quickly.

"Thank you, Warner." Lilia said hurriedly before he left.

Lilia took her time dressing, putting on a tee shirt and jogging pants, one of many she had asked him to pack for her. She then sat to eat the meal Warner had thoughtfully brought and take her pain killers.

Knock, knock… she heard the sound on her closed door. "Come in, Warner."

"How are you doing? Did you eat? Take your meds?"

"Yes, I did, thank you for everything, Warner. I really appreciate it."

"I brought up your briefcase, laptop, and purse. I forgot I had them in my office." Warner continued, "I'll be going into the office tomorrow. Susan will be here around eight a.m. I forgot to tell you the television is in this bookcase," he said walking over to open the doors so she could see. "The wifi password is written on this piece of paper," he placed it on the table beside her. "I don't know what you will want to do tomorrow." He walked back to the door, "Do you need anything else?"

"No, Warner. Thanks, I'm fine."

"Okay then. I'll give you a call tomorrow to check in on you."

"Okay. Goodnight, Warner."

"Goodnight, Lilia," He said taking her finished meal away.

# CHAPTER 13

After meeting Susan, Warner's housekeeper, and eating breakfast, the day was quite boring and unadventurous for Lilia. She tried to work on her laptop, but it gave her a headache, so she mostly watched or listened to the tv and walked around trying to exercise a little. Susan had promised to help her have a proper bath in the afternoon before she began preparing dinner. She couldn't even use her cell phone as she'd forgotten to ask Warner to pack her charger. She had no one to call anyways.

Around lunchtime, Susan appeared at Lilia's room door with a phone in her hand. "Ms. Lilia, Mr. Warner is on the phone for you, dear."

"Thank you, Susan, but as I told you this morning, please call me Lilia." She walked over to take the phone from her.

"I won't but thank you, dear." Susan smiled turning away from her and heading towards the stairs. "I'll be back in an hour, dear, to help you get into the bath."

"Thank you, Susan." Lilia said, "Hello," she said, putting her phone to her ear.

"Lilia. How are you?"

"I'm doing fine thanks, Warner. How are you? How's everyone in the office doing?"

"Why haven't you been answering your cell phone?" He asked, ignoring her other questions.

"My phone's dead. I forgot to ask you to bring my charger from my condo. I have one in my desk at the office. Do you mind bringing it for me? It's in my top drawer."

"Of course. I'll bring it home."

"Thanks. How are things in the office, Warner?"

"All is okay. I've had some catch up to play on this Wilkins case. I'm about to meet with John to see what he has. Then I have a meeting with Shawn and Chris. I'm going to ask if the police have contacted them about your attack."

"I haven't heard anything from the detectives." Lilia offered.

"You wouldn't have, as your phone hasn't been on."

"Oh yes, that's right." Lilia remembered.

"I'll come home after meeting with Shawn and Chris, so you can get your charger. I'll work from my home office."

"Are you sure?"

"There's nothing here I need to be here for... if I'm needed there. Am I needed there Lilia?" Warner pushed gently.

"I wouldn't say no to your company. Susan is very kind; however, she's extremely formal and efficient."

Warner laughed gently, "Yes, I've been trying to get her to call me Warner for years. She insists on 'Mr. Warner' and keeping a very scheduled household. Breakfast is ready at eight a.m. sharp, dinner is always ready at five p.m., and she leaves at five thirty p.m. Every day."

Warner continued, "She normally leaves midday and returns in the afternoon, but I did tell her about your injuries and asked if she would stay all day for a week or so until you no longer needed assistance."

"Oh Warner, you didn't have to do that."

"It was either her or me. And I didn't think you wanted me helping you with personal matters, like bathing… dressing." Warner took an audible deep breath, "I don't think I could handle it for that matter."

"Warner…" Lilia's voice trailed off softly.

"I can't even handle thinking about it, Lilia." Warner stated.

"Warner," Lilia stopped him, "I'll see you later?"

"Yes, I'll see you later. Goodbye, Lilia."

"Goodbye, Warner."

Lilia hung up and realized how hot that suggestive conversation had made her. Just the thought of Warner looking at her nude body, helping her dress, touching her skin, had her overheating. She was certainly glad that Susan was going to be helping her into the shower soon. She definitely now needed a cold one. She would tell Susan that cold water was better initially as it was good for healing her bruised ribs.

A couple of hours later, with her shower completed, Lilia tried again to check her email, quickly before a headache again set in. That completed, she took her pain medication and settled back to close her eyes and relax in the sitting area.

"Ah-hem."

"Ah-hem!"

She roused herself at the sound, and asked, "Was I sleeping?"

"I do believe so, since I've come to check on you twice and you haven't moved. I figured I should wake you as it's almost time for dinner."

"Have you been here long?"

"I've been in my office working for a couple of hours. I took the liberty of plugging in your phone for you so it would have some juice when you woke up."

"Thank you," Lilia braced herself on the chair wincing as she sat up.

"How are you feeling?"

"The same, thanks. The pain killers help take the edge off, but they do make me sleepy."

Warner sat in the chair across from her, "I'm sure you need the sleep. The nights can't be easy."

She looked at him in surprise, "No, they aren't. I'm up every four hours or so…" She trailed off, "How was your day? Did you meet with John? Shawn and Chris?"

"I didn't end up meeting with John."

"Why not?"

"I got a call to meet up with a detective that I know. He was actually one of the detectives that made the Wilkins arrest. We go way back and have kept in touch over the years. We were in university together. I decided to go into practicing law and he decided to protect and serve." Warner looked at his hands, like he was considering something.

"Warner? What happened?"

Warner looked at her for several long seconds then sighed, "Some hikers were walking the trails along the Don Valley River. Their dog started barking over a pile of leaves, and when the hikers investigated, they found a decomposing body."

Warner took a deep breath and sighed rubbing his hand over his shaved head and handsome but strained face, "They suspect it to be the missing bail bondsman, Sean Hindson, but the autopsy will confirm." Warner looked at her, worried at how the news would affect her.

"Oh no." Lilia sighed and closed her eyes, "that poor man. His poor family." She shook her head. "Did they say how he died?"

"They haven't released anything formally yet—they have yet to even notify the family—but I was told they suspect foul play."

Lilia laid her face in her hands.

"Why don't you check your messages. See if the detectives contacted you." Warner suggested, plugging out and passing her the phone.

"Are you trying to distract me?"

"Was I that obvious?"

"Absolutely." Lilia stated putting her passcode into her phone.

"I'm going to bring up your dinner, okay?"

"Warner," Lilia paused nervously, "Will you stay and eat with me?"

"Of course." Warner said leaving the room for her to check her messages in private.

Lilia quickly logged into her phone to find; *big surprise* she thought, *no messages!* Lilia made a mental note to contact the detectives in charge of investigating her attack tomorrow to let them know where she was and how to contact her when needed.

Just then, Warner walked back into the room balancing two trays of food in his hands, handing one to her carefully and placing the other on the table. He then produced two bottles of water that were tucked in his trouser pockets. "There we are," he declared smiling.

"Thank you, Warner, it looks delicious."

"That's all Susan. She is a wonderful cook." He said sitting down digging into his food.

They ate in silence, pondering their own thoughts for a while. Setting his food down to drink some water, Warner then said, "Did you hear anything from the detectives?"

"No, they didn't call. I'm going to contact them tomorrow to let them know where I am, in case they're trying to locate me."

"You shouldn't tell too many people where you are, just in case you were targeted for some reason."

"Who would I tell, Warner? I don't have friends. The people I know are the ones at Hale & Cross. Did you tell Shawn and Chris I was staying with you?"

"Yes, it was the only way they wouldn't put a security detail on you, remember? Anyways, they're the only ones from the office that know if you didn't tell anyone."

"Alright. I'll call them tomorrow to let them know how I am too." She said, taking a bite of her delectable meal. "Susan can really cook. I better not gain weight during my stay here."

Warner laughed, "Just eat in moderation, and make sure you walk around, when you can. Did you ice today?"

"Of course. I don't want to look black and blue forever." Lilia smiled.

"Good. I asked Susan to also make sure she kept ice packs accessible for you, every hour or so."

"You sure have asked Susan to do a lot. I don't want her or you to go to extra work having me here," Lilia said.

"Listen to me, Lilia: everything I have done, or have asked Susan to do, it's because I wanted to. If you haven't guessed it already, I care for you... and I want to make sure you're safe. I don't know who attacked you, I only know someone hurt you, and I don't want them to get another chance." Warner finished and stood, "Now, if you're finished eating, I will say goodnight. Do you want tea or something else?"

"Warner." Lilia's words stopped him, "Thank you." Lilia took a deep breath, and avoided his eyes as Warner watched her expectantly, "I... I care for you too." She finished, finding courage to make eye contact with him.

"Goodnight, Lilia," Warner bent over and paused before gently kissing her on her cheek and picking up her tray of half-eaten food.

Lilia placed her hand against her burning cheek and said, "Goodnight, Warner."

# CHAPTER 14

The next few days passed by uneventfully. It seemed as though she would spend each day waiting for five thirty p.m., when Warner would join her for dinner. Every day was the same: Lilia iced her bruises, worked a little, exercised a little, and listened to Susan talk about all of the characters in the soap operas she loved to watch as Susan sat with her after lunch. Then, before dinner, Susan would help her into and out of the shower.

Lilia felt alarmed about how much she actually looked forward to having dinner with Warner every evening. The feeling of excitement and anticipation of waiting to see him was so new for her.

Even though the time they spent together was short, she enjoyed hearing him speak about his day—not because she missed being in the office, but because she enjoyed listening to his voice. She would ask him lots of questions just to make him stay longer each night, but he would always say that he didn't want to tire her out, take their trays, make a comment about her not eating enough, kiss her cheek, and say goodnight.

After Susan helped her out of the shower and she began to get dressed, she was startled out of her thoughts of Warner by the sound of her cell phone ringing. Lilia hurried to her phone as quickly as she could, given her still sore body.

"Hello?" she answered expectantly.

"Hello, may I speak with Ms. Lilia Bennett?" the male voice answered.

"This is Lilia Bennett."

"Ms. Bennett, this is Detective Collins."

"Detective Collins, thank you for returning my phone call. I know how busy you must be. I had just called to update you with where I was staying if you needed me for anything."

"Yes, I got your message, thank you. I'm calling to let you know that we are investigating some leads in your case. We got footage from one of the security cameras provided by your firm. The footage shows the image of a man wearing a baseball cap in the garage around the time you were attacked." He took a breath and continued, "He manages to avoid being caught by the camera, either looking the other way or avoiding the camera completely. We suspect he knew where the cameras were."

"Are you able to identify him?" Lilia questioned nervously.

"Not yet. But we think it may be someone you know."

As Lilia listened to him speak, she heard a soft knock on the door and saw it being gently pushed open by Warner, who then poked his head in. She gestured for him to come in and watched him push the door open more with his foot, with their two trays of food perched in his arms.

"Someone I know?" Lilia repeated. *It's the detective*, she quietly mouthed to Warner. He nodded, and quietly sat in the chair across from her after setting their trays down. "So, you don't believe it was a random attack."

"No, we don't. How are you feeling? Are you well enough to come down to the station to look at the footage? If not, we can come to you."

"Yes, would you be able to come here? I'm not able to drive as of yet, so that would be easier." Warner tilted his head to the side and looked at her curiously.

"Tomorrow work? Around two o'clock?"

"Yes, that would be just fine. See you tomorrow. Thank you, Detective Collins." Lilia hung up the phone.

"What's going on? I got some of it from your end of the conversation."

"They have a photo of him. The guy they think attacked me. The detective said he seemed to be familiar with where all of the cameras in the garage were because he avoided looking directly into any of them. They think the attack was personal." Lilia placed her hands gently against her face. She felt so numb she didn't feel any pain as she touched her face.

"They want to see if I can ID him tomorrow."

"Here? Is that why you said you couldn't drive?" Warner paused, offended. "Why would you say that—you know I would take you."

"I didn't know what your workday looked like. I don't want to inconvenience you. I asked them to come here."

Warner just stared at her in silence, "What time tomorrow?"

"Two o'clock."

"Okay. I'll be here."

"Warner, don't you need to be in the office? Or in a meeting? In court?"

"I need to be here with you." Warner looked directly into Lilia's eyes.

With that statement Lilia started to feel anxiety spill over her. It must have shown on her face, because Warner leaned over and took her hand.

"Look at me," He said softly waiting for Lilia to look at him, "You're okay. You're safe here. I'll be here with you. You are so strong. You can do this. I know it," he affirmed to her.

"I'm afraid Warner."

"Of?" Warner asked her.

"That it's someone I know."

"Whoever it is. He will be discovered. Trust that. Trust that I'm here for you. Whatever you need." He sated while his thumb softly caressed the top of her hand.

"Oh, Warner," Lilia turned her hand over in his, gently squeezing it. "Thank you. You don't know how much that means. I don't have anyone really..." Her voice trailed off.

"You have me now." Warner stated and squeezed her hand, smiling gently, "And we now have cold food that I have to heat up again for us to properly enjoy all of Susan's cooking." He stood up and bent over, kissing her gently on the cheek. He then picked up their plates of food and walked towards the door, "I'll be right back."

While he was gone, she tried to get her composure back by standing up and walking around the room, but all she thought of were his words to her. She stopped to gaze out of the window and as she stared at his immaculate gardens, she realized that she honestly believed him when he said she could trust him. She hadn't been able to trust anyone in a very long time… She hadn't let anyone in close enough to trust them.

Of course, she'd had boyfriends before, but she had never really let them get too close. The pain of how it felt to lose her parents was always in the back of her mind. She didn't want to risk loving someone and losing them again. Now, with spending so much time with Warner, she realized how lonely that was.

"Are you okay?"

She turned around to see Warner standing next to the chairs, the plates of food on the tables beside them. She was so lost in her thoughts; she hadn't heard him return.

"Yes, I'm okay now. How long have you been back?"

"Not long. You were so deep in your thoughts, I thought I'd give you a minute or two. But I also didn't want to have to go back downstairs to warm up the food again." Warner smiled, "Are you ready to eat?"

"I sure am." Lilia stated walking over to her seat.

They both began eating in quiet, enjoying the food that Susan had prepared… as usual.

"How was your day today? Have you heard any more news about Sean Hindson? Melinda? What about Wilkins? Have you met with John yet?"

"You miss being in the office, don't you?" Warner stated more than asked. He wiped his mouth with his napkin and continued, "Okay, for your first question, my day was okay. I haven't met with John yet, I was supposed to meet with him tomorrow, but I'll email him and push it to Monday. I haven't heard any more about Hindson. I haven't had any new information, and no," he stressed, "I do not want you investigating anything. Take time to heal. And with that… how are you feeling today?"

"I'm okay. I'm starting to feel better. Less sore, even though I look a mess. In line with what Dr Webber said to expect. I don't need the pain killers as much now. I am taking them at wider intervals."

Warner smiled, "I'm glad to hear it. And you don't look bad, just slightly wounded. You'll be healed before you know it." He continued, "Now, what else were you interrogating me on?"

Showing indifference to his choice of words, Lilia said, "I also asked about Melinda and Wilkins?"

Warner smiled again, "Shawn and Chris have arranged Melinda's memorial."

"When is it?"

"Tuesday." Warner stared at her.

"Don't worry, I won't go. As much as I want to pay my respects, I don't think I'll be well enough. And I will still look pretty beaten up." Lilia chuckled.

"I just don't want you to push yourself." Warner explained.

"I know. Thank you for caring."

"I do." Warner continued, "What can I say about Wilkins…" he trailed off, "I haven't met with him since the last time, but I'm glad that he remanded himself into custody. The streets feel a lot safer with him off of them."

"Yeah. So, it wasn't him."

"Wasn't him what?"

"It wasn't Wilkins that attacked me. If he hadn't been in jail, I would have thought it was him."

Warner sighed.

"You thought that too, didn't you?" Lilia questioned him.

"I did."

They both grew quiet again, "I should let you get some rest now." He said rising to his feet, "it's getting late."

He approached her, seated, and bent over, resting one hand on the armrest to brace himself. Lilia immediately felt her heartbeat speed up and her body warm up. His hand lightly touched her chin, his finger gently lifting her face to raise her eyes to his.

"Do you trust me?" He said softly.

"Yes, I do, Warner." Lilia sighed closing her eyes, ready to feel his lips against hers.

Warner's head bent even closer, and she felt his lips softly caress hers. As he felt her respond, he deepened it, running his hand gently along her jaw line to the back of her neck, gently caressing her.

Lilia raised her hand to caress the side of his face and heard him groan. When he ended the kiss and backed away slowly, Lilia forced her eyes open to look at him, and saw that his eyes were still closed.

"W-W-Warner?" Lilia stammered.

He opened his eyes and looked at her, took a deep breath and said, "I'll take the dishes down. Goodnight, Lilia. I look forward to seeing you tomorrow. I'll work from my office downstairs, so I'll be home if you need me, okay?"

"Okay," Lilia said managing to get out the one word.

Once Warner turned and left the room, Lilia raised her hand to her chest, over her heart, hoping she could calm it down just by willing it so. By the time Lilia made it into her bed and under the covers, she had replayed the kiss with Warner over so many times in her mind, her heart maintained a steady quick rhythm, until she eventually fell asleep.

# CHAPTER 15

The next day passed quickly, as she felt both anxious and restless waiting for two o'clock and Detective Collins to arrive. Warner came up to the sitting room to join her for lunch around noon, greeting her with a kiss on the cheek and asking her if she felt well enough to meet the detectives on the main floor or if she wanted them upstairs in her sitting room. She decided that she would brave the stairs after lunch and join everyone on the main floor for the first time since her arrival.

After they ate, Warner left her to change her clothes. "I'll come back in, say, twenty minutes? To help you down the stairs?"

"Twenty minutes is more than enough time." Lilia said, "Thank you, Warner."

Lilia dressed slowly, picking out the dressiest jogging suit she had. She combed her hair, slowly putting it back into a low ponytail, which was the easiest style to do considering her bruised ribs were still healing.

She heard Warner knock on the door, announcing his presence. "I'm ready," she called out, "You can come in."

He opened the door and waited for her to join him. "How are you feeling?"

Knowing he was asking about meeting the detectives, she answered, "I'm nervous. I don't want to be able to identify him, and yet I do so this can be over. You know what I mean?"

"I understand that."

When they approached the stairs, Lilia paused and Warner said, "One step at a time. I'll be right here." He took her arm in one hand and placed the other one on her waist at her back. "Ready?" Lilia nodded.

Once they finally arrived on the main floor, Warner helped Lilia into a chair in the sitting room. "Are you okay?"

"I'm okay. A little sore, but okay."

"I asked Susan to get some ice packs ready for you. Do you want them?"

"Yes, thanks for thinking of it."

"I'll get them."

Warner left the room and when he came back, he stated, "The detectives are here," He handed her the ice packs.

"Thanks, Warner." Lilia said placing the ice packs on her complaining ribs. "I just need a minute." Lilia closed her eyes in bliss at the instant ease.

"I'll bring them in, okay?"

"For sure."

Warner walked out of the room, leaving Lilia alone with her thoughts. She spent a lot of time thinking about things she never in her life thought she would. One realization she'd come to was that as life could be so short and tomorrow not promised, she needed to live it. In the past, she'd thought it was better to remove relationships from her life so when they ended she wouldn't be hurt. Now she knew differently. And she planned to act differently when she was finally feeling more like herself. When it didn't hurt to move.

"Lilia is waiting for you in here." She heard Warner speaking to the detectives, before she saw them walk through the door.

"Ms. Bennett." Detective Collins said as he approached Lilia, "Thanks for meeting with us. How are you feeling?" He asked as he reached out to shake her hand.

"I'm still sore but healing more every day. Thank you for asking. I'm glad to. I want to help you find who did this."

"You remember Detective Gregg?"

"Yes, I do. It's nice to see you again, Detective." Lilia reached out to shake his hand as well.

"You as well, Ms. Bennett."

The detectives both took a seat across from Lilia, and Detective Collins placed the folder he was holding down on the table.

"Would you be comfortable with us taping our session, Ms. Bennett? As we're not at the station, we need to have the documentation if you are able to ID the man in the photo."

"Yes, of course."

At that, Detective Gregg pulled out a recorder and placed it on the table in front of them.

"Detective Collins and Gregg, attending an interview with Ms. Lilia Bennett." Detective Collins continued explaining that they were not conducting the interview in the station and the purpose for the interview. "Present also is Warner Reid, colleague and friend of Ms. Bennett's, attending at her request. Is that all correct, Ms. Bennett?"

"Yes, that's correct," stated Lilia.

"Ms. Bennett, this is the stilled photo from the security footage obtained from Hale, Cross & Associates, who voluntarily provided the footage." Detective Gregg picked up the folder from the table and passed it over to Lilia. He continued to narrate as Lilia paused before opening the folder. She looked up and her eyes found Warner's, who nodded at her and mouthed quietly, *You can do this. I'm here*.

Lilia looked back down at the folder and began to open it slowly.

"Oh!" Lilia said in surprise as she felt chills and shock run through her body.

"Ms. Bennett?" Detective Collins called out, though Lilia didn't quite hear him. "Can you identify the person in the photo, Ms. Bennett?"

"Oh no," Lilia couldn't make any other words out.

"Lilia!" Warner said worriedly, taking a step towards her. Detective Gregg held an arm out to stop him from coming any closer.

"Lilia, you can do this, please. You need to tell the detectives," Warner pleaded.

"Warner," Lilia started, tears in her eyes, "it's Jeff."

"Jeff?" Warner asked.

"Jeff whom? Ms. Bennett, we need a first and last name if you know it. What is the name of the man in this photo?"

"You think he attacked me?"

"This is the only footage we got of his face. Every other camera angle, including the footage of the actual attack is of the clothing, but it's the same person. Ms. Bennett, are you saying that you know this person?"

"Yes, I know him." Lilia said looking at Warner, one tear rolling down her cheek.

"Tell them, Lilia." Warner said quietly.

"It's Jeff." Lilia stated, "Jeff Sanders."

"And who is Jeff Sanders to you, Ms. Bennett?"

"He's a security guard at the firm. At Hale & Cross."

Detective Gregg immediately got up and walked out of the room with his phone in his hand and begun dialing.

"Thank you, Ms. Bennett. I understand how hard this was for you, and I'm going to ask you to confirm for me. Please look at the photo again and just confirm the identity of the person you see."

Lilia looked down at the photo one more time and wiped the tears from her eyes.

"I am confirming the identity of the person I see as Jeff Sanders, security guard at Hale, Cross & Associates. I know him as working the night shift. When I would leave the building, I would see him at the security desk or doing rounds in the parking garage." Lilia stopped, then started again now angry, "Why?" She looked at the detective, "Why did he do this to me?"

"We will do our best to find out, Ms. Bennett. Thank you for your time." Detective Collins turned off the recorder and spoke again, now gesturing that Warner could join Lilia. Warner hurriedly walked over to her and placed a comforting hand on her shoulder.

"Detective Gregg has gone to put an APB out for Jeff Sanders as a person of interest, see if we can locate him and pick him up for questioning."

Lilia nodded, finding comfort in Warner's support, while Detective Collins rose to his feet pocketing the recorder and taking the now offensive folder from her.

"I'm going to see them out and I'll be right back, Lilia. Okay?" Warner said, and Lilia nodded again.

"I'll be in touch, Ms Bennett. I'm sure we'll have answers soon and I hope you heal quickly."

"Thank you, Detective."

Warner walked out with the Detective, then returned within minutes. He knelt down in front of her and placed his hands on her knees. "How are you feeling? Are you okay?" he asked.

"I just can't believe it, Warner. I spoke to him every day. Why would he attack me?"

"I don't know, Lilia, but we're going to find out." Warner stated, rubbing her knees gently.

"Have you seen him?" Lilia asked, "Has he been at the office?"

"I don't think so. I haven't really been looking. I've been leaving early most days. Honestly, I've been trying to get home for dinner by five p.m. every day." Warner made eye contact with Lilia and smiled.

Lilia smiled back at him, "I've enjoyed having dinner with you every day too."

"Do you want to call Shawn? Find out if he's been at work? Or do you want me to call him?"

"Do you mind calling? I don't really feel like talking about it in depth."

Warner got off the floor to get his phone out. As he dialed, Lilia said, "Please tell Shawn not to say anything. I know I'm not wrong in my identification, but what if the police are wrong and he didn't attack me, and he just happened to be in the garage? I don't want him to lose his reputation or his job because of mistaken identity." Lilia said trying to give him the benefit of the doubt.

"Innocent until proven guilty, eh?" Warner said, "The detectives said that the person you identified was the same person, wearing the same clothing, as the person that attacked you." Warner shook his head and rubbed his hand over his head and face.

"What, Warner?" She now knew that he rubbed his head and face when he was annoyed.

"I don't have what you have."

"And that is?" She said, prepared for a fight.

Warner looked at her, "Your grace." He said quietly, "I'll call Shawn, just to find out if he was there and let him know the state of the investigation. I'll tell him not to say or do anything about it, as you don't want him convicted before his trial. You just want to keep him and Chris informed. Okay?"

"Thank you."

"I'll come back to help you back upstairs so that Susan can help you with your shower."

"You knew she was helping me every day?"

"Of course," he smiled and left the room.

When Warner returned, Lilia was walking around the room slowly.

"What are you doing?" Warner asked.

"Exercising. I usually try to do some type of activity before Susan helps me shower. I find it helps me sleep."

Warner's eyes squinted, "I don't remember the doctor saying you should exercise."

"What did Shawn say?" Lilia blatantly changed the subject, then turned to look out of the window.

Warner shook his head and answered. "I had to wait while he contacted the security department and logged into the payroll system to find out his attendance." He started, sitting down in the chair that Lilia had vacated.

He sighed, "Lilia," he said her name to get her attention, so she turned around to look at him, "Jeff Sanders hasn't been at work since your attack. He called in sick the next two days, then requested a leave of absence."

# CHAPTER 16

"What does that mean?" Lilia said looking at Warner, "What are you saying?"

"I'm not saying anything, Lilia. Whatever happened, for whatever reason he hasn't been at work," Warner paused, "If he had anything to do with your attack—" Warner stopped, not finishing his sentence, his hands clenched at his sides.

"Warner," Lilia said walking over to him and reaching out slowly to touch his hand, "It can't be Jeff. He's always been kind to me," Lilia said thoughtfully.

Warner looked down at her hand touching his and slowly unclenched his fist turning his hand into hers so that their fingers intertwined. They looked into each other's eyes, and Lilia continued, "Jeff always seems to watch out for me, he's so friendly. He's married with children. He brought me donuts…" She reasoned, trailing off as she realized she never actually received any donuts.

"It seems like you're trying to find excuses for yourself as to why he couldn't have done it. None of those excuses are reasons though. You know that, right?" Warner stared at her.

"I know. I just don't want to believe that anyone I know could do that to me."

"I understand that. But if he had anything to do with it…" He shook his head, "the police will find out. Shawn is calling the detectives to let them know he hasn't been at work." Lilia sighed as Warner continued, "And I am going to call John. I have several missed calls from him. Will you give me a minute?" He said as he walked out of the room with his phone in his hand.

While he was on his call, Lilia decided that she try to make it upstairs by herself, as she was feeling less pain and feeling more confident. She wanted to see if she could work, check her email and voicemail.

It took her some time to get there, but she was almost to the top of the staircase when she heard Warner calling her name.

"Lilia, why didn't you wait for me? Or ask Susan to help?"

Lilia didn't stop and took the last two remaining steps before she turned around at the top.

"I'm starting to feel less pain, Warner. Going up is much easier than going down the stairs anyways, and I wanted to get started on some work."

Warner remained at the bottom of the stairs, shaking his head. "I'm going to the office. The investigators found something. John wants to show me."

"Do you know what it is?" Lilia questioned.

"He wouldn't tell me over the phone. He wants me to see it. I'll see you when I get back. Do you need anything?"

"I'm alright, thanks. Susan is here. We'll be fine. Thanks." Lilia smiled at Warner and said, "See you later."

"See you when I get back."

Lilia turned and walked to her sitting room, now turned office, to check her email. She also sent one to the associates Grace and Carl to let them know she was ready to help them work on any cases. She had contacted Carl by phone earlier in the week to thank him for saving her and to let him know that she was doing okay.

Once Grace had responded, making the obligatory *hope you're doing okay and we're all thinking of you* and *hope you come back soon* statements, she then listed all of the work she needed done. Lilia smiled and was grateful for the work. She felt needed. Back where she belonged.

No sooner had she started working than she heard Warner's voice calling for her from downstairs. She looked at the time and saw that hours had passed since she had first begun. Suddenly, knocking on her door replaced the sound of her name being called.

"Come in, Warner." The door opened and taking one look at Warner's face, Lilia asked, "What happened?"

Warner came in and sat down beside Lilia. "Lilia," Warner started, staring at her.

Lilia grew more worried, as she waited for Warner to release the information that was causing him stress. "Warner?"

"I met with John." Warner began, "Shawn asked him to go through all of the security videos from the last month or so. They used facial recognition software to track Jeff Sanders whenever he was in the building." Warner looked directly into Lilia's eyes, "Most days he was in for his scheduled shifts, in and out on time." Warner then reached out to take Lilia's hand in his, "There were two times that he was at the firm when he wasn't on shift. John double checked the schedule. Both times he went into your office."

"That can't be true," Lilia said in disbelief.

"It's true, Lilia. I saw it myself." Warner continued insistently, "Once you almost caught him. You arrived just as he was leaving. You stopped and spoke to him."

"Oh my gosh," Lilia said in resolution, "that must have been the day he said he had donuts."

"Yes! He walked in carrying a box. He walked around the floor offering it to everyone before he entered your office."

"Do you remember anything missing? That day he left with something. It seemed like there was a bulge under his coat. In the footage, you can see it falling out at the bottom and he pushes it back."

Lilia thought back trying to recall the day. "That day... I noticed... my briefcase was on my chair and the files were disorganized inside. I thought I'd lost it." Lilia said thoughtfully, "That was the day we were meeting with Wilkins. I was so out of it afterwards."

"Was anything missing, Lilia?" Warner said insistently.

"I don't know. I didn't notice anything…"Lilia said, "I'll have to check my briefcase, my office… a lot has happened in the last few days Warner. I need time to think."

"I'm sorry. I don't want to put pressure on you, but we need to find out to know what he wanted."

"I know. I want to know too. I'll check my briefcase."

Warner got to his feet, "I'll get you something to eat while you're checking."

"I'm not hungry, Warner."

"You need to eat." Warner said insistently, "I'll be right back."

Lilia began going through every file, trying to recall exactly which cases she had been working on for all of the associates. Seeing that each file was there, she didn't notice that any were missing. *There has to be something I'm missing.* Lilia thought to herself. "Just check again," she said softly to herself.

Opening each file, and going through them thoroughly one more time, Lilia realized that a couple of items out of one file was indeed missing.

"Warner!" Lilia shouted, then cringed at the pain she'd caused herself.

"I'm right here," he said as he walked in carrying a plate of food, "Did you find something?"

"It's Wilkins."

"Wilkins's file?"

"Not his whole file, just all of the photos. All the pictures of him that John gave me! From when we tried to alibi him and John found proof he was in town when the witnesses were murdered."

"And you're sure you didn't leave them in your desk? Or give them back to John?"

"I normally keep each file organized. I can't be totally sure they aren't in my desk until you check tomorrow." Lilia said with a smile.

"I'll definitely check tomorrow. And if they aren't there, my next call is to John."

# CHAPTER 17

The next morning, Lilia waited impatiently for Warner's call. He left early to go straight to her office to look for the missing photos.

"Come on, Warner." Lilia whispered at her phone willing it to ring.

Instead of a ring, there was a knock on the door, "Come in!" Lilia called.

"Good morning, Ms. Bennett. Mr. Warner said to be sure to bring you breakfast this morning, since you didn't eat last night. He said not to trust you to come down for it." Susan said entering the room with a tray full of food in her hand.

"I wasn't hungry." Lilia answered feeling chastised.

"Well, I won't be blamed for not feeding you. I'll be back in thirty minutes to take your empty plate." Susan demanded placing the tray down on the table, then walking out.

Lilia tried not to roll her eyes as she knew Susan was following Warner's directions, but instantly got distracted by her ringing phone.

"Warner?"

"Lilia."

"Well? Did you find them?" She questioned.

"No. I couldn't find them. I looked everywhere." He continued, "I'm going to call John and let him know to start looking for any connection between Sanders and Wilkins."

"Will you also let Shawn and Chris know?"

"I'll go see them after I put John on it."

"Alright. I'm going to call Detective Collins and see if they've had any luck finding Jeff. If not, maybe there's a way we can weed him out." Lilia said thoughtfully.

"Don't do anything, Lilia. Leave it to the cops. And John. Let them handle it." Warner said.

"I won't do anything…" Lilia said, "Unless it's something that could really help."

"Lilia," Warner said warningly.

"Gotta go! Let me know what John says!" she said quickly. "See you for dinner!"

Lilia disconnected before Warner could say anything else.

Lilia then found the detectives card to give him a call.

"Collins." He answered.

"Detective Collins?" Lilia asked, "this is Lilia Bennett. I just wanted to get in touch to see if you were able to find Jeff Sanders."

"I'm sorry, Ms. Bennett, he hasn't turned up yet. When we find him, we'll bring you in to ID him."

"Our internal investigation team found some information I'd like to tell you about, Detective." Lilia filled him in that they suspected Sanders of taking information from her office.

"That's very interesting, Ms. Bennett. Please have that evidence sent over to me as soon as you can."

"I will." Lilia continued, "Also, Detective Collins... I have an idea I wanted to pass by you quickly. I think it could help get Sanders come out of hiding."

"Please leave it to us, Ms. Bennett. We have eyes out looking for him. I don't want you to put yourself in harm's way. Please just have that information sent to me so we can investigate further."

"Okay, Detective." Lilia answered. She hung up, irritated, thinking, *If they aren't going to find him, I will. I just need a little help…*

As opposed to calling Warner, Lilia decided to text him. *Hi! I know you're busy filling everyone in, but when you have time, can you give me a call please? I spoke with Detective Collins. I have an idea!*

*Yes, I am busy. I said not to do anything.* Warner texted back.

*I haven't done anything. Yet. I need your help.*

When Lilia got no response back, she didn't know whether to take it as a good or bad sign.

Half an hour later, Susan was happy as her breakfast was eaten and Lilia was nervously anticipating Warner's phone call. Hours went by and instead of calling her, Lilia smiled as she looked up from her laptop to see Warner leaning against the door jam.

"Okay. So, what's this idea of yours?" Warner said with a sigh.

# CHAPTER 18

"Hello, Mrs. Sanders?" Lilia said speaking into the phone, while Warner sat watching her. "Hello? Who is this?"

"Mrs. Sanders, this is Ms. Candice Crawford from the HR department at Hale, Cross & Associates. I wanted to speak with Mr. Jeff Sanders, please?"

"His job? Jeff isn't here. What is this about?"

"Mr. Sanders requested an emergency leave of absence, effective immediately. Our company policy, in the event of an emergency, is to continue to pay the employee for at least a month so that they, and their family can be comfortably supported during the leave. We just need him to come in, sign the paperwork, and accept the cheque," Lilia lied.

"Jeff isn't home and hasn't been home for a couple of days. I don't know when he'll be back. He was going to visit his mother in Montreal. Can I come in and accept the cheque? I'm his wife."

"Unfortunately not, Mrs. Sanders. It must be signed by the employee. I will put a note on his file that you were contacted about it. Maybe you can contact him to let him know that the cheque is waiting for him? Unfortunately, if he doesn't come in to sign off on the cheque within the next ten days, we will consider that a refusal of payment."

"I've tried to call him, and he hasn't answered the phone. We could really use the money; Jeff just took off to his mothers."

"I'm sorry, Mrs. Sanders. Can you contact him again, or his mother? Get word to him about the cheque." Lilia stated.

"I'll try."

"Thank you, Mrs. Sanders. Please take care." Lilia said, hanging up the phone.

"So that's how you do it. You're good." Warner said after she made sure the phone was disconnected.

"Now, we hope that she contacts him and that he comes into the office."

"We need to contact Shawn and John, let them know the plan. John can put his people in the security team so that they know if he comes."

Knock, knock. They both started as there was a knock on the door. "Susan?"

The door opened and Susan came in balancing two trays of food. "Are you two ever going to stop working? I've had your dinner ready for quite some time now waiting for you to come and get it, Mr. Warner. You know I like you to eat my food fresh!" Susan scolded.

"I'm sorry, Susan, we were working and lost track of time." Warner said.

"Yes. I know you did. First, Ms. Lilia was working so hard I didn't want to disturb her, then you come home, and you work even longer," she continued.

"Thank you so much, Susan. We do appreciate you. You shouldn't be working so late though." Warner stated.

"Oh, not to worry. My George has plans tonight. Out with his friends so I'd be going home to an empty house tonight anyways," Susan explained, referring to her husband. "Once you have finished eating, I can see if Ms. Lilia needs help with her shower, and then I'll make my way home."

"I should be fine, Susan. The last couple of nights I've barely needed your help. I've been feeling stronger and stronger every day."

"Yes, that's true, Ms. Lilia, you have been doing it mostly on your own, but I'd hate to leave you just in case you needed me."

"It's okay, Susan," Warner said, "If an emergency happens, I can help her." They both looked at Warner in shock. "I'll keep my eyes closed," he continued with a chuckle, "Look, I'm sure Lilia will be just fine, Susan. She climbed the stairs all on her own today like a champ." Lilia smiled.

"I should be able to go back home soon I think, since I'm able to take care of myself, and I don't have stairs at my place," Lilia stated.

"You still have to be able to drive, and…" Warner started, but was interrupted by Susan.

"Alright then, since you have it all under control, I'll leave you to eat, and I'll be going then, Mr. Warner."

"Thanks again for bringing up the food. I'll make sure your kitchen is clean." Warner smiled.

"You do that. Goodbye." Susan said leaving the room.

"Now back to this nonsense of you moving back home." Warner said looking at Lilia.

"What do you mean nonsense? I am getting more and more self-sufficient every day. My facial bruising is clearing up, so I should even be able to show my face back at the office soon."

"It's not just that, Lilia." Lilia looked at him questioningly. "Someone attacked you, and that person is free, whether it's Jeff Sanders or someone else," Warner said seriously.

Lilia nodded slowly, "There is that."

"Right now, here is the safest place for you. At least until he's caught."

"Yes, I agree, Warner."

"Great, now let's eat this food while it's still 'fresh,'" Warner smiled, mocking Susan.

"Let's. I just realized how hungry I am!"

After they had eaten for a while in comfortable silence, Lilia said, "Once I am feeling up to it, I would like to go back to work though."

"We can do that."

"Would you be able to take me back to my place first? So, I can get work clothes, and possibly my car if I'm okay to drive?"

Warner looked at her for a moment, chewing slowly, "Clothes of course, I think we should wait until the doctor clears you to drive though. When's your appointment?"

"Tomorrow, actually." Warner stared at her again with a questioning look on his face. "I asked Susan to take me. I had figured you would be at the office, so…." Lilia's voice trailed off.

"Lilia, I definitely would like to be there."

"I know that, now."

"Do you want me to take you to your appointment?"

"If you want to come and you are not busy."

"No, Lilia. Do you want me there? If you wanted me there and I had an appointment I would cancel it. Do you want me there?" Warner asked her again, staring directly into her eyes.

"Yes, Warner. I would like it if you came." Lilia said looking back at him, "I'll let Susan know in the morning that you'll take me."

"I'll work from home tomorrow and we can go. What time is your appointment?"

"One o'clock."

"I'll make myself available by twelve, then we can go, okay?"

"Great. Thank you."

"You don't need to thank me. I want to be with you. I want to make sure you're okay."

"I'm going to be okay, Warner." Lilia reached out to touch his hand as it rested on his tray, balancing it.

"Let's see what Dr. Webber says." Warner said smiling, reaching out to place his other hand on top of hers, rubbing the top with his thumb, "Are you finished your supper?"

"Yes, thank you." Lilia said.

Warner took her tray and balanced them both, "I am going to go downstairs and clean up Susan's kitchen now."

"Okay, I'm going to have a shower."

"Call me if you need anything. I'll check on you after the kitchen sparkles."

"Okay, I will." At Lilia's response, Warner smiled and left the room.

Lilia moved as quickly and as safely as she could through the showering process, determined to be ready in her jogging pants by the time Warner came to check on her.

And when he knocked, she had just finished getting dressed, and was just settling in the seating area reading a book on her tablet.

"What are you reading?" Warner asked.

"A book about time management for attorneys."

"Ha!" Warner laughed, "Of course you are!"

Lilia just shook her head, "As you can see, I was fine. I showered on my own, barely any pain."

"Good. Glad to hear it. Now that I know you and the kitchen are sparkling clean, I will be in my office doing a bit of work. I'll call Shawn and John in the morning to let them know what we're up to."

"Alright. Goodnight, Warner."

"Goodnight, Lilia," Warner said as he came closer to her, leaned over and grasped her chin gently. She raised her head to him, closing her eyes, ready to accept his kiss.

She felt his lips ever so gently touch hers, his tongue gently licked her lip, requesting admittance, which she granted, slowly opening her lips to accept his.

She heard his quiet groan as she felt him pull away from her slowly, "It's getting harder to stop kissing you," Warner moaned.

Lilia smiled shyly, "I haven't asked you to, have I?"

Warner smiled and shook his head, "You better be careful with those playful words. I may take you seriously the next time you let me kiss you."

Lilia smiled and said, "You should. Goodnight, Warner."

"Goodnight, Lilia. I will not sleep tight."

Lilia smiled at Warner's back as he walked out of the room closing the door behind him.

* * *

The next morning, Lilia didn't see Warner, though he filled her thoughts as she worked and got ready for her doctor's appointment. At precisely twelve o'clock, Lilia heard Warner knock on the door.

At Doctor Webber's office, Lilia was examined and then waited with Warner to hear the doctor's assessment.

"Your bruises are healing very nicely, Ms. Bennett. It is obvious that you have been icing and exercising. As you continue to feel better you should be able to resume your regular activities."

"That's great to hear, Doctor. I wanted to ask you if I can drive?" Lilia asked and she heard Warner breathe out loudly beside her.

"Once you feel up to it, you should be able to do short drives, twenty to thirty minutes. Once you're able to move your legs up and down comfortably with no rib pain, try a short drive."

"Thank you, Doctor," Lilia stated.

"You're free to go, unless you have any other questions. If anything comes up and you want to make another appointment you can; just give my assistant a call, and she'll book you in."

"Thank you," Lilia repeated, "I don't have any questions. I feel better every day."

"Good, good," Doctor Webber said, "Take care, Ms. Bennett, Mr. Reid."

"Take care, Doctor."

Once Warner settled her in the car and then got into the driver's side he asked, "Do you want to stop by your place and get some of the things you wanted? Work clothes and stuff? Or are you too tired?"

"I feel fine. We can go. I'd like to check my place, get my things."

"Let's go then."

"Did you get to call Shawn and John this morning? Tell them what we did?"

"What we did or what you did?" Warner smiled and looked over at her quickly, "Yes, I did. I told them that we could hopefully expect for Jeff Sanders to show his face at the office. John said he'd handle it. I left it at that.

I don't know what he's planning. I'm not questioning a former Marine."

"John was a former Marine? That explains so much."

"I'm surprised you didn't know. I thought you knew everyone's personal story in the office."

"John is a little intimidating, and he's a man of very few words. I don't think we've ever had a conversation that wasn't about a case."

"It definitely took me a couple of years to get more than a one-word answer from him." Warner said as they pulled and parked in front of her building.

As they entered the lobby, Lilia greeted the concierge, "Hi George! How are you? How is your family?"

"My family and I are doing quite well, Ms. Bennett. Thank you for asking. How are you? I was told that you were going to be away for a while due to injury. Are you returning today?"

"Not yet unfortunately, George. I've just come to pick up a few more items. This is my friend, Warner Reid. He's going to help me collect some things."

"Good afternoon, Mr. Reid. Oh, and Ms. Bennett, there has been an envelope couriered for you, I'll just get it for you. And there have been quite a few notes made from the evening concierge of a gentleman coming by asking for you."

"Thank you, George. Did anyone get identification from him? Was there a message left?"

"No, just notes that someone was asking for you. It may have been the same man that was here a couple of days ago when I started my shift. When I came in to relieve

Ben in the morning, we stopped a man from trying to go up in the elevator. He was trying to convince another tenant to use their fob to let them onto your floor. When we approached him, he left."

"Are there security cameras here?" Warner asked.

"We do have cameras that back up onto the main hard drive every twenty-four hours. I don't have access to them, unfortunately."

"George, Ms. Bennett was attacked and has relocated for her safety. We will be informing the police to get access to the security footage. What day was he here?"

"Oh no! I'm so sorry, Ms. Bennett. I had no idea! He was here two days ago."

"Did he have any prominent features that you can recall?"

"Not really, he was wearing a baseball cap, and a large coat which covered his frame," George replied thoughtfully, "And he did have some cuts and bruises on his face."

"Thank you, George. If he comes back again, please contact the police."

"If you can find out who we need to contact for the security camera footage, we'll go upstairs, pack her things, and be back down in about a half hour to get it from you. Does that work?" Warner asked the now flustered concierge.

"Yes. I'll get on it right now. Please let me know if I can do anything else. I'm truly sorry that this happened to you, Ms. Bennett. I'll do whatever I can to help."

"Thanks, George. We'll be right back."

They took the elevator up to Lilia's condo in silence, and upon entering Lilia asked Warner, "Do you think it was him? Do you think it was Jeff?"

"I don't know Lilia, but it seems probable that it was. For some reason, Jeff attacked you. And he didn't succeed—he could still be looking for whatever it is he wanted, and he thinks you have it."

"But what could I have that Jeff could want?! I don't have anything."

"Even if you don't have anything, he thinks you have it, which makes keeping you safe very important."

"This is just too much… Can we just get my stuff and go?" Lilia made her way to a closet and removed a suitcase from it.

"Here, let me help you. The doctor just said you were recovering. Do you want to reinjure yourself?" Warner took the suitcase away from her, "Take out what you want to take with you, and I'll pack it, okay?

"Okay," Lilia said making her way to her closet.

After packing work clothes and more odds and ends that she thought she'd need for the next couple of weeks, they went back to meet George at the concierge desk.

"Ms. Bennett, here is your mail. I took the liberty of collecting it from your box for you, as well as your couriered package. This is the information for security's head office, you can contact them for the security videos." He handed everything to Lilia.

"Thank you for your help, George. I really appreciate it." Lilia said placing everything into her bag.

"I hope you feel better soon, Ms. Bennett, and that the police find the guy that hurt you."

"Take care, George." Warner said leading Lilia to the door.

After Warner helped her into the car and put her suitcase in, he asked her for the contact information, so that he could call John with it.

"I thought you were going to give it to the police?"

"The police will take too long. John can get the information and if we find out it is Jeff Sanders, we can give the evidence to them. What if it just happens to be someone you know. A long lost relative?" Warner said picking up his phone to call John.

"I don't have long lost relatives; both my parents were only children."

"What about grandparents? Nobody?"

"Nope, all deceased. No family that I know of. Are you going to make that call so we can go?"

"Yeah," Warner said quietly, while he dialed John's number. "John. It's Warner Reid. I have some information I need you to follow up on." Warner told John what happened.

Warner then grew silent, while John spoke to him.

"Okay," Warner said, "I'll let Lilia know. We'll come in tomorrow."

"What did John say?" Lilia asked when Warner got off the phone.

"He discovered something he wants to tell us about. About Sanders."

"He didn't tell you what it's about?"

"No, but will you be okay to go in with me tomorrow?"

"Yes, definitely. I'm glad we went to get my work clothes."

Once the arrived at Warner's place, Susan greeted them at the door.

"I was just about to leave, Mr. Warner. I have left your dinner in the oven, please eat while the food is fresh. I'm sure Ms. Lilia is just starving right about now. I don't know why you would keep her out all day." Susan accused.

"Thank you, Susan. We will eat right away. I'm quite hungry, aren't you, Lilia?" Warner asked, ignoring all of the other things Susan was saying.

"Yes, I am. Thank you so much, Susan. I'll just wash up and head to the kitchen."

"I'll put your suitcase upstairs and then meet you."

"I hope your appointment went well, Ms. Lilia."

"Yes, it did, thank you. The doctor said I was recovering quite well."

"Well, that's great news, though there was no doubt."

"Thank you, Susan. I'll be going into work with Warner tomorrow."

"Well, don't let him work you too hard. Goodbye, Ms. Lilia."

"Have a great evening, Susan." Lilia said, Susan already out of the door.

A few minutes later, Warner came down the stairs and said, "I just got off the phone with John. He has secured the video footage from your building's security department, and he is having the team review it as we speak. He'll fill us in tomorrow."

"Wow, John works fast."

"He and his team are the best. Shawn and Chris only work with the best."

"Does that include you?"

"I am one of them." Warner said confidently. "All of my clients were convicted because they were guilty and we pleaded out, or they're walking free because they were innocent. Wilkins, now... He may break my record." Warner said, sitting down to join her at the kitchen table.

"Nothing's changed with him?"

"Of course not," Warner stated, taking a sip of water, "If the witnesses in his case were still alive, we would have gone to trial already. Unfortunately, he sees their deaths as his 'get out of jail free' card." Warner continued, "If we find proof that he had something to do with their deaths, that he and Sanders worked together..." His voice trailed off.

"You can't do anything about it, Warner."

"I know," He sighed.

They ate the rest of their meal in silence, then Warner cleaned the kitchen while Lilia went upstairs to shower and change. Just as she had finished responding to emails and opening the mail George had given her, she heard a knock on the door.

"Come in, Warner."

Opening the door Warner said, "I just wanted to check, see if you needed anything?"

"I'm fine. I'm looking forward to going in tomorrow."

"Shawn and Chris will be glad to see you." Warner continued seriously, "We'll only stay for an hour or so, just long enough to meet with John, then I'll bring you back."

Lilia took a breath, getting ready for a fight, "I think I want to go back to work."

Warner stared at her for a second before saying, "What?! Why?!"

"I'm practically healed. I feel like I'm not being used to my fullest being here. I'm not practicing law."

"I thought you were helping Grace and Carl research their cases?"

"I am. It's not the same. I need to be there physically working, Warner."

"I think it's too soon. With Jeff still out there…"

"I think if I'm at the firm, it could help flush him out. If he's looking for me and he knows I'm there., he's more likely to show up."

Lilia's comment was met with silence, so she continued, "I'll go to and from work with you every day, so I'd never be alone, but he won't know that. We could catch him, Warner."

Lilia then got up from her seat and walked over to the table where she had put her mail. She picked up a letter and walked over to Warner handing it to him.

"I need this, Warner. I need to practice law," Lilia said as Warner opened the letter.

"You passed."

"Yes," Lilia said with a smile, "I have to submit the Admission Application to the Board, but yes, I passed the Bar exam." She continued, "I will submit the application and tell Shawn and Chris tomorrow."

"Congratulations, I knew you could do it." Warner walked over to her and gave her a kiss, "I don't have to like it—you going back to the firm—but I understand."

"You do?"

"Yes, I do," Warner took her hand, and kissed her again, a little less chastely this time, and Lilia smiled, "when do you want to start?"

"I think I should be fine by next week. All of the facial bruising should be gone by then. Hopefully, I'll have been granted admission by then as well too."

"Okay. We should let Shawn and John know. John will need to step up the security once you start to keep a close eye on you."

"I'll let Shawn know tomorrow when we meet."

"If you are going back to work next week, there's something else we should discuss before you go back."

"What's that, Warner?"

"Can you sit down, please?" Warner sat down across from Lilia as she took her seat.

"What else do we need to talk about, Warner?"

"I think we need to talk about what is happening, with us, I mean."

"Oh… ummmm…"

"Listen, Lilia, we don't have to define what we are or what we are doing, but I do want to make my intentions clear. I can wait until you are ready to do the same, but don't torment me," Warner began, taking her hand in his, "I want to actively pursue this—us. I want to find out what we could become to each other. I know that we could be amazing for each other if you'd give us a chance," Warner continued. "But we do work together and I, currently, am your superior, so I don't want you to feel pressured to choose one way or another. If you want to wait until you are granted admission and become an associate, we can do that too," Warner sighed, "Will you say something? Take me out of my misery please?"

"If you would stop talking, maybe I could say something too," Lilia laughed.

"This is funny to you? Me putting my feelings out there?"

"Warner," Lilia stopped him from talking, "I feel the same, but I don't know if I can do this. I don't know if I'm ready; I've never even been in a serious relationship before. I've never let anyone get too close to me. Losing my parents hurt me and I've never wanted to risk my heart… it hurt too much." Lilia tried to pull her hand away from his, but Warner wouldn't let her.

"Just knowing that you feel the same is enough for me. You'll never know if you are ready if you don't try. You can trust me." Warner raised his hand to her chest, resting over her heart, "Trust me with your heart. I'll protect it and you—I swear. Just try. Give us a chance. That's all that I ask."

Lilia placed her hand over his and said, "I'll think about it. I promise, Warner."

Warner leaned into Lilia, gently placing his lips against hers, moving his hand from her chest to her neck, pushing into her hair bringing her gently closer to him. He deepened the kiss, his tongue caressing her lower lip.

Her mind went numb as she lost herself in his kiss and forgot what it was she was supposed to be thinking about.

As he pulled away slowly, he said against her lips, "I will be thinking about that all night." He rested his forehead against hers and played gently with her hair.

He pulled away from her slowly and stated, "Since you're going to be here for a while, I think you should have a desk in here."

"A desk? Warner, what are you talking about?"

"So, you can be completely comfortable. Have an office space, a desk to sit at."

Lilia felt lost as she was still trying get the muddled feeling out of her head after that kiss.

Warner stood up and walked to the door, "You know my intentions, Lilia. I intend for you to trust me with your heart. I trust you with mine. When that happens, we will then inform HR that we are in a relationship. Okay?"

"I'm so confused, Warner."

"Goodnight, Lilia, and congratulations again. You deserve it, you've worked extremely hard for this moment."

"Thank you, Warner," Lilia said quietly as Warner closed the door quietly behind him.

# CHAPTER 18

When Lilia woke the next morning, the first thing she did was submit her application to the Board of Law Examiners. Once that was completed, she got ready and went downstairs to wait for Warner.

"Good morning, Susan."

"Good morning, Ms. Lilia, do you want some breakfast before you leave?"

"I'm actually fine, Susan. I'm too excited to eat. I passed the Bar!"

"Okay. That's great news." Susan said as Warner entered the kitchen.

"It is great news. She deserves it." Warner stated.

"Thank you, Warner."

"Are you ready to go?"

"If you are."

"I'm glad I didn't go to any trouble making you break-fast." Susan said sarcastically, standing in front a tray of cut fruit and poached eggs.

"Leave it for tomorrow, Susan. We'll have it tomor-row." Warner said taking Lilia gently by the elbow trying to hustle her slowly out the door before they received Susan's scorn.

Lilia heard Susan complain as they left, "Leftover poached eggs? What is that man thinking? I'll just take it home to my George then."

Lilia and Warner were still chuckling as they got into his car.

As they drove Warner said, "I called John to let him know we were on our way. He'll meet us in Shawn's office."

"I can bring you back home afterwards." Before Lilia could protest Warner continued, "I have to meet a client so it's not out of my way."

Lilia smiled and nestled into her seat for the rest of the ride.

Warner pulled up to the front door of the firm, stop-ping the car. Confused, Lilia asked, "Aren't you going to park?"

"From now on, when we come and go, John will have someone at the door. They'll wait with you while I park. You are not to walk in the parking lot for the near future. We can't chance it."

Lilia nodded, "Thank you. I don't know if I'm ready to go into the garage yet either."

"I'm glad you agree." Warner said then went over to her side to let her out of the car. He made sure she was in the care of the security guard and then went to park.

Arriving back to her side quickly, Warner accompanied her to Shawn's office. "I'll leave you with Shawn and then come in a bit later with John. Sound good?"

"Definitely."

"Lilia!" Carl said, coming out of his office, "How are you feeling? Are you coming back?"

"Hi, Carl." Lilia smiled, "I'm meeting with Shawn to discuss it. Probably next week. I'm starting to feel normal again."

"Well, you're definitely healing well. Seeing you that night." Carl shook his head, "It was horrible. I'm so sorry. If I had gotten there sooner…"

"You got there just in time, Carl. I'm so grateful." Lilia said, trying not to cry.

Carl smiled, "It'll be great to have you back. It hasn't been the same without you."

"Thanks, Carl." Lilia said, as he waved goodbye and walked over to the other offices.

Lilia turned again to Shawn's office and asked his assistant to let him know she was there.

"Lilia! It's so great to see you! I've been getting reports on your recovery from Warner and your emails. It's great to actually see you recovering. This can't have been easy for you."

"Thank you, Shawn. It's great to see you too. It has been difficult, but I'm definitely getting better. I'm self-reliant now, and my bruises are all healing." Lilia continued, "I think I'm ready to come back to the office next week."

"So soon? Are you sure?"

"Yes, I'm sure. You know that Warner and I made a play to get Sanders to come into the firm?"

"Yes, both Warner and John have been keeping me informed of everything going on."

"I think being in the office could lure him in, under the guise that he is coming for the fake cheque. I'm also feeling very detached from the office. I do need to get back; working from home is not the same." Lilia took a breath, "And I have good news. I passed the bar exam, and this morning I applied to the Board for admission." Lilia ended off with a smile.

"Well, Lilia, congratulations, though I didn't doubt you would be successful." Shawn continued, "If you want to start next week, we will welcome you back. Please don't overdo it. And let John know when you're coming in. I understand we are meeting with him and Warner so I will let him know to put his people in security. Just a few extras he trusts to keep an eye on you."

"Thank you, Shawn, I won't overdo it."

Shawn interrupted, "I have another stipulation; you are not to be in the parking garage at all. We will employ a driver to take you to and from home. Since your attack, we've added security at night to assist with walking employees to their cars. Everyone has to be out of the office by seven p.m. Security comes up to escort all stragglers out to their cars."

"Wow, that sounds wonderful, Shawn. I am sure everyone feels safe and appreciates it."

"We have heard great feedback from the staff. Do you agree to my terms?"

"I agree. But I won't need a driver. I am going to continue to stay at Warner's house for the time being. I would not feel completely safe at my condo. I will drive in and out with him each day, at least until Sanders is caught. Hopefully that happens quickly."

"Agreed. Chris and I will certainly do anything we can to help."

"Thank you, Shawn."

"John and Warner should be in shortly. John is going to update us on everything his team has uncovered." Shawn said just as his assistant called to let them in.

After they all greeted each other, Shawn asked John for an update.

"John, tell us what you've found."

John nodded and began, "We got the footage from your condo, Lilia. We determined that the man trying to gain access was Sanders. I uploaded his image to our facial recognition software to compare the footage of Sanders in the parking garage for verification that they it was the same person, so that we could present the evidence to the police."

Warner stood up said, "Good. There's proof it's him. We can get it to them today."

John held his hand up to Warner, indicating that he wasn't finished. When Warner sat back down, John continued, "When we put his image into our facial recognition software, it pulled up all of the matching images that were stored in the software. We still had the images stored of the man that was with Wilkins in Brantford."

"Where Lucille Diaz was found." Lilia confirmed softly.

"Yes." John stated, "The software indicates a 90 percent biometric match between all of the images."

"Sanders is the man with Wilkins? Is that what you're saying John?" Warner asked.

"It's a possibility. Facial recognition isn't one hundred percent accurate when subjects aren't looking directly at the camera or hidden by shadows."

"Oh my..." Lilia said softly, "It was a part of the Wilkins file that I think went missing from my briefcase."

"When Sanders was in your office?" Shawn asked.

"Yes," Lilia said looking at him.

"Two members of my team went to Brantford this morning. They have stills of the footage and photos of Sanders and Wilkins. They are going to see if there are witnesses that can place them together."

"As soon as you hear from them, let us know." Shawn said.

Just as John was getting up to leave, Lilia thoughtfully said, "Wait." She continued, "if they could have been..." Lilia didn't know how to say what she was starting to suspect. "Sanders and Wilkins..." She looked up at Warner, "Melinda? Sean Hindson? Could their deaths be linked too?"

The three men exchanged glances. "I'm on it." John said and stalked out the door.

"It can't be." Lilia said shaking her head, "There has to be a mistake. Not Jeff."

Warner leaned towards her from his chair to take her hand in his. "He attacked you, Lilia. He went to your condo. There's no mistake in that."

"He just can't be involved with Wilkins." Lilia said insistently, "There must be an error with the software. John said it wasn't one hundred percent."

Warner gently rubbed his fingers over hers, looked into her eyes comfortingly and said, "Let's wait and see what John can confirm before we decide anything." Warner didn't know who she was trying to convince. "Right, Shawn?"

Warner looked up to find that Shawn had left the room. He smiled and looked back at Lilia, "Are you ready to go?"

"Maybe we should stay? Wait to hear from John." Lilia shook her head and got to her feet.

"John or Shawn can call just as easily as they can tell us in person." Warner answered. "Today was a lot."

Just as they walked out of Shawn's office, they met Shawn about to come back in.

"I just heard from John. The investigators found eye-witnesses that can place both Wilkins and Sanders in Brantford. Together and separate. He's sending them and a few others to do the same where his other victims were found."

At hearing the news, Lilia reached out to hold onto Warner's arm. Warner put his hand on top of hers.

"He's still trying to access CCTV footage from around Melinda's place. The police have seized most of it so it's going to be difficult."

"Thanks, Shawn. I appreciate your help." Turning to Warner, Lilia said, "I'm just going to check my office before we leave. See if I need anything else."

"I'll meet you at your office." Warner responded.

Once Lilia was gone, Warner said, "You disappeared."

Shawn nodded, "You looked like you two could use a minute. I'm sure this has been upsetting for her."

"It has, but I'm learning she's a strong woman."

"And smart. I'm glad she's on our team. I'd hate to go against her in court." Shawn said as Warner smiled.

"Let me know if you hear any more from John, okay?"

"Of course. I'll fill Chris in later. He's meeting with a client."

"Thanks. See you, Shawn."

Shawn nodded and said, "Bye, Warner."

Warner went to meet Lilia at her office so he could take her home.

They rode home in silence, each of them lost in their thoughts. Lilia's were filled with disbelief and Warner's filled with anger.

Once they arrived, Lilia went straight up to her room. She had hoped that they would have heard from John by now.

Lilia settled in to distract herself with work when she heard a knock on the door.

"Come in."

Warner walked in with a tray, "I brought you lunch, you should eat. You didn't have breakfast."

"I'm not very hungry." But knowing she should eat, she smiled and said, "Thank you, Warner."

After eating a little bit of food, Lilia asked, "Are you going back to the office?"

"No. I'll work from here. I have some phone calls to make."

"Have you heard from John yet?" She asked though she knew he hadn't.

Warner shook his head.

"Do you think he did it? Jeff? Do you think he could have… murdered all of those people?"

"I think that so far there is enough video evidence to make him a suspect." Warner said.

"What are you saying Warner? Why would he kill them?" Lilia stood up and started walking around the room.

"He attacked you, Lilia." Warner stood too, "He was stopped. How do we know that he wasn't trying to kill you too?"

Lilia turned to look out the window as her mind turned, "But why? What reason would he have?" She asked herself more than she was asking Warner.

Lilia continued speaking to herself, "If it was, that would mean he would have to have some connection to Luke Wilkins." Lilia turned around to face Warner.

"We have to find that connection Warner. And we have to find him. We have to find out what I had to do with it. Why attack me?"

Warner smiled as he watched her mind work, "Already on it. I called John to tell him to start looking into connections between Wilkins and Sanders. Also, to see if there is any CCTV footage of either of them in the vicinity of Callie Simmons and Linda Graham's places. John has already given the police the footage of Sanders at your condo."

Warner continued, "John is trying to find out if Sanders had any connect to Melinda. He couldn't get his hands on any video footage of Melinda's place because the police seized it all already."

"We need to find him." Lilia looked at Warner, "And I know how."

# CHAPTER 19

"No Lilia."

"Warner, the only way we are going to flush him out is to make him think he can come after me. I need to go in and out of the office alone."

Warner got out of his seat, and walked over to her, "That's too much of a risk, Lilia. Do you hear yourself?"

"I wouldn't really be alone." Lilia continued, "When he shows up, John's team comes out of the shadows and grab him."

"No. Just wait. He has no idea we are investigating him at this point. Let's just see if he goes to pick up the cheque. Before we start thinking of other ways to get you injured again. Okay?"

Lilia was silent.

Warner stepped in closer and took her hands in his, "Please, Lilia."

Lilia nodded, "Okay. I'll wait."

"Thank you," Warner smiled and leaned over to kiss her, before checking the time.

"I've gotta go. I'm late for a phone call appointment with a client."

"I'll see you for dinner?"

"Yes. You'll see me for dinner." Lilia smiled.

Warner quickly kissed her again, then picked up their half-eaten food and left the room.

A couple of hours later, Susan knocked on the open door, "Ms. Lilia, your desk will be delivered within the hour. Do you know where you want it to go?"

"Desk? What desk?"

"Mr. Warner said a desk was coming today for your sitting room."

"Oh. We just spoke about that briefly. I didn't know he was actually going to order one."

"Mr. Warner always does what he says."

"Yes, I'm beginning to realize that."

An hour and a half later, Lilia had organized the room, and was working at the new desk, when she turned to see Warner leaning against the door jam.

"Hi," Warner said.

"Hey," Lilia said, "Thanks for the desk."

Warner entered the room, walked towards her and bent to kiss her on her cheek, "Glad you accepted it." He said smiling.

Lilia shook her head and sighed, "How did everything go today?"

"John just called me. He had one of his guys watching the Sanders house. Jeff was spotted going inside."

"I guess he's not in Montreal visiting his mother then."

"Let's just hope they want the money bad enough that he shows up at the firm. John and his team will detain him and hold him for the police. Then we can find out why he attacked you, why he was in Brantford with Wilkins." Warner paused, "Hopefully by then John also has more information, more proof."

"What else can we do? I feel like we are leaving everything to John, his team, and the police."

"We just have to continue doing what we are doing. Calling his wife pretending to be HR was a really good idea by the way." Warner said with a smile.

"If only it actually works."

"I have a feeling it will, Lilia." Warner continued, "Ready for dinner?"

"For sure, but I'll come down and sit at the table."

"Wow. A formal dinner." Warner said laughing, "A date?"

"It's a date." Lilia smiled.

When Lilia was seated at the table, Warner brought two plates of food to the table and announced, "Well, she made one of my favorites for us tonight. Lasagna!"

"I think you have lots of favourites," Lilia said, laughing, and taking her plate from him, "At least three times a week you say that Susan made one of your favorite meals."

Warner laughed, "Susan can turn any meal into my favorite," He then began digging in.

After a few minutes of practically inhaling his food, Warner looked up to see Lilia staring at him, "You really enjoyed that lasagna," she stated smiling.

Warner smiled, "I did."

"So, what's happening with the Wilkins case?" Lilia asked bringing them back to work related topics.

Warner shook his head, "Not much. The prosecution has requested another stay of proceedings, as the medical examiner has yet to determine the cause of death for Callie Simmons and Linda Graham. They are considering bringing more charges against Wilkins."

"If John's team can't find anything then you know the prosecution won't," Lilia paused, "And of course, no change with Wilkins right? He doesn't want to plea."

"Luke Wilkins spent the ten minutes I gave him only asking me about one thing, so I ended our meeting."

"What did he keep asking you about?"

"You, of course," Warner stated.

"Oh my gosh. What did he say?"

"You don't want to know," He replied with disgust.

"Ugh," She groaned, "I'm glad we ate already. I lost my appetite."

"Me too," Warner said.

"I think that I'll call the detectives tomorrow. See if they've made any progress with my case. If they have information we don't." Although she knew that they probably wouldn't say much, she still wanted to ask. The police tended to release information on a need-to-know basis.

"It definitely can't hurt."

After they finished dinner, Warner went to clean up the kitchen, while Lilia went upstairs to shower. When they were both finished, Warner came up to check in on her.

"Are you tired?" Warner asked.

"No, I'm not, I was just going to read my book before bed."

"Do you want to hang out and talk instead?" He said leaning against the door jam.

"Sure, come on in." She responded. "What do you want to talk about?"

"Anything and nothing." He said taking a seat, "Anything that's not related to work."

"That could be a long list." She said chuckling.

"How about if I start. What made you want to be a lawyer, why criminal, why defence and not prosecutorial?"

"One, that's a big question. And two, it's kind of work related, but I'll answer anyways." Lilia began by telling Warner about how she grew up, her home life, hoping that would explain why she decided to become a lawyer.

"We didn't have a lot growing up, financially, I mean. I never knew it though." Lilia smiled. "My parents always protected me, and provided a loving environment, but I knew." Lilia continued, "They worked so hard. The only thing I could do for them was to be successful. So, I got good grades."

Warner nodded, and reached out for her hand, gently encouraging her to continue.

"It wasn't the greatest of neighbourhoods, and I saw the kids around me dropping out of school, getting involved with drugs and crime. The kids I went to elementary school with were in juvenile detention before I graduated high school. My parents made sure I had choices."

"By the time they died, I knew I wanted to go to law school. They didn't see me do it, though. They died before I got my acceptance letter." Lilia didn't notice Warner move closer to her, until she felt his fingers wipe the tears off her cheeks.

"I'm sure they would be—they are—so proud of you Lilia." Warner insisted softly, comforting her.

Lilia smiled in acknowledgment. "When they died, I decided I wanted to be a prosecutor. It was a car accident. A hit and run. The police suspected it was a drunk driver." Lilia continued, "I wanted to be a prosecutor so that I could put people like him or her, cowards, away for life."

"They weren't caught?" Warner asked.

"No. And I was so angry at this invisible person for so long."

"What changed? It must have been something significant." Warner asked.

"It was Hale & Cross. And Melinda." Lilia answered simply, smiling.

"What?" Warner said, "How?"

"In law school, we had a case study about a teenage drunk driver. It was a pro bono case, and Melinda was the defending attorney."

"The People versus Paul Billings." Warner cited.

"You know the case."

"I do. It was one of Melinda's finest moments."

"Billings was a sixteen-year-old kid who was headed down the wrong path. If Hale & Cross hadn't taken on his case, he would be in jail, or back in jail, not in a high school equivalency program, counselling, and getting on the right path."

Lilia smiled and said, "I did some background on Hale & Cross. I found out how much groundwork was being done in low-income communities. Education programming, after school programs, sports programs... building children up like my parents did for me." Warner nodded in understanding.

"It was then I decided I wanted to become a defence lawyer. I wanted to help stop people from becoming destructive. Tearing apart people's lives. I wanted to be able to help children, teens... give them opportunities so they don't turn to crime." Lilia said quietly, "Become drunk drivers."

Warner reached out for her hand, offering her support, and, squeezing it gently, said, "Is that what led you to Article at Hale & Cross?"

"Yes. And Melinda." Lilia explained, "After that case, I began studying more of her cases. Even going to sit in the courthouse to watch her if I could. She was so dynamic. She could make a jury think a guilty man was innocent. She did so much research. It was like she knew what the prosecution was going to say and already had a rebuttal prepared. I admired her. I wanted to learn from her. I respected Chris Hale and Shawn Cross. The firm and sense of community they had built. That's why I applied to Article at Hale & Cross. I wanted to learn all I could from the best."

"And now you're one of the best." Warner said smiling.

"I just got admitted," Lilia said smiling, "Because of this attack, I haven't even been able to enjoy it."

"You're almost one hundred percent. This week will be over before you know it. You'll be practicing in no time, with your own clients, asking others to research for you. Though I'm not sure anyone can meet your standards."

"That sounds far too much like Melinda. I was never able to meet her standards. She was so good, but I don't want to ever make anyone feel the way she made me feel, Warner."

Warner began caressing her hand with his thumb, "And you won't. You have high standards, sure, but you're compassionate and caring. I know you'll be an excellent mentor and boss. Even if you might be demanding," he finished with a twinkle in his eye.

"What about you? What made you decide to be a criminal lawyer?"

"Well, my reasons are more traditional. My father and mother were both lawyers. My older brother went to law school, then so did I, and so did my sister, whom you thought was my wife. All different types of law, working in firms, but my sister and her husband have a private practice."

"A whole family of lawyers?" Lilia said with a smile. "What types of law does everyone practice?"

"Unusual, right?" Warner answered. "My father recently retired but practiced civil law. My mother, family law, but is now also getting ready to retire. Older brother, tax law. And my sister and her husband's area of practice are labour and business law, respectively."

"Does your older brother have a family? I know your sister has two children, right?"

"Four children, two boys and two girls. My brother is determined to remain a bachelor, much to my mother's chagrin."

"And you, Warner? What do you want?"

Warner looked directly into Lilia's eyes and said, "I want it all. With the right woman. Marriage, children—if it's in the cards. I want to raise our children, grow old together, and then visit with our grandchildren in between travelling to different countries after we retire."

"You have it all planned out."

"I do. Right down to the children's names."

Lilia smiled, shaking her head, "I'm not even going to ask. I hope your wife has some say."

"You will." Warner said with a smile.

Lilia laughed, and Warner asked, "Do you? Want it all? Marriage and kids?"

Lilia sighed, "I don't have to have it. But with the right person I think I'd want it."

"Have you thought any more about the possibility of us?"

"Yes… I have…" Lilia answered slowly.

"And?" Warner paused expectantly, "What do you want to do? I hope you know what I want."

"I know what you want, Warner." Lilia took a breath, "I want it to. I want to see what can develop." Warner smiled happily. "Would you stop smiling." Lilia demanded.

"I will. Eventually." Warner said, "We'll have to go into HR, and let them know. Is that okay?"

Lilia took another breath, "I guess so."

"Thank you for trusting me. Letting me in. Telling me about your family."

Lilia nodded, "It was easy to open up to you. I haven't told anyone all of that before."

Warner nodded in understanding and leaned in to kiss her softly on the forehead. "I'll see you in the morning."

"Yes, goodnight, Warner."

Warner stood up holding Lilia's hand and raising her also to her feet, leaning in for another goodnight kiss. Their kisses now seemed to come so naturally. As she rested her hands around his waist, she felt his hands move up her arms to cup her head gently. He always moved so cautiously; she could tell that he was nervous about hurting her.

He ended the kiss as gently as he'd begun it and slowly backed away from her, his hands being the last to break the connection.

Softly he said, "Goodnight, Lilia," as he eased out of the room, closing the door behind him.

# CHAPTER 20

The day finally came when Lilia was well enough to return to work. She was completing all tasks on her own, even assisting Susan with meal preparation, when she was allowed in the kitchen. She had continued doing low-impact exercises twice daily and had been lifting her legs alternately for twenty minutes as the doctor suggested.

She emailed Shawn, Chris, and John to let them know she was ready to return and got confirmation that they were prepared with the added security.

They had continued having their evening meals together in the kitchen, so Lilia decided that she would let Warner know that evening at dinner. *Hopefully Susan made one of Warner's favourite meals and he'll be in such a good mood he won't argue,* Lilia thought to herself.

Just as she was about to wrap up and shut down her computer, she was alerted to a new email. She decided to read it before going down to the kitchen to help Susan with dinner.

The email was from the company that delivered the desk.

*That's weird that they would email me. Isn't Warner the contact?* Lilia thought. But maybe he provided my email as a contact.

Also weird that the company would use a free email account and not a business domain name. Warner would have used a reputable business.

Lilia continued reading the email, which stated that something was missing from the desk and they would like to send someone with the missing piece tomorrow. She had been using the desk for over a week and hadn't noticed anything wrong with the desk. She pushed it back and forth just to be sure that it was sturdy and made a mental note to ask Warner about it during dinner.

As Lilia organized supper with Susan in the kitchen, she let her know that she intended on returning to work tomorrow and wouldn't be there for lunch.

"You look ready. But Mr. Warner is not going to want you to go back so soon. Mark my words." Susan warned.

Just as they finished preparing the meal, in walked Warner. Lilia steeled herself for the conversation they were going to have.

"Good evening, ladies," Warner greeted, "I could not have come home to a more pleasant sight. Two beautiful women in my kitchen." They both stared at him, prepared for him to say more, "I am not saying another word," holding up both of his arms in surrender. "I am now going to wash up before I get into trouble," he said leaving the kitchen.

"He's lucky," said Susan, "he was about to get a whole lot of this tomato sauce right on his high-priced suit."

Lilia laughed, "And this salad bowl right on top of his head." Lilia continued, "Will you eat dinner with us before you leave tonight, Susan? The dinner looks delicious." Lilia hoped her answer would be yes, cowardly wanting to delay having a conversation with Warner.

"I will, actually. George is working late again tonight, so I will eat here. Your company is much better than my own." Susan smiled at Lilia, while she took out three plates to serve everyone's meal.

"This tomato sauce is so good, Susan. I can't believe you make it from scratch," Lilia said.

Entering the kitchen, Warner said, "Your tomato sauce is the best. My favourite!" and Lilia rolled her eyes.

"Every meal of yours is his favourite, Susan."

"I like eating with you both. You give me much more praise than my dear George," Susan said smiling.

As they sat down to eat Lilia asked, "Warner, I wanted to ask you. When you had the desk delivered here, did you give the company my email address as a contact?"

"No, I gave them mine. Why?"

"The delivery company emailed me. They said there was a piece missing from the desk and they want to deliver it tomorrow. The desk seems fine to me. I thought it strange that they would email me and not you."

"That is odd. Did you notice the email address?" He questioned.

"Yes, it came from a free email account."

"I'll email the company tomorrow and find out. There shouldn't be anything."

"Okay, thanks," she said as they finished their meal.

Just as Susan began clearing the table, Warner said, "Oh Susan! No. Please. My two favourite women prepared the meal. I'll clean up." He set his charming smile on Susan.

"Oh, Mr. Warner," Susan said coyly, "I'll say goodnight then. See you tomorrow." She turned to Lilia and whispered, "Good luck."

"Good luck with what?" Warner asked, not missing a thing.

"I'll help you clean up."

"No, you sit down and tell me what you need luck with."

"As we were preparing dinner, I let Susan know that I wouldn't be here for lunch tomorrow. I'm planning on going back to work. She said that I looked ready, but that you weren't."

"Oh really? Is that what Susan said?"

"Yes."

"Okay. Did you already let John know to increase security?"

"Absolutely. I received confirmation from him and Shawn."

Warner simply nodded staring at her.

"Aren't you going to try to talk me out of it, Warner?"

"Absolutely not. If you think you're ready, you must be. Who am I to tell you you're not? My concern is for your safety. I have to trust that John is taking care of it. Taking care of you. I have two meetings tomorrow so I will not be in the office for much of the day. But I'll take you and pick you up. Can you leave around four p.m.? I've grown quite used to having dinner together."

"Yes, of course. I enjoy having dinner with you each night. I'll be ready to leave at four p.m." Lilia replied, shocked at his compliance.

"Great. Go on up. Let me finish cleaning up here and I'll join you in your sitting room," Warner said, "Can you forward me the email that you got? I'm going to check its validity."

While Lilia was in her room, she forwarded the email to Warner, showered, and then began preparing for tomorrow. She pressed and laid out her suit and packed her briefcase. She felt like she was a child excitedly getting ready for their first day of school.

She was still in the bedroom when she heard Warner milling about in the sitting room. She entered and, seeing him sitting in the chair, she went over and did what she had never done before—bent down and kissed him gently.

As she pulled away, her eyes locked in on his shocked face, "What's wrong?" she asked.

"Nothing whatsoever." He stood and kissed her again.

Lilia smiled, "Sorry for taking long. I was getting ready for tomorrow."

"Are you ready?"

"I think so. I had just finished pressing my clothes when you came in."

"From now on, anything you need cleaned, give to Susan. I have a company pick up, launder, and press all of my suits once a week."

"I couldn't do that, Warner."

"While you are staying with me, you can, and you will." He punctuated his words with a peck on her lips. "If you give it to her on Thursday mornings, they pick it up and have everything back by Monday."

"I feel like I'm always saying thank you."

"Then stop saying thank you and just accept."

"I promise to try."

"All you can do is try." Warner continued, "I'll let you finish getting ready for tomorrow, I'm going to work a bit. Did you send me the email?"

"Yes, I did," Lilia continued, "What time should I be ready tomorrow? You're always gone by the time I come down for breakfast."

"I usually eat at eight a.m., then head to the office. Will that be okay? Or is that too long a day?"

"No, that's fine Warner. I'll be ready."

"Goodnight," Warner said, leaning down for their goodnight kiss, which started soft and gentle as he normally kissed her. The kiss soon became more unrestrained with Warner's hands exploring her body slowly, moving from her shoulders, down to her hips and around her back.

His lips continued to explore hers as his hands explored her upper body, trying to be gentle. Lilia allowed her hands to explore his body as well, moving from his hips to his chest, while enjoying the feeling of warmth and electricity everywhere his hands touched. Lilia heard someone moan, and felt Warner pull away slightly and his hands stilled, "Am I hurting you?"

"I'm fine Warner, you don't need to stop."

"Oh Lilia," Warner groaned, "I need to stop while I can."

Lilia tilted her head back up to her to bring their lips back together for a short kiss before easing slowly away from him.

"You're right. It's hard to stop." She said with a slow smile.

"I'll say goodnight now. See you at eight a.m." He gave her a last, chaste kiss on her lips and turned to walk out of the door.

"Goodnight, Warner."

# Chapter 21

Lilia got up early the next morning, or simply got out of bed because she couldn't sleep anymore. Between thoughts of Warner and excitement for going back to work, she barely closed her eyes. This day would be different though. She had to remain aware and constantly vigilant. Upon entering the firm, her first stop was to meet with Shawn and Chris, to discuss her new position, and most likely everything going on with Sanders.

As she walked down the stairs with her laptop and briefcase, she heard Warner say from the bottom of the stairs, "Hey, you should have let me bring those down for you."

"If I let you do that, then would I be well enough to be going into the office?"

"Thank you for the closing argument, counsellor." Warner said as Lilia smiled.

"Have you eaten yet?" Lilia asked.

"Yes," Warner replied, "I wasn't sure if you had snuck down earlier this morning to avoid me."

"I was tempted. But only because I didn't want to be reminded of it. I need to be focused today, not feeling flustered, the way I felt all last night."

"We both had a rough night then, hmm?"

"Let me grab a bagel, and then we can go."

"I have to go get my briefcase and laptop. I'll be ready in a bit."

Once she had eaten, she made a stop in the bathroom to freshen up and then met Warner at the front door.

"Ready?"

"I think so."

"Should I give you a 'knock 'em dead' kiss now? I don't think you'll want me to kiss you at the office."

"No, I certainly won't." Lilia closed her eyes and tilted her head up to him for a kiss.

"Mmm," Warner whispered, "cream cheese, yum."

"Oh Warner," Lilia broke away from his kiss, laughing.

"Sorry." Warner said, "We should probably go to HR sooner rather than later."

"So soon?" Lilia asked.

"I don't know if I'm going to be able to see you every day at work and not touch you or kiss you, which I'm sure our colleagues would notice."

"Isn't it inappropriate to do that at work?"

Warner looked at her, his face deadpan, "Let's get in the car." He said shaking his head.

Lilia laughed walking past him through the front door.

Once the car pulled up outside of the office building, Warner asked her to wait while he called John. "We're outside" Warner said quickly. At that, another car pulled up behind them, and a man got out. Warner looked at Lilia and said, "You can walk up to your office with him. He's one of John's guys. I'm going to park, and I'll come check on you in your office."

Lilia smiled and said, "Thanks. I have a meeting with Shawn and Chris once I get settled, so I could be in with them."

"I'm supposed to be in that meeting as well, so don't start without me."

"You're going to be there?"

"Of course."

"Okay, see you inside," Lilia said, getting out of the car.

"Knock 'em dead." Warner said, smiling.

Lilia smiled and greeted the gentleman waiting for her.

"Don't acknowledge me, ma'am. We don't want anyone thinking we are together. I'll follow you at a slight distance," he said quickly and quietly.

Lilia took a deep breath as she started to realize how vulnerable she was. She began the walk to the elevators, not making eye contact with anyone she passed on the way. She didn't glance towards the security desk, it reminded her of Jeff Sanders.

Lilia exited the elevators and once the doors closed, she glanced behind her to see that the gentleman that had accompanied her up in the elevator was already gone. She barely noticed the door to the stairwell swing quietly shut.

Walking in, she felt slightly back to normal, seeing the morning bustling of the assistants, law clerks, and associates that were already in the office. She stopped at Carl's office, before going to her own, wanting to say hi to him before anyone else, but his office was empty.

Once in her office, Lilia settled in quickly, and then called Shawn's executive assistant to let him know that she was ready to meet when he was. Several minutes later, she was called to his office.

She walked over to Shawn's office, where she saw his assistant sitting outside, "Welcome back, Ms. Bennett, you can go right in. They are waiting for you."

"Thank you, Mrs. Smythe," Lilia said walking to the open office door, knocking to make them aware of her presence.

"Come in, Lilia." Shawn said as they all rose to their feet, Chris coming over to greet her with a handshake.

"Welcome back Lilia. You are a welcome sight. I'm so glad to see you doing so nicely. You are looking well."

"Thank you, Chris. I'm excited to be back and get started." Lilia nodded at the other members in the room, "Shawn, John. It's so nice to see you both again. Warner." She acknowledged, also nodding at him.

Shawn gestured for everyone to sit down and as Chris lead her to her chair, he said, "And congratulations. Shawn told me you've received your admission by the Board. Wonderful news in the midst of all this…" He gestured with his hands in a stressful manner, trying to find the proper word, "stress."

They were all quiet for a moment, before Shawn broke into everyone's thoughts by clearing his throat. "This is a very stressful time. With Melinda's death, and your attack, Lilia," Shawn shook his head, "We'll continue to do what we can to help the police find justice for both you and Melinda. Finding Jeff Sanders will hopefully provide some answers, and you are very strong to come back while he is still on the loose." Shawn paused and continued, "John has joined us to give us an update. John?"

"My team has been looking for connections between Sanders and Wilkins. We haven't been able to find any so far. There are no familial connections nor do their lives seem to intersect except for this firm. We haven't been able to access any of the video footage at Melinda's. The police already have the footage, but I have contacted the detective and let them know of our suspicions of Sanders. Given that he attacked one of our staff, maybe he attacked Melinda too. I didn't mention possible connections to Wilkins."

"And what about Sean Hindson and the other two victims? Did you find any video footage of Sanders or Wilkins with them?" Lilia asked.

"We found footage of a man who has the same build as Sanders in the vicinity of the victims. But unfortunately, we were not able to access enough footage to accurately identify him. We tried the facial recognition software without success." He continued, "With Hindson, we are still looking, because we don't know exactly when Hindson went missing or from where, it's a lot more to go through. We have switched gears and are tracking Hindson instead."

"Thanks, John. Let us know as soon as you get anything."

"Of course, Mr. Cross." John said making his way to the door.

"John, how many times do I have to ask you to call me Shawn?"

"I will not, Mr. Cross." John said directly, while Shawn sighed as John left the room.

"For John not to find anything on Sanders… That is surprising. Sanders definitely knows how to disappear." Chris said.

"Lilia," Shawn began, "We know that you can now practice but with all that's going on we aren't going to give you any new cases yet. We want you to finish assisting Warner, Carl and Grace with the rest of their cases. They are still overwhelmed with Melinda's case load."

"Definitely. Thank you, Shawn."

Lilia went back to her office and got to work. Before she knew it, it was three o'clock. She had told Warner that she would be ready to go by four p.m. She decided she would quickly eat the fruit that she'd brought and then go through her email again, flagging the items that would need her immediate attention tomorrow.

"Have you had enough for your first day? Are you ready to go?" Warner asked from her office door.

"Hi." Lilia smiled. "Yes, I'm ready. I'll just pack up."

"How did it go?"

"It was okay. I'll fill you in on the details in the car." Lilia continued, "How was your day?"

"I just had meetings. Nothing big happening."

Lilia packed up her bags and walked with Warner out to the elevators.

Once they got to the security desk, Warner asked her to remain in the lobby while he got the car. He subtly gestured to a man standing behind her. Lilia turned to see the same gentleman from the morning standing off to the side, directly out of the line of site of the entrance doors.

Warner pulled the car up in front, and Lilia quickly climbed in settling herself in the car.

"Physically, how was your day? Was it too much or were you okay?" Warner asked.

"I was fine actually. I met with Shawn and Chris. They want me to concentrate on the cases we already have until all of this Sanders stuff is settled."

Warner took a quick glance at her and then looked back at the road while he drove. "That sounds like a good plan. Are you okay with it?"

"Yeah, I am. I just… I've waited so long to get here, and because of Sanders…" Lilia's voice trailed off.

Warner's hand reached over the centre console of the car to take Lilia's hand in his, "So how was your day?" Lilia asked.

After a pause he began to tell Lilia about his day, telling her about the meetings he had with his clients. He went on to talk about the complexity of each case, and Lilia shared some ideas on how he could move forward, citing case studies that had set precedence.

"How do you have so much information, just stored in your mind like that?" Warner said as Lilia smiled, "Now, your turn."

Lilia told him everything about John's meeting with her, Shawn and Chris.

"Okay, so we wait."

"Yes, we wait," Lilia sighed as they pulled past the security gates of Warner's home.

They entered the house, and both headed to their respective spaces to wash up and change, before joining Susan in the kitchen for dinner.

Lilia joined Susan in the kitchen and helped her plate all of their dishes. Susan told her that she would join them for dinner again. Lilia really enjoyed Susan's company and found her quite funny. Once Warner joined them, they all sat down and began to eat Susan's delicious meal.

"How was your day Susan?" Warner asked after he paused from eating to take a breath.

"It was quiet without you Ms. Lilia. I've grown used to having you here to chat with during the day." Susan said.

"I'm sorry Susan, I really did need to get back to work though, I'm feeling better."

"Yes, of course... Oh that delivery man came today. You were talking about it yesterday. He said he needed to see Ms. Lilia about the missing desk piece."

"What?" Lilia questioned.

"Yes, he said he'd emailed you to let you know that he was arriving. I told him you were at work and that I would give the piece to you, but he said he had to give it directly to you for some reason. That it needed to be signed off on

– but he didn't have any paperwork with him. So strange he was."

"Did you email the company Warner?"

"I did. They said there was no missing piece. They confirmed with the delivery company. I thought it was just one of those phishing emails." Warner looked down at his plate for a moment and then looked up, "Do you remember what he looked like Susan? If I showed you a picture of someone, could you tell me if it was the same person?"

"Oh yes of course!"

Warner got up leaving the table and came back within minutes holding a piece of paper. He handed it to Susan saying, "Is this him Susan? Is this the man you saw?"

Susan studied the photo for a minute, and said "Yes, I do believe that's him, only," she paused, "He had a few scars on his face. They were red scars, obviously not stitched up properly."

Lilia looked from Susan to the photo, reaching out to take it from her hand, "Warner?"

"Jeff Sanders." Lilia said as Warner looked at her.

"If you hadn't gone to work today…"

"How did he get passed security though?"

"Well, security called in, and they said it was the delivery company, I remembered you speaking about them last night, so I cleared them to pass the gate." Susan continued, "I assumed you had emailed the company and had gotten it straightened out."

"Of course, you did Susan," Warner said laying his hand on her shoulder, "Don't worry, you did nothing wrong." He sighed, taking a seat beside Susan to explain,

"This man is very dangerous. We suspect that he is the one that attacked Lilia. I thought she'd be safer here. If anyone else comes round looking for Lilia or trying to gain access to the premises when I'm not here, do not permit them. Okay Susan? For your safety as well as ours. We don't know what he's capable of anymore."

"Oh, my goodness!" Susan gasped, "I never will again, Mr. Warner! I swear on my George that I won't let anyone in here again." Susan continued, placing her hand on top of Lilia's, "Oh, Ms. Lilia, you poor poor dear. Had you been here... what could have happened?" She said not really expecting an answer.

"I am going to see if I can access the security camera footage. From my property and the security team. If I can get a clear ID on him, I'm going to provide it to John and the police," Warner stated walking out of the kitchen.

"Oh Ms. Lilia, I can't imagine how you are feeling with all that has been happening."

"I'm alright, Susan. I'm just trying to make sense of it all and I don't know if I will until he's caught, and we can hopefully get some answers."

"Well, just know that I'm here for you if you need anything, Ms. Lilia. Even just an ear to listen."

"Thank you, Susan. Why don't you get going—it's getting late. I'm sure George is home by now, and you should take the leftovers home for him. There usually aren't any, the way Warner packs your food away."

"I'll just clean up the kitchen then."

"No, no, Susan. I'll clean up the kitchen. I'd really rather be cleaning than to be thinking about this."

"If you're sure, dear. I'll go home, as I'm sure by now George is waiting for me." Susan said, starting to pack the leftovers.

"Thank you for all of your help today and everyday Susan."

"Goodnight, Ms. Lilia."

Lilia cleared the table, washed the dishes, and cleaned the kitchen. She was feeling tense and uneasy as it was definitely obvious that Sanders was still trying to get to her. This feeling of unease made her hands itch and desire to be busy and this resulted in a sparkling clean kitchen. Once she was finished and she could find nothing else to clean, she decided it was time to find Warner.

She realized she'd never been in his office before, so she wandered around the first floor until she found it, knocking on the open door gently to get his attention since he was on the phone.

He looked up and gestured for her to come inside. "Yes, the footage is from my home security system and from a company that secures my community." He covered the mouthpiece for a second and mouthed the word *police* to her. "Yes, I can have the company send it to you. Can I give you their contact information as well?" He paused listening, "Would you recommend that she do that? Even though there's an open investigation with him as the main suspect?" He paused again, "Okay, I'll let her know. Thanks again, and please feel free to contact me or Ms. Bennett at any time if any more is required." Warner said hanging up.

"What did they say?"

"Well, I sent them the security footage from the camera from the house and told them that Susan could Identify him. You heard about the security company. They suggested that you go to the court and file a restraining order against Sanders."

"Wouldn't they actually need to be able to find him to serve him the order for me to actually file a restraint?" Lilia ran her hands through her hair feeling agitated.

Warner smiled, "Good point, and the length of time it would take. Hopefully, John and his team will find him first."

"I hope so, Warner."

"Do you want to talk after I clean up the kitchen?" Warner said standing up.

"I already cleaned up and I think I'm just going to go to bed Warner. It's been a long day."

"You cleaned up? Thank you."

"It's the least I could do, Warner. You've been letting me stay here, taking care of me, helping me... so much, I'm just really grateful."

"I care about you. I want to take care of you, keep you safe."

"I know, and I care about you too." Lilia walked over to him, placed her hands on his arms and stretched up to kiss him gently on his lips. As she kissed him, she felt his hands lightly touch her shoulders and down her arms to settle gently on her hips.

Warner slowly pulled away saying, "See you in the morning. Goodnight, Lilia."

"Goodnight, Warner."

# CHAPTER 22

Lilia got used to the routine over the next two days with Warner dropping her off at the front door and having the same gentleman, who's name she didn't even know, follow her up to her floor. She was told that someone also made rounds in the office during the day, but she was never able to spot who it was, which didn't surprise her given the expectation of invisibility.

A couple of the cases that she had been assisting Carl and Grace with were soon going to trial, and they had begrudgingly begun to ask the law clerks to do more of the foot work when they found out that Lilia passed the Bar. The Wilkins case was also slightly halted by the investigations into the deaths of the witnesses and the resulting stay of proceedings, which Warner had indicated he didn't expect to be lifted soon.

With all of this, her workload had begun to get lighter and with no additional news from John's team about all of the ongoing investigations, she was feeling redundant, so she decided to email Shawn and Chris to request a meeting. She needed to work. Either a case to assist with or her own, with someone to oversee her if they felt discomfort. Shawn's response came within hours, stating that he and Chris would meet with her at three o'clock.

Just before her meeting, Lilia was just getting ready to leave her office when her cell phone began ringing. Seeing that it was Warner, she answered it, just as Shawn arrived in the doorway of her office, "Hello, Warner?" she said questioning.

"Are you in your office?" Warner asked.

"Yes of course. Where else would I be? I am about to have a meeting with Shawn and Chris. Shawn just walked into my office and is waiting for me."

"Stay with Shawn and Chris. I'll be right there."

"Warner, what's going on?"

"I'm sure Shawn is going to tell you. I'll be there in five mins." Warner said disconnecting the connection.

"Shawn?" Lilia questioned, placing her phone on her desk.

"Let's go to my office. Chris is waiting for us there." Shawn said, turning in the direction of his office with Lilia following close behind.

Once they arrived, Shawn gestured for Lilia to sit in a chair. "I'll stand," Lilia responded, "Chris," She acknowledged, "What is going on?"

Shawn cleared his throat and began, "John called me, just before I came to your office. His team apprehended Jeff Sanders."

"What? Where? When?" Lilia had so many questions and didn't know which she wanted answered first. She sank into the chair beside her as she didn't think her legs would hold her.

"Here. Today." Shawn stated, as Warner walked quickly through his office door.

Warner went straight to Lilia's side, placing his hand on her arm asking, "Have you told her yet?"

"Just now." Chris said.

"They have him in a security office downstairs, holding him until the police arrive." Shawn continued, "John said that they seized a gun."

"He was coming to kill me?" Lilia asked.

"We don't know that." Warner said, rubbing her arm gently, "We'll hopefully know more if John and his team get him to say anything, or when the police question him."

Just then Shawn's cell phone rang, and he picked it up, "John." He said, and then listened. They all waited for him to share the information. "Okay, thanks. See you in a bit." He disconnected and then placed the phone down on his desk.

"The police have arrived and have taken him into custody. The detectives are coming up to meet with us. John is coming with them."

"What happens next?" Lilia asked.

"They'll probably let you know about his charges, ask if you want to make an additional statement. We'll see." They all waited quietly for John and the detectives to enter, lost in their own thoughts. Soon enough the anticipation was over.

After everyone was introduced, Detectives Collins and Gregg confirmed that Jeff Sanders had been arrested on the outstanding warrant for assault. They asked if they would be able to see Carl Jeffries, to see if he could be accompanied to the station to formally identify Jeff Sanders as Lilia's attacker. Chris immediately left Shawn's office to locate Carl, so that he could join the detectives.

Shawn stated, "As you know we want to help in any way we can. This happened in our office to one of our employees, by one of our employees."

Carl and Chris rejoined them in the office. "Carl is prepared to come down to the station immediately to see if he can identify the person that attacked Lilia, Detectives."

"Mr. Jeffries, we appreciate your help with the investigation. Your previous description of the person you saw, in addition to possibly identifying the man in custody, will help us with the case." Detective Collins continued, "Detective Gregg will bring you down to the station and then give you a ride home afterwards."

"We can send a car to bring you in in the morning Carl."

"It's okay. I'll have my wife meet me at the station and drop me off in the morning. I want to do everything I can to help." He looked at Lilia, remembering.

Warner placed his hand on Carl's shoulder, "She's doing okay now Carl. She's recovering."

Lilia stood up and hugged Carl, "You protected me. You stopped it from happening Carl. Thank you."

Carl hugged her back, and then turned to walk out with the detectives. Before leaving, Detective Collins turned to Lilia and said, "We'll let you know if we need you to make another statement."

"Thank you, Detectives."

Once it was only John, Warner, Shawn and Lilia left, Shawn said, "Looks like your plan worked. By telling his wife there was money here for him."

"Maybe. He was either here for the money or to try to get to Lilia." Warner said then filled him in on their housekeeper telling him Lilia had returned to work.

John began, "We tried getting something out of him when we had him. He wouldn't talk. We'll see what the police can do."

"Do you have any more on IDing Wilkins or Sanders at any of the witness's deaths? Or on accessing any footage from Melinda's condo?" Warner asked.

"I was just about to get an update from the team when Sanders walked into the building. He hadn't even gotten to the security desk when we intercepted him."

"Okay, update me as soon as you have something."

John nodded and walked out of Shawn's office.

Warner held his arm out to Lilia, "Ready to go?"

"Before you do, I'd like to speak with both of you a moment." Shawn said and Lilia looked at him curiously.

"It's quite obvious to me at this point that there is more than just a working relationship between the two of you." Lilia looked at him in shock. "I ask that you disclose the relationship to HR so that it can be documented."

Warner sighed, "We aren't in a relationship, Shawn."

"Not yet then." Shawn said, "Now, Lilia. Can we meet tomorrow? About your email."

"Of... um, yes, of course." Lilia stammered, still thrown off by the previous comments made by Shawn.

Warner placed his hand on her elbow, signaling for her to rise from the chair she had been sitting in. She got up and walked in a fog to her office, packing her things, while Warner waited at her office door. "Are you okay?" He asked.

"I'm just trying to process all that's happened." She was silent for a moment, "How did you know about Sanders being picked up?"

"I was on my way in from a meeting. It must have been about seconds after it happened. I saw John's team taking someone into the security office." He paused, "I called John to find out what happened. He wasn't answering so I waited until he did. He told me he called Shawn, so I called you and made my way up."

"It was that. It was when you came to me." Lilia said with realization.

"What are you talking about?" Warner asked.

"Why Shawn thought that we were in a relationship."

Warner smiled, "That's actually not the first time Shawn has said something."

Lilia looked up in surprise, "What? To you? When?" She stuttered.

"When you were in the hospital. They said that they could see how I felt about you. How I reacted when I heard about your attack. Chris said that you looked at me the way that his wife used to look at him." Warner smiled softly, "And that I should try dating you first." Lilia stood staring at him stunned, with her bags in her hands. "Ready to go?" Warner asked her.

Lilia stayed silent all the way to his car. He assisted her into it and went around to the driver's side. After driving for a little while, he said, "I would you know."

"You would what?"

"Like to date you." Warner said.

"Oh," Lilia replied with a slight smile.

"Now that Sanders is caught, I would like to take you on a date. Out to dinner. Will you go? No work being discussed?"

Lilia paused before saying, "Yes, Warner. I'd like that." Lilia said, and glance over at him when she heard a deep sigh come out of him, as though he'd been holding his breath.

"How about tomorrow night? I'll let Susan know we won't need dinner." Warner said smiling.

"Tomorrow night would be fine."

"Great. I'll pick you up at six o'clock." Warner said and Lilia smiled.

# CHAPTER 23

As Lilia got ready for her date with Warner, she recalled her conversation with Carl upon seeing him in the office that morning. She had asked his assistant to let her know the moment he came into the office so she could ask him about his experience at the police station.

When Carl knocked on her office door, she hadn't expected him. She had been waiting for his assistant to call her. "Carl," She said with surprise, "I was going to come see you."

"I thought I'd come see you. I knew you would want to talk. My wife just dropped me off."

"Thank you, Carl. How are you? How did yesterday go?" She inquired.

"The detectives made it surprisingly easy. They explained everything before it happened. I had to wait a while as they had to wait for the lawyers to arrive." He

241

smiled. "But once everyone was there, it went quickly. They had a bunch of guys lined up with red hats on. I picked him out, but for sure his lawyers will say that it's because he worked here. Sadly, I didn't even know who the guy was before this. But I'll testify to that. I don't mind admitting I'm self-absorbed." He said with a slight smile.

"I don't know everyone who works in this building. I didn't know who you were until Melinda yelled at you." Carl admitted and then coughed into his hand, slightly embarrassed. Lilia smiled at him, letting him know that it was fine, and after chatting a little more, Carl made his excuses as he had to get ready for a meeting with a client.

Choosing a casual but stylish dress, Lilia put it on, admired herself in the mirror, and decided she would wear it. Seeing that she only had ten minutes before Warner would "pick her up," she put on her make up quickly. Once she was ready, she left her room to walk down the stairs, seeing Warner waiting at the bottom for her.

"I'm sorry to keep you waiting," Lilia remarked.

"You look beautiful." Warner responded, "And I wasn't waiting long."

"Has Susan left already?"

"Yes, she said that she would see you tomorrow." He said offering her his arm. "Shall we go?"

"Where are we going?" She asked as he helped her into the car.

"I hope you like seafood as we are going to a very romantic seafood restaurant that I heard about but have never been to."

"Oh, that's nice. I like seafood."

"Before we get to the restaurant, I'd like to ask you one work related question."

"Breaking the rules already, Warner?" Lilia asked playfully, and Warner laughed, "What's your question?"

"How did your conversation go with Shawn and Chris? You mentioned that you were going to talk to them about increasing your caseload."

"It went well, actually. They had said they didn't really want to give me anything because of Sanders. But now that he's been arrested, they said if I feel I'm ready to handle it, they'll discuss giving me my first case." She continued. "They're going to ask Grace to oversee me. They were going to ask you but, given our circumstances, they feel 'it would be best to ask someone without bias' quote unquote." Lilia stated.

"I wouldn't be biased towards you!" Warner said, slightly offended. Lilia crossed her legs in the seat next to him and he glanced down. "A little distracted maybe, but certainly not biased."

Lilia laughed, "Oh, I heard from the detectives too. Sanders has his bail hearing tomorrow."

"Hopefully he'll be refused bail and they can keep him off the streets."

"Yes, hopefully." Lilia said thoughtfully. "I wanted to speak to you about that as well."

"About what?"

"If he's refused bail and he's in jail," She trailed off, "I think it's best for me to go back to my place."

Warner sat in silence, for a few moments. "Why?"

"If we are now formally dating Warner, I just don't feel right living with you. Please try to understand."

"I understand." He said pulling into the parking lot of the restaurant, "Why don't we wait and see how tomorrow goes, and then we'll talk about it, okay? Let's just enjoy our date."

The evening was fantastic. There was no more work talk, and the conversation didn't stop until the waiter brought their food. They both grew silent, admiring their food and then savouring their first bites. Lilia closed her eyes to fully enjoy the flavourful lemony scallop and scampi dish she had selected. When she opened them, she saw that Warner had been staring at her smiling.

"How's your meal?" she asked.

"Not as good as yours apparently," he smiled, "Truthfully, this salmon confit is excellent."

Once their dinner was finished, Warner asked her to share dessert. Even though she didn't necessarily have a sweet tooth, she agreed, as she didn't want the night to end just yet. As they shared the decadent caramel cream pie, Lilia thought about how much she enjoyed their evening. How much she enjoyed working and spending time with him. She smiled shyly at her thoughts as she met his gaze.

"I won't ask you what you're thinking about, because I don't think you're going to tell me." Warner laughed.

"And you'd be right." Lilia smiled again.

Their evening soon came to an end, and they spoke of everything and nothing all the way back to Warner's home. Once inside, Warner placed his hands gently on her shoulders and pulled her closer into him so he could kiss her. "Thank you for a wonderful evening, Lilia," Warner said gently against her lips. He then pulled back and stepped away from her, with Lilia looking at him in surprise, "Only a kiss on the first date." He said smiling.

"I had a wonderful time, Warner. Thank you."

"Goodnight, Lilia."

As Lilia got ready for bed in her room, she replayed the evening in her mind, grateful for Warner's entry into her life, although she also recognized the horrific reason it happened. The firing and murder of Melinda Kent. Having that thought subdued her and she tried to settle herself to sleep.

# CHAPTER 24

On the drive into the office the next morning, Warner asked Lilia about the bail hearing happening later in the day.

"Do you want to go?" Warner asked her, "I'll come back to the office to pick you up on my way if you want."

"No. I don't want to. I'd rather wait to hear. Will you call me when it's done?"

"Of course," Warner said as they arrived at the office. Although Jeff Sanders had been apprehended, Warner continued to let her out of the car in front of the office building, waiting for one of the security guards to walk her into the office

After an hour or two of work, Lilia made her way down to Warner's office. Knocking gently on his door, she waited for Warner to look over at her.

"Why do you still let me out at the front door? Instead of parking in the garage and us walking in together?"

Warner pushed the file he was looking at to the side and replied, "Although Sanders has been caught, we don't know if he was working with someone."

Lilia nodded in agreement saying, "Are those still John's men accompanying me?"

Warner didn't speak, so Lilia prompted him, "Warner?"

"No, they aren't. They are a new private security team."

"Who commissioned them? Was it Shawn and Chris?"

"No. I did. I needed to be sure of your safety."

"Warner…" Lilia was lost for words.

"It's done Lilia. I won't undo it. Until this is over, they stay." He paused, "Okay?"

"Yes, okay." Lilia said, "Thank you."

"You don't need to thank me. I need to do this." Warner began packing up his files, "Now I have to go if I'm going to make it in time."

"Are you going to the bail hearing now?"

"Yes, I'll call you when it's over."

Lilia nodded, "I'll see you later then."

"Yes, Lilia." Warner said as he stood up, "I'll be back by four p.m. to take you home."

"See you then, Warner," Lilia left, returning to her office and her work.

Although she had work to do, her thoughts were on the bail hearing, and she found her eyes continuously drawn to the time. Once a few hours had passed, she checked her phone making sure it was turned on. When he still did not call, Lilia believed that it must mean bad news. To distract herself, she contacted Grace to see if she had time to go over the case that Shawn and Chris had assigned her.

An hour or so later, after meeting with Grace, Lilia went over all of the notes that Grace had made on the case file. Just as she was finishing up, her phone rang. She held her breath as she picked it up to check who it was.

"Hello, Warner."

"Lilia," Warner answered, "How are you doing?"

"I'm alright," Lilia said impatiently, "Just sitting here waiting on your call. What happened?"

"Bail was denied." Warner stated as Lilia let out a sigh of relief, "Judge said he was a flight risk since he disappeared for so long." Warner paused, "Are you okay?"

"Yes. Thanks for calling. I was getting nervous; it was taking so long."

"Sorry. I stuck around to speak with the prosecutor to see if I could get any more information. He was called into a meeting, so I didn't get anything."

"I have his information. I was going to contact him as well, find out what they need from me."

"Alright. Let me know if you need anything. I'm headed to a meeting with a client. I'll be back to pick you up on time."

"Sounds good. Bye Warner."

Lilia looked for the prosecutor's business card, placing the call to his office, but he wasn't available, so she left a message with his assistant.

With Lilia's head buried in files, she was surprised by her phone alarm alerting her to the time. It was three fifty p.m. and time for her to head down to meet Warner. She packed up the files and her laptop, put on her coat and headed down in the elevator.

As Warner held open the car door for Lilia, she heard her phone ringing, so she rushed to settle herself to answer it.

"Hello," Lilia answered expectantly, looking over at Warner as he settled into the driver's seat.

"Ms. Lilia Bennett? This is Charles Caufield from the Prosecutors Office."

"Mr. Caufield! Thank you for calling me back."

"I was to contact you anyways, Ms. Bennett. I wanted to arrange to meet with both you and your colleague, Carl Jeffries, to go on record with your statements."

"Yes, of course. Let me know when and I'll be in your office."

"My assistant will contact you with a date and time; however, I also wanted to let you know that after the bail hearing, Sanders's lawyer contacted my office. He said he wants to talk; he wants a deal. He said he has information for us."

"What?!" Lilia exclaimed and, at that, Warner indicated and then pulled the car quickly over to the side of the road.

"We are going to meet tomorrow and, depending on what he gives us, he may plead guilty, and then there is no need for you to testify."

"Will you let me know before you accept the deal?" Lilia asked.

"It will all depend on the validity of his statement and level of discretion needed with what he discloses. I will let you know if I can."

"That's all I can ask. Thank you for your call, Mr. Caufield." Lilia stated hanging up the phone.

Warner stared at her waiting for her to repeat the conversation. Lilia paused and then told Warner what was said before he resumed driving again.

"What are you thinking?" Lilia asked.

"I'm thinking about the information he has. Whether he's giving up an accomplice, or if he's confessing to more crimes…" Warner's voice trailed off.

"I was thinking the same thing. If he has an accomplice… You were right to be cautious." Lilia said closing her eyes.

She felt his hand rest on her leg, and he began to rub it gently. "Don't worry. He's in custody. If he is giving up his accomplice, that's one step closer to you being free from me."

She looked over at Warner quickly, to see him smiling. "Warner, it's not about being free from you…" she started as she placed her hand on top of his.

"I know. I was kidding. I understand that you want your independence back, and now that we are officially dating, you need separation. I get it," Warner paused, turning his hand over to hold hers, squeezing it gently, "and that will happen soon I'm sure. With whatever information Sanders has to divulge."

After arriving at his house, Lilia finished washing up to get ready for dinner. Warner entered the kitchen just as Lilia began sharing out their dinner plates.

Warner came to stand beside her placing his hand on her hip and leaned over to kiss her on her cheek.

"Did Susan go home already?" Lilia asked after he pulled away.

Warner smiled, "Don't worry, she won't catch us making out." Warner continued, as he turned to pour them each a glass of wine, "She left, as George was going to be home for dinner tonight."

Lilia smiled too, shaking her head as she walked their plates over to the table, joining him with the wine. After enjoying Susan's spectacular cuisine, for a few moments, Lilia paused, taking a sip.

"Why does Susan always cook like she's cooking for the Queen? This food is just…"

"Incredible." Warner completed her sentence, "Always." Taking his last bite of food, Warner further explained to Lilia, "When I hired Susan, it was just to help me around the house. When I became an associate at Hale & Cross it got so busy, I decided to hire someone for the house-keeping and laundry—get to the things I no longer had time for." Warner paused taking a generous sip of wine, "After about a month, Susan decided that I wasn't eating because she never saw me eat, and from that day on she began cooking and my stomach as never been happier."

"I am definitely going to miss Susan's meals when I move back home, Warner."

"You don't have to miss anything, you know." Warner said and Lilia laughed, shaking her head at him.

Changing the subject, Warner said, "I met with Wilkins today. He got attacked in jail. He claims it was a guard who did it. He doesn't know which one, he only saw the uniform and there were no witnesses—big surprise. He wants me to apply for a transfer to another jail, as his 'life is in danger'."

"Was he badly beaten?"

"He has bruises on his face and body, but he didn't have to stay in the infirmary. I'm waiting for the medical report, which I will use to apply for the transfer tomorrow."

"Do you believe him?"

"I believe that he was beaten. Do I believe that he was beaten by a guard? Not really. There is a reason he wants me to apply for the transfer though. It would be nice to figure out why before it actually goes through."

"Well, it's either getting him away from something or someone or getting him closer to it. Did he ask to be transferred to a specific jail?"

Warner smiled, "No, he didn't."

"So that should mean that he wants to get away. From whom or what?" Lilia's head began turning. "Maybe you should check out who else is in that cell block. Perhaps a friend or family member of one of the victims?"

"I called John to ask him to look into in on my way to pick you up today. I told him to call me as soon as he had something, so hopefully in an hour or two. We know how fast John and his team works."

"Yes, we certainly do. Regardless, you'll still have to put in the transfer, keep your client safe for trial."

Just as Warner was about to agree with her, his phone rang. "And there it is." Warner said looking at his phone. "It's John. Right on schedule. Excuse me." Warner said, rising from the table. "Hello, John," he answered.

As Warner spoke to John, Lilia began clearing the table. Before she had finished, Warner had returned and began taking the dishes out of her hand. "I'll clean up."

"We'll clean up together." She smiled, "Well, what's the verdict?"

"John couldn't find anyone with a connection to Wilkins or any of the victims." Warner shook his head. "I don't see another reason he would want out unless he really was attacked and feels threatened."

"What about a connection to any of the guards? Did John check them out too?"

"He did, without me even having to ask, and he couldn't find anything there either."

"So... next step?"

"Continue with the transfer request. I want to apply to transfer him to a maximum-security prison."

"Would he agree to that?"

"It's the next closest prison. That will be my reasoning anyways." Warner said, drinking the last of his wine, and then continuing to clean.

"Hopefully, Caufield calls you tomorrow with some good news." Warner said, changing the subject.

"What news would be good?"

"Good point. Hopefully what Sanders has to say is worth it."

As they finished cleaning, Lilia dried her hands and said thoughtfully, "It makes me nervous to think that he could be working with someone, and that someone is still out there."

"I know. I hope you feel safe here with me. I will do my best to protect you Lilia."

"I know, Warner. And I do feel safe. I feel like someone is always watching me." Lilia chuckled, "Most of the time it's you. But that's okay too." She smiled, walking over to him and placing her hands on the sides of his head and staring into his eyes, as he stepped towards her. His hand raised to her hips and she watched his eyes slowly move down to gaze at her lips. "You're right. I catch myself watching you a lot." Warner said softly, as he moved his head down closer to hers. Lilia felt the air being sucked out of her as she felt his lips finally caress hers.

She felt his hands exploring her body as his tongue explored her mouth. They kissed for what seemed like forever, and when she felt him start to pull away, it wasn't long enough. With her eyes closed, she felt his lips grace her forehead.

"Oh Lilia," he moaned quietly, "It's getting harder and harder to stop."

"Warner…" Lilia moaned. She allowed her hands to fall to his chest, naturally putting more distance between them. "Goodnight, I'd better go. I have some notes to go over tonight."

"Yes, I'm sure I have some work to do as well." Warner said putting a little more distance between them. "Why don't you go up, and I'll finish cleaning up down here?"

Lilia smiled, "Okay," she tiptoed to kiss him on his cheek. "Goodnight."

# CHAPTER 25

The next day, Lilia did some research on the case she had been given by Shawn and Chris. So far, Grace had done more work than she had. The last couple of days had been so overwhelming that she needed to get focused on establishing herself at the firm. She certainly didn't want Shawn or Chris to regret giving her a case so quickly.

Lilia's client Amy Parker was accused of defrauding thousands of people through a fictionalized funding donation page. Amy and her boyfriend Kraig Duncan created a page, claiming that Amy had been left stranded as her car had broken down on her way to pick up her children from daycare. On their page, they claimed that a homeless man gave her the last of his money to catch a cab to get to the daycare in time to pick up her children. Thousands of people donated over $30,000, meant to thank the homeless man, which the couple squandered away, spending it on themselves, as they didn't have children.

Lilia was also waiting to hear if more charges would be laid as the police were now also investigating allegations of past donation pages that Amy and Kraig may have posted, allegedly scamming others.

Grace had already attended the initial arraignment the week before, and although the judge had granted bail, Amy was not able to post the $25,000 bond, so she was remanded into custody, to be held until the trial.

Hours later, as Lilia finished going through the copies of material and evidence provided by the prosecution and Grace's notes on everything, she agreed with Grace that if Amy was offered a plea bargain she would encourage her to take what was offered to avoid going to trial. Once she was finished, Lilia sent Grace an email to confirm their appointment to meet with Amy Parker the next day to go over her options. Lilia had yet to meet Amy, so hearing the information from Grace would be better as they had already developed some sort of trust.

Before she knew it, her alarm sounded, and it was time to pack up to meet Warner for home.

As they drove, Warner asked her if she had heard from Charles Caufield regarding the meeting with Sanders.

"No, I haven't heard anything yet. I'm practicing patience." Lilia said smiling.

"I wish I had a little bit of that."

"What? Patience?"

"Yes. I don't know if you've realized it yet, but I don't have a lot of patience."

"Oh, yes. I had realized." Lilia laughed.

Once they finished cleaning up after eating dinner together, Lilia excused herself to get some work done.

Instead of working, Lilia found herself thinking of how much had happened in the last couple of years since taking the articling position at Hale & Cross. When she began at the firm, Melinda Kent had been a mentor, only to become an adversary. She had passed the Bar and was now an associate at the very law firm that she had almost resigned from.

Two years ago, she never thought that she would trust a man, trust anyone enough to get as close as she had gotten and was continuing to get to Warner. But Warner, with his determination and caring heart, had been slowly creeping in, and taking a hold of hers.

She began to work a little on the Parker case before getting ready for bed, hoping to find precedence to help set expectations with sentencing if they were able to plea bargain. She planned to go over everything with Grace before their meeting with their client.

The next day, Warner dropped Lilia off to meet Grace outside of the prison, reminding her to ask Grace to drop her off outside of the office before parking.

"Warner, I'm okay to walk with Grace inside the building from the lot. I'll text John and ask him to send your security to the lot to watch us. Is that okay?"

Warner squinted his eyes at her. "It'll have to do." He said as Grace walked up to them.

"Grace, is Lilia okay to go back to the office with you?"

"Of course. I have another meeting, but I'll drop Lilia off at the office on my way."

Warner smiled knowing he'd gotten his way by accident, "That's great. I'll see you both at the office later." Warner pulled out of the lot.

During the meeting with Amy, Lilia, and Grace discussed the evidence against her and went over what would happen next. If she plead guilty and decided to accept a plea bargain, or if she plead innocent and went to trial. They also discussed sentencing, with either scenario. Amy seemed to understand it all and also understood that with all of the evidence against her, she should take the plea if offered. Amy asked them if they knew what her boyfriend had chosen to do, and Grace told her that it didn't matter. It would only matter if they decided to go to trial and he was offered a deal to be a witness against her. Grace looked at Lilia.

"You also have to be prepared if they come with that deal for you." Lilia said.

"What do you mean?" Amy asked.

"If Kraig decides to go to trial, they may ask you to be a witness against him, in exchange for a lighter sentence. We have to expect that Kraig's lawyers are having the same discussion with him." Lilia continued, "With all of the evidence against you, we have to advise you that it would be beneficial to make a decision and be the first to go to them with an offer."

Amy placed her face in her hands and Grace continued, "They're also investigating prior allegations against you and Kraig. They could be looking to charge you with more, so we need to prepare for that. If you have anything you want to admit to, you can confess, and we can plea for all of your convictions to run consecutively." Amy looked at her blankly, "At the same time." Grace explained. "But you have to be honest with us. We need to know it all."

Amy was silent for a long time, and Lilia and Grace gave her time to think. She placed both hands on the table and entwined her fingers before she began speaking. She cleared her throat and looked at them both, "We did it two other times. We made up different stories, and then we moved after we got the money. This time we didn't move. I guess we got too comfortable." She looked down. "We should have moved, then we probably wouldn't have gotten caught."

Lilia looked at Grace, and then looked back at Amy. "Tell us about it. About each time."

"The first time we created a memorial and funeral donation page for my mother, who died from breast cancer. We got over $10,000 for that."

"Is your mother… ?"

Amy looked right at Lilia and said, "My mother is alive and living in Burlington." Amy continued, "The second time, it was Kraig's dying father. We asked for help in making his dying wish come true. We got about $25,000 for that. We decided to change to a homeless man because of the 'pay it forward' crap. There were already so many pages of people asking for money for sick people or to pay for people's funerals, we decided that people would be more likely to give to a homeless man and a mother for her kids."

Amy continued, "So can we ask for a plea? I'll confess to all of that if it gives me less time." Amy looked down. "I know one of the witnesses. She was my friend and I told her everything. We were trying to get her to help with the next one."

Grace cleared her throat, "We'll arrange for a meeting with the prosecutor's office. We will come back to you with the best offer."

Lilia stood, and reached to shake Amy's hand, "Thank you for your honesty, Amy."

Grace drove Lilia back to the office in silence. Once they pulled up outside of the building, Grace put her car in park.

"I've been a criminal lawyer for over fifteen years now, and sometimes it still shocks me how cold and selfish people can be. I've defended murders, thieves, embezzlers…" Grace trailed off. "I'm glad she's willing to take the plea. That would be a difficult case to take to trial and expect to win." Grace continued, "Why don't you contact the prosecutor and make an appointment to meet. Let me know when it is, and we can go together."

"I'll call when I get upstairs and email you with the details."

"Great. See you later, Lilia."

Once in her office, Lilia immediately contacted the prosecutor to set up a meeting. And just as she got off the phone with his office, setting up a meeting for the next morning, her cell phone rang.

"Lilia Bennett." Lilia said answering her phone.

"Ms. Bennett, this is Charles Caufield calling from the prosecutor's office. Do you have time to meet?"

"Yes, but is it about my testimony or about Sanders taking a plea?"

"I'd really rather discuss this in person, Ms. Bennett."

"If he's pleading out, and you're accepting the deal, I'd really not rather waste my time coming in."

"He's willing to give us his accomplice, Ms. Bennett. Or rather, the person who ordered him to kidnap you."

"Kidnap me?"

"Yes. Can we discuss this in person, Ms. Bennett?

"Today?"

"If you can meet today, that would be fine. Anytime."

"Five o'clock?"

"Of course. I'll see you at my office at five p.m."

Getting off the phone, Lilia sat in stunned silence. She could not believe what he'd just told her. *Sanders was trying to kidnap her, and someone had gotten him to do it? Who and why?* Snapping herself out of it and checking the time, she decided to call Warner to see if he was available to go with her after picking her up at four o'clock.

"Lilia? You okay?" Warner answered immediately.

"Yes. No. I don't know, Warner."

"What happened, Lilia?"

"Caufield called. He wants to meet with me at five o'clock. Can you come with me Warner?"

"Of course. What did he say?"

Lilia told him and at the end her voice broke as she felt a tear roll down her cheek. "What if he had…"

"Don't think about that Lilia. He didn't succeed. I'll pick you up in front as scheduled at four o'clock and we'll go meet with Caufield."

"Yes. Okay."

"Don't worry. I'll be there soon."

"Thank you, Warner. I'll see you soon." Lilia said hanging up the phone.

Warner pulled up outside of the law firm, and Lilia was already waiting. She had found it hard to concentrate after getting off the phone with Warner, so she packed up her stuff and had been waiting at the door for at least ten minutes before he pulled up.

"Were you waiting long?" Warner asked after she had settled in his car. "I'm not late, am I?"

"No. Not at all. I just couldn't think, so there was no point pretending. I just came down here to wait."

"How are you doing?"

"I'm a bit nervous. Anxious is a better word really. I just want to get this over with."

"Understood." Warner said quieting, realizing she needed silence.

They drove the rest of the way to Caufield's office in tense silence, with Lilia fidgeting with her clothes and bag until Warner slowly reached over and held out one of his hands. She looked at him in surprise, and then placed one of her hands in his, squeezing it gently and smiling softly.

"Thanks," she whispered softly.

"Anytime," he answered, using his thumb to caress the back of her hand gently.

Once parked, Warner came around to assist her. Once she was standing in front of him, he placed his hands on her shoulders and looked into her eyes.

"I'll be with you, every step of the way. It's going to be okay."

Warner walked with her inside, making their way to the prosecutor's office. Once there, Lilia found the assistant and let her know that she had a meeting with Charles Caufield.

"Your name please?"

"Lilia Bennett and Warner Reid."

The assistant picked up her phone and said, "Mr. Caufield, I have a Lilia Bennett and Warner Reid here to meet with you." After a moment of listening to the voice at the other end, she said, "Yes, of course sir."

She rose from her chair and said to Lilia and Warner, gesturing to the door just behind her desk, "Please follow me." She knocked gently and then opened the door walking inside. Lilia and Warner walked past her into Caufield's office.

A large brooding man rose from his desk and walked around it to shake Lilia's hand, "Lilia Bennett. It's very nice to meet you, though I wish it were under different circumstances." He then turned towards Warner, "Warner Reid." Caufield said with obvious respect, "Nice to see you again." They shook hands and Caufield gestured towards the two chairs directly in front of his desk. "Please sit down and we can get started."

Lilia took a seat, sensing Warner sitting beside her, as her gaze was focused on Charles Caufield.

"As I told you on the phone, Ms. Bennet, I met with the defendant, Jeff Sanders, at his request. He wants a deal. He's offering the identity of the individual who told him to kidnap you. He clearly stated that he was supposed to kidnap you—it wasn't supposed to be an attack. He implied that he was threatened to execute this act against you, and he also implied that there were more crimes that he and the other individual had committed." Caufield continued, "His lawyer explained to him that the sentence for kidnapping is harsher than the sentence for assault, yet he continued talking."

"What does he want?" asked Lilia.

"He's meeting with his lawyers about it. They are going to come back with what charges they want taken off the table." Caufield looked directly at Lilia and said, "I want you to be prepared that if what he has good, and can be verified, and if he gives us the person that wanted him to kidnap you, we may look at not charging him for attempted kidnapping or assault in your case."

"So, in exchange for his testimony against the leader, you would let him walk? Not being charged with anything?"

"No. We will charge him with something." Caufield said earnestly, "Depending on the information he gives, of course."

"And you'll charge the leader, the orchestrator with everything? Including attempted kidnapping?" Warner clarified.

"In exchange for his testimony." Caufield finished nodding.

"Will you keep me informed?" Lilia asked.

"Only as it doesn't interfere with the investigation."

Lilia stood, "If that's all, I think we should go."

Warner stood, resting his hand on Lilia's back, nodding at Charles Caufield.

"Thank you, Mr. Caufield, I look forward to hearing from you when you have something." Lilia stated.

"Thank you for meeting with me, Ms. Bennett." Caufield nodded at Warner, and Warner led Lilia out of the room.

Once they settled in the car, Warner waited before he started it, and looked at her expectantly.

"It's just like you thought, Warner. Sanders had an accomplice, and we'll just have to wait and see who the mastermind is."

"Just wait. And what happens while we wait? We just stress about your safety?"

"Warner…" Lilia closed her eyes.

"I'm sorry," Warner said placing his hand on hers, which was resting on her lap, "I don't want to make you feel worse."

"I'm already afraid and nervous Warner, your comments don't change that." Lilia stated, "I'm just… I don't know…" Lilia said shaking her head.

"I'm going to do everything I can to keep you safe." Warner said, "Lilia, look at me." Warner placed his hand on Lilia's chin, raising her eyes to his. "I promise you."

Lilia smiled softly, nodding slowly, "I know, Warner."

"Ready to go?"

Lilia nodded, "Yes. Let's go."

Warner started the car and aimed it towards his house. "Tomorrow, I'm going to contact John, and ask if there's anything more we can do. I'm also going to increase security."

"Increase?"

"Yes. Right now, I've got two guys following you. I'm going to increase it depending on what John says."

"There are two guys? I've only ever noticed one."

"That means they're doing their job."

"I guess that's good." Lilia acknowledged as they pulled up in front of his house.

As they walked into the foyer, Lilia said to Warner, "I don't think I'm very hungry tonight, Warner. I think I'm just going to go straight to bed."

"You don't want dinner?"

"No, thank you. I just want to be alone for a little while."

"I understand. If you want dinner in your room, let me know. You should eat."

Lilia smiled and started up the stairs. When she'd made it halfway, she heard Warner say her name stopping her, "Please don't shut me out, Lilia."

"I won't, Warner. I just need a moment. To process this."

"Ok. I'll see you in the morning. Goodnight."

"Goodnight, Warner."

Lilia went upstairs and got lost in her thoughts. She was afraid. And because of that fear, she let go of her independence, living with Warner, being watched by his security detail.

She just wanted to shut all thoughts of it out for one night, so she decided to take a hot bubble bath, something she didn't treat herself to often, as she never seemed to have time. Lilia put on some music and got into the steaming hot water, resting her head against the side, closing her eyes.

Feeling herself shiver, Lilia's eyes popped open to realize she had fallen asleep in the now cold bathtub. Lilia got out quickly and hopped into the shower to allow herself to quickly wash and warm up.

Once finished Lilia entered into the sitting room, to see a plate of food covered, with a note from Warner, stating, "Just wanted to make sure that you had something to eat, if you got hungry. Leave whatever you don't want outside of your door and I'll come pick up the plate."

Lilia smiled thoughtfully at Warner's attentiveness. From the beginning he had been taking care of her, and even as she, in not so many words told him she needed space, he gave it to her while still being attentive to her needs. She uncovered the still hot food, now feeling slightly hungry, and wondered when he'd brought it in, as she hadn't heard a thing.

After eating, she decided she would take her plate downstairs and wash up herself. Warner had done so much for her, she wanted to pass by his office to thank him for bringing her some food. After cleaning, she knocked on his office door.

"Come in, Lilia."

Lilia opened the door, "Hey."

"Hi. You doing okay?" Warner asked.

"I'm okay. I think I just needed a warm bath and some me time."

Warner smiled as Lilia continued, "Thank you for dinner. It was just what I needed, even though I didn't know it." Lilia paused, "So, what are you working on?"

"I was just going over the details of Wilkins transfer tomorrow."

"Did you get him transferred to a maximum-security prison?"

"Yes. He wasn't too impressed, but he wanted out, so he took it."

"Did you ever find out who he's running from at the prison?"

"No. John was trying to do a background check on as many people as he could, but there wasn't enough time."

"That's too bad."

"Yeah." Warner paused, "I don't know what it is, but my gut is telling me that he may not be running from something. There's a reason he wants out. I just don't know what it is."

"I'm sure you'll find out soon enough."

"How is your case going?"

"Grace and I are going to meet with the prosecutor tomorrow. We're trying to plea. A girl and her boyfriend charged with fraud."

"Ah. The couple accused of creating fictionalized stories online?"

"Yes. That one."

"Why are you pleading?"

"This is the first time they were caught, but not their first time doing it. A different story each time."

"Whoa. I see. Good luck with it tomorrow."

"Thanks. Grace has been great. She's done a lot on the case but has really let me lead. Something I never got to do with Melinda."

They were both silent for a moment. "A lot has happened in the last couple of months, hasn't it?" Warner continued, "It's completely understandable that you'd feel overwhelmed."

Lilia nodded, as Warner rose to his feet and walked around his desk towards her. He reached out for her hands and Lilia placed hers in his. His eyes locked on to hers and he leaned in to kiss her on her forehead. He pulled back and rested his forehead against hers.

He spoke softly, "I've got your back, all day every day."

Lilia smiled, "I know." She stated, "You have never made me question that. Thank you."

"You'll never have to question how I feel about you. Whatever you want to know, just ask." Warner leaned back to look in her eyes again. Lilia looked into them and saw the depth of his feelings. She wasn't ready to ask, nor was she ready to identify what she was feeling for him.

"When you're ready. I'm here." Warner said, leaning in and kissing her lightly on the lips. "Goodnight. I'll see you in the morning." He said releasing her.

"Goodnight, Warner." Lilia said leaving his office and returning to her room.

# CHAPTER 26

As Lilia and Grace exited the prosecutor's office, Grace said, "You should be extremely proud of yourself. You did a great job negotiating. You certainly didn't need me here."

"I definitely needed you, Grace. You had to make sure I didn't screw it up."

"If anything, I wonder if that poor guy is wondering if he got screwed. I can't believe you were able to get a reduced sentence, and, with her testifying against the boyfriend, no future charges on any past crimes."

"Ask for what you want, and you just might get it."

Grace smiled, "You got it."

"We still have to get her to confess in writing and agree to testify against him."

"She'll agree." Grace stated, waving her hand in the air in dismissal.

They got into Grace's car and drove back to the firm. Once arriving outside of the office, Grace said, "Let me know when you are meeting with Amy and I'll go with you, even though you don't need me."

Lilia smiled and shook her head. "Thanks, Grace. Are you free to go this afternoon? I can arrange to meet with her."

"Let's get it over with. I'll head to my office and reorganize some stuff and we can head over."

"Great. Two o'clock?"

"I'll make it work."

Lilia nodded and they both returned to their offices to get some work done. Lilia made arrangements to meet with Amy and finish some research on a couple of Carl's cases.

Two o'clock came very quickly, and Lilia left the office with Grace to meet with Amy.

When Lilia realized that she wouldn't be able to return to the office in time to meet Warner at four p.m., she excused herself from Grace, leaving her to continue recording and documenting Amy's confession. She turned on her phone to send him a quick text, and noticed that she had several missed calls, most from Warner, and one from Charles Caufield.

"Lilia." Grace called her over, "I think Amy is finished."

Lilia quickly texted Warner saying she was with Grace, that she would be later than four o'clock, and she would call him on the way back to the firm. She turned her phone on silent and returned to Grace and Amy. All documents completed, Lilia and Grace left the prison, and made their way back to the firm.

Once Lilia was settled in the passenger seat, she told Grace that she needed to check her messages. Looking at her phone once more, she noticed that she'd missed more calls from Warner and a text saying to call him immediately. Before she could call, her phone rang again, displaying Warner's name.

"Hello," Lilia said glancing over at Grace.

"Lilia. I've been trying to contact you."

"I know. I'm with Grace. We are on our way back to the firm."

"I'm at the firm. Can you ask Grace to pull up to the front of the building? I'll meet you there. Don't check your messages. I'll explain when I see you. Okay?"

"Warner, what are you talking about?"

"Just get here safely. Don't check your messages."

"We'll be there in ten minutes."

"Okay."

"What's going on?" Grace asked.

"I'm not too sure. Warner seemed stressed about something. Would you mind dropping me off at the front? Warner is going to meet me at the door."

"For sure. Great job with Amy. I have to meet with the prosecutor tomorrow about another case, so I can bring the agreement to his office."

"That's great. Thanks, Grace."

"No problem." Grace said as they pulled up to the front of the firm.

Before the car stopped, Lilia saw Warner at the front door with a security guard. As soon as the car stopped, Warner opened her door, grabbed her bags and hustled her out of Grace's car directly into his.

"Warner!" Lilia said with exasperation, "What is going on?!"

"You didn't check your messages?"

"I didn't. Can you tell me what's going on?"

Warner was quiet.

"Warner?"

"I'll tell you when we're safe at home."

"Seriously?" Lilia looked at Warner incredulously. "Safe? At home?"

"Lilia." Warner stated, stopping her from talking anymore.

Lilia quietly sat in her seat, trying to wait patiently until they arrived at his house, thinking that she should have checked her messages when she was with Grace.

Once they arrived at his house, Lilia turned to him in her seat, "Okay, we're here."

"Inside." Warner stated. He got out of the car and walked over to let Lilia out of the passenger side.

Once inside, Lilia turned to him and said, "Are you quite finished ordering me about? Can you just tell me now?"

"Let's go to the sitting room."

Lilia followed him into the sitting room and sat down in one of the seats, while Warner walked to the window and stood looking out.

"Caufield called me. He tried to get in touch with you, and since he couldn't get you, he called me." Warner started. He turned and began making his way over to her, "He got the name of the mastermind from Sanders." Warner sat down beside Lilia and took her hands into his.

"Who, Warner?"

"It's Wilkins, Lilia. Luke Wilkins. He made Sanders try to kidnap you."

"What? Wilkins?"

"Yes. Sanders confessed to it all. Wilkins was the master behind them all. He made Sanders kill the witnesses, Callie Simmons, Linda Graham, and Lucille Diaz."

"Oh Warner." Lilia looked at him incredulously.

"There's more, Lilia. Jeff Sanders was Wilkins's tool. He made him get rid of anyone in his way, including Sean Hindson, the bail bondsman, and, Lilia," Warner paused, "He's the one who killed Melinda, Lilia. Sanders killed Melinda. Melinda wasn't getting him out of jail and wouldn't recuse herself. Wilkins wanted you as his lawyer. He thought you would automatically be assigned if Melinda was out of the way."

"Sanders confessed to this?"

"Yes, he confessed. He said Wilkins threatened him. Threatened to rape and brutalize his wife and daughters, then kill them if he didn't."

"How did Wilkins get to Sanders? How would they have met?"

"Sanders said that Melinda had paid him to do odd jobs for her on occasion. Drive her places, investigate things, be her personal security. He met Wilkins on one of those trips."

Lilia was silent so Warner continued.

"Sanders said Wilkins was obsessed with you, since that first time you met him with Melinda. That's when he got to Sanders. Wilkins called him once from jail and told him there would be notes left for him. Instructions. And if he didn't do them… Wilkins made him steal your files on him to see what we had. Everything was on behalf of two goals. Getting Wilkins out of jail and getting him access to you." Warner closed his eyes, "He even made Sanders get a cabin. That's where they were going to take you." At Lilia's gasp, Warner reached out to take Lilia's hands in his, and held her gaze in his, "You're safe. You're safe, with me." Warner then raised his hand to her face and wiped the tear off her cheek, then continued, "There's more."

Lilia closed her eyes, and laid back against her seat, "How could there be more?"

"Lilia." Warner said, bringing her eyes back to his. "It's Wilkins. He escaped. During the transfer today. The prison guards were attacked when they stopped at a light. It was a planned attack, he had people waiting to break him out." Warner finally finished while Lilia sat in shock.

"Lilia." Warner ran his hand up and down her arm. "Are you okay?"

"Are the prison guards okay?"

"They were killed trying to stop Wilkins from escaping."

Lilia shook her head sadly, "What did Caufield say?" Lilia then asked.

"They have an APB out for Wilkins. They have warrants to charge him will all the murders and your attempted kidnaping."

"What happens next?"

"I spoke with John while I was waiting for you." Warner continued, "I had already increased your security detail to three men, so now I'm increasing it to four."

"There were three men following me today?"

"Yes, invisible and making sure you stayed safe."

Warner paused, "John also suggested you lay low until Wilkins is apprehended."

"'Lay low,' what does that mean?"

"Stay out of harm's way. You can stay here. Work from here instead of going to the office."

"So, you leave every day and I have to stay here alone?"

"You won't be alone. Susan will be here with you. I'll even station one guy to be inside with you."

"Ugh," Lilia said.

"This is your life, Lilia. We don't know how many men Wilkins has access to. He obviously still had connections on the outside to get to Sanders and to orchestrate his escape."

"Yes. Of course, you're right, Warner. Do Shawn and Chris know yet?"

"I notified them when I got into the office after having no luck getting in touch with you."

"I was with a client."

"Yes, I found out after speaking with the security guys following you."

"Ah."

"Shawn and Chris are getting me and the firm recused from the Wilkins case based on the grounds that he is wanted for Melinda's murder and your attempted kidnapping."

"Good." Lilia shook her head and then placed her head in her hands, sighing. "I need to call Shawn, and Grace."

"Okay," Warner sighed, "Do you want some privacy?"

"I'm just going to go upstairs. Thanks, Warner."

"I just wish I could do more."

"You've done so much, Warner." Lilia said, "This is just too much for me." Lilia said, "I'm going to head upstairs," she said shaking her head and leaving the room.

Lilia's thoughts began turning as she walked up the stairs. She felt so out of control right now—her head was spinning—and she needed to get some of it back. Entering the room, she decided that she would start by at least feeling like she could control her employment. She found her cell phone and called Shawn first.

He explained that he'd already had calls to John and to the chief of police to make sure that she was being protected. Lilia told him that Warner had already commissioned a security service and Shawn responded that he wanted to make sure there were more eyes on her.

"The chief of police is going to increase patrols by Warner's house at my insistence. You're staying there, right?"

"Yes, Shawn, thank you."

"And don't come in; it's best you stay put until Wilkins is caught, that bast—" Shawn stopped himself from using the foul language and cleared his throat. "Sorry, Lilia," He cleared his throat again.

"No. That's quite alright, Shawn,"

"I also asked John to put his people on finding Wilkins. They're on it."

"John and his team are excellent at what they do. And Shawn," Lilia paused, "I really do appreciate all you and Chris have done."

"Chris has already spoken to Grace to finish trying the case you are working on, only to find out that you got a plea bargain?"

"Yes. Grace and I agreed that it was the best outcome considering she had undiscovered past crimes that they could still charge her for."

"Yes, Chris and Grace brought me up to speed this afternoon. In exchange the client will testify against the boyfriend. Good work. Grace will finish up the case for you, even though it's basically concluded."

"Thank you. I was going to call Grace next, actually."

"Now there's no need."

"I've been feeling so out of control since the attack happened, Shawn, and you, Chris and Warner have been doing so much for me, to protect me… I feel so grateful."

"We all want you safe, Lilia. We're all looking out for you." Shawn finished.

"I know, Shawn. I'm going to give John a call and ask him if there's anything I should be doing. I don't like just sitting waiting for something to happen."

"That's a good idea. I'm sure he'll have advice. Take care, Lilia. Talk soon."

"Take care, Shawn."

After texting Grace to let her know that she appreciated her taking over the rest of the Amy Parker case, she contacted John. John just confirmed what everyone else said.

"Sit tight, Ms. Bennett." John said, "Until we have eyes on Wilkins. Right now, you and Sanders are unfinished business. Sanders is in custody. We just have to keep you safe until he and his accomplices are apprehended." John said matter-of-factly.

"I can't just sit here idly by," Lilia started.

John interrupted with a serious voice. "My team is on it. Give us time."

"Okay. I hear you. I'll stay put. I trust you guys will get him."

After that, Lilia heard the phone disconnect, and she wasn't surprised that John hung up without acknowledgement.

After taking a shower, putting on sweats and taking some time to herself, Lilia decided to lay down and close her eyes for a moment, not intending to fall asleep but, somehow, she did.

Lilia woke up to hunger pangs. I can't have been asleep for too long, she said to herself. But, upon checking her phone, she saw how wrong she was. It was well after eleven o'clock at night. She had slept for several hours.

Making her way quietly to the kitchen, she wondered if there was any of Susan's dinner left. She looked in the fridge and began pulling different items out of the fridge to put a plate together. Once she warmed it up, she put everything away and sat down to eat.

Finishing her last bite, she noticed a shadow entering the room out of her peripheral vision. She got up quickly and backed up.

"Lilia, it's me, Warner," he said turning on the lights, filling the room with brightness.

"Oh, Warner, you scared me."

"I'm sorry. I was working in my office and heard you in here."

"You were awake? I was trying to be quiet. I thought you were sleeping."

"I'm glad you ate. I came up to check on you and you were knocked out."

Lilia took her plate to the sink. "I'm sorry if I disturbed you from your work."

"You didn't." Warner paused, "You doing okay?"

Lilia nodded drying her hands on the towel by the sink after washing up. "I spoke with Shawn. He's extremely supportive. Same with you. And John."

"You spoke to John?"

"Yes. I wanted to know if I could do anything. I feel like you all are doing something, and I just have to hide out here."

"We all just want to keep you safe."

"I know and I appreciate it." Lilia continued, "It's just been a long time since I've had to rely on anyone."

"You have me now. I want you to feel like you can rely on me, okay?" Warner walked up to her and placed his hands on her shoulders and looked directly in her eyes, "Okay?" He said again when she didn't answer.

She stared in his eyes, "I know I can trust you, Warner."

Warner then leaned down closer to her, tilting his head, and waited for her to raise her lips to his. As soon as she touched her lips to his, she felt her lips burn, and that heat very quickly moved to other areas of her body. Immediately she felt the need to touch him. She needed to feel him, touch him, so she raised her hands to his waist moving them upwards, massaging his torso, and then moving around to his back, pulling him in closer to her.

She felt him inhale deeply, before his arms moved around her, pulling her in closer to him. Her lips opened in response letting his tongue in to explore. Just as she was feeling herself get lost in his kisses, their hands exploring each other and, just as she realized that she wanted more, she felt him pull away from her. She took a deep breath, her lips felt bare and cold. She opened her eyes to find Warner's eyes seeking hers intently.

"Do you trust me, Lilia?" Warner asked and as she nodded slowly, Warner clarified and said, "No, do you trust me with your heart?"

Lilia stared at him, trying to think through the fog in her brain.

"Don't think. Feel. Do you trust me with your heart, Lilia? I need to know before we go any further." Warner paused, "I trust you with mine."

Lilia closed her eyes, pushed the doubt out of her head and told herself to take a chance. Taking a deep breath

Lilia said softly, "I trust you, Warner. With my heart. I trust you."

She opened her eyes in time to see Warner's slight smile, as one of his hands raised to gently rest on either side of her face, and the other in the small of her back. "Thank you." He said as his head lowered to hers again connecting them once again, the hand on her back pulling her closer. He slowly pulled her in tight against him, her body arched backwards over his arm as she pressed into him.

He broke the kiss to gaze at her. Her eyes were only half open as she felt drugged by his lips. He pressed his lips deeply against hers again and moved his hand from the side of her face to gently touch her neck and along her arm, to graze against her breast. She instinctively leaned her body towards his hand, encouraging him to touch her, giving him permission to touch her more intimately, and he did, caressing the side of her breast through her clothes. She allowed her hands to explore his body more, moving them from his back to his chest.

She felt Warner's hands move to the bottom of her sweater, reaching underneath, and finally touching her skin, his hands exploring the skin at her waist and slowly moving upwards, gently caressing it.

His hands paused, stopping just underneath her breast. She felt his lips pull away slowly from hers and with her eyes still closed, she heard him say, "Are you sure?" Warner asked her.

"Yes," Lilia said when she found her voice. "Are you?" She questioned.

"I want more than this." Warner stated as he moved in to put his lips against hers. "I want all of you." He said with his lips against hers. "Can you give me your heart, Lilia?"

Warner's hands moved up to cover her heart over her breast, and his other hand moved around to her back to hold her to him. Lila felt her arms move to the front of his shirt and she began undoing the buttons. She wanted to feel his skin in her hands. How she wanted this, to finally feel him.

"Yes, Warner. I want yours too."

Once his chest was finally free to her, she pulled away from his lips to watch her hands explore his chest. Warner bent down to whisper in her ear, "Are you sure Lilia?"

Lilia nodded, "I'm sure."

Warner ran his hands down her arms to take her hands in his. He began walking backwards to lead her to his room. Closing the door behind them Warner brought his hands to her hips, slowly bringing her closer to him. Continuing to look into her eyes, he brought their lips back together.

Running his hands up along her torso, Warner raised her shirt, slowly bringing it over her head. "You're beautiful." Warner said, and she felt beautiful under his gaze.

Warner looked directly into her eyes and said, "I don't want just tonight, Lilia. I want it all. I want all of you. Mind, body, and your heart. Are you ready for that?"

"I think we can arrange that," she said flirtatiously.

"I'm serious, Lilia," Warner said placing his hand on her chin and bringing her eyes back up to his, "Do you want all of me?"

"Yes, Warner. I do." Lilia gasped.

Warner's lips came down to hers in relief and Lilia heard him breath, "Thank God."

"Oh Warner," Lilia breathed and gave all of herself to Warner.

They made love, tenderly and full of passion, and time held no meaning. They enjoyed each other's bodies for what seemed like an eternity and an instant. As they lay in bed, exhausted, Warner caressed Lilia's back as she moaned in satisfaction.

"Lilia?" Warner called her name to see if she was awake.

"Mmm? I'm sleeping," she mumbled, her eyes closing.

Warner smiled, "I love you and I'm going to take care of you."

"Mmmmmm…" Lilia said, barely hearing him as she fell asleep, not feeling his kiss on her forehead.

# CHAPTER 27

Lilia awoke the next morning and kept her eyes closed as memories of the night before came back to her. She lay there, trying to be still as she figured out what she should do, when she felt Warner's arm wrap around her waist and pull her in closer to him.

"Mmm," he moaned, "are you just going to lie there and not say anything?"

"I wasn't sure if you were awake."

"I am," he responded, kissing the back of her neck.

Wrapping his arm right around her, Warner rolled her body onto his.

"Warner!" Lilia exclaimed, as he placed his hands on the sides of her face and brought his lips to hers. Lowering his head, he said, "Last night meant something to me, Lilia. No regrets. No shyness. No turning back, okay? It's us now, we." He ran his hands over her shoulders and down her back taking the blanket with him so that her back was exposed. "Are you okay with that?"

Lilia smiled, "Are you asking me to be your girlfriend?" She asked running one hand along his jaw line.

Warner smiled, "Check the yes box for yes…" He paused waiting.

Lilia looked at him smiling softly, "Well, I guess, since you asked so nicely."

"You guess?" Warner said, getting a devilish look in his eyes as she felt his body harden. "I wonder how I can convince you?"

Rolling her over so that she was beneath him, he said, "Let me know when you're sure."

Over an hour later, Lilia woke again at the sound of the door opening. She opened her eyes quickly, and hurriedly pulled the covers over her head.

"First, good morning. Second, why are you hiding from me?" Warner's voice came to her through the covers.

Lilia slipped the covers off her head, "I thought you were Susan." She said, "Good morning."

"Well," Warner said, sitting on the edge of the bed, "Susan hasn't arrived yet, as it's just after seven o'clock in the morning." Warner continued, "Susan is not in the habit of entering my room when I'm home without knocking first. I went downstairs to make sure we didn't leave anything in the kitchen, so she wouldn't get any surprises." Warner leaned over, waiting for her to welcome his kiss.

Lilia leaned over towards him, meeting him for his kiss.

He leaned back and smiled, "I think we have time before Susan comes, for me to come back to bed?"

"No, we don't. I have to get to my room and shower. And you have to get ready to go to work."

"I'm going to work from home today. I have no pressing meetings, except to meet with you." Warner smiled devilishly.

Sitting up, Lilia said sternly, "Warner." She shook her head, then continued, "And I'll be fine here with Susan. You don't have to keep watch over me."

"It's not about keeping watch Lilia. After last night, I just can't seem to stand the thought of being away from you." Warner looked away from her.

Lilia smiled and said, "Last night was very special to me too Warner…"

"I hope you're not about to say thank you." Warner said.

Lilia's eyes widened and Warner laughed shaking his head, "Come on, we have an hour before Susan comes. We have time to shower together."

"The way you would want to shower, I would probably still be in there when Susan came." Lilia said, "I think I'd better shower by myself." Lilia took her sweatshirt from him, placing it over her head and getting out of bed. Warner stood next to her and pulled her into his arms.

"Maybe you should move your stuff in here," Warner said thoughtfully.

"Warner," Lilia responded, "you know I'm moving back to my place when all this is over, right?"

"We'll see." Warner replied kissing her on the lips, and sliding his hands underneath her sweatshirt, touching her intimately, "I'll make sure you don't want to."

Lilia closed her eyes, appreciating his touch. Removing his fingers, he placed his hands on her behind, squeezing it gently and then giving her a little pat. "Come on. Go get showered, babes. I don't want you to get mad at me if you're still in here when Susan comes."

Lilia's eyes widened again at his audacity, picked up her tights, and turned without response to walk out of his room.

After showering, she got dressed and presented herself for breakfast. As Warner had said he was working from his home office, she hoped that meant that they would eat breakfast together.

She walked into the kitchen, seeing only Warner, "Where's Susan?" Lilia asked.

"She's here. She's doing whatever it is she finds to do around the house." Warner leaned over to take her by the waist to pull her into his arms for another kiss, "Just so you know, as your boyfriend, I would now like to be greeted with a kiss."

"We just saw each other." Lilia responded, pulling away quickly, looking for Susan.

"That was over a half an hour ago." Warner continued, "And Susan knows about us already."

"What?" Lilia was incredulous, "You told her? Already?"

"When I came into the kitchen, she basically said that she knew we spent the night together. When I asked her how she knew, she said the dopey look on my face gave it away." Warner shook his head, "She said I always looked at you like I wanted you. This morning I looked satisfied. That's how she knew. Old bird."

"Warner!"

"He calls me 'old bird' to my face, when I bother him. No surprise for him to say it behind my back, Ms. Lilia." Susan said coming into the room. "Glad to see you have the same dopey look as him though. It's about time you two did it."

"Susan!" Lilia exclaimed while Warner chuckled.

"See why I call her 'old bird'?" Warner said, "What's for breakfast, Susan?"

"Working from home today? You usually take breakfast to go."

"Actually, we need to talk to you about that, Susan."

"Okay, okay, sit down. I've made omelets. We can talk while we eat."

After explaining to Susan all that was going on, with Wilkins being responsible for Lilia's attack and escaping from prison, Warner told Susan that he had ramped up security at the house, and that Lilia would be staying there.

"I will completely understand if you want to take a leave until he's caught, Susan. With Wilkins loose, we don't know if he'll try to make an attempt on Lilia here, and you could be at risk." Warner said.

"Well, Mr. Warner, I know you protect your own, so I know that Ms. Lilia will be protected while she is in this house. I certainly don't want Ms. Lilia here all day by herself, so of course I'll be here. I've worked for you for over five years now, and today was the hardest for me to get in here, all the security guards and police asking me questions." Susan got up from the table now agitated, muttering to herself that she felt like a criminal just trying to get to work.

Lilia smiled, and Warner reached out to take her hand, squeezing it, before letting her go so they could both start eating.

After finishing their breakfast, Lilia asked Warner if he needed help on any of the cases he was working on. She also planned on emailing Carl and Grace, to ask them if they also needed assistance. Since her case was being finished by Grace and this whole Wilkins drama, Shawn and Carl hadn't had a chance to give her anything new, and Lilia hated being idle.

Warner told her that he could use some help, so she should come to his office around ten o'clock.

Leaving the kitchen, to check her emails and email Grace and Carl before meeting with Warner, she overheard Warner saying to Susan, "I think we'll order our dinner tonight Susan…" She thought that was odd, since Warner loved Susan's food over any restaurant food, but she placed it out of her mind.

At ten o'clock, she knocked on Warner's office door. "Come in, Lilia."

As she opened the door, Warner said getting out of his chair, "You don't have to knock; you're always welcome in here."

"I will always knock on a closed door, Warner. What if you are in a private meeting or on a private call?"

Warner rolled his eyes, "Okay then, I'll leave the door open when I want you to come in." He said taking her computer and notebook out of her hands and placing them on the chair. He took her into his arms and began kissing her.

After enjoying several kisses, then detaching her lips from his, Lilia said, "I thought you wanted some help?"

"I do." He said taking her hands and placing them around his waist, so he could pull her closer into him.

Lilia felt him harden, "Warner!" Lilia said in shock.

"I've been thinking of you all morning. Last night was amazing." Warner closed his eyes and moaned.

"It was amazing." Lilia said leaning in to kiss him again, then stepped away quickly.

"But we can't do that now anyways; Susan's here, and what about all of that extra security that you talked about? Aren't they here?"

Pulling her back to him, Warner said, "I sent Susan home for the day. I told her we would be ordering out tonight. And the extra security is effective at twelve noon. So, we have roughly two hours before I have to admit them onto the premiscs." Warner finished speaking by the time she realized he had undone all of the buttons on the front of her blouse, exposing her to him.

Warner smiled, bringing her hands to his shirt, "Your turn." Lilia smiled and began to undo his buttons.

"Really, Warner? Here in your office?"

"I want to make a memory with you in every room in this house." Warner said bringing his lips to hers as he pushed her shirt over her shoulders, so it dropped to the floor. "Can I help you? You also don't need this." He said undoing her bra.

"Warner," Lilia breathed and got lost in him all over again.

Sitting, quite satisfied, on his lap in his office chair, Warner ran his hand up and down caressing her back.

"You didn't hear me last night, because you fell asleep, but I want you to hear me now, Lilia." He placed his fingers on her chin, so she was looking into his eyes when he said, "I love you."

She rested her hand on his chest and rested her head down on his shoulder saying, "Warner."

"No, I don't want you saying something because I did." Warner started, "I said it because I've known it for weeks now. I wanted you to know how I felt." Lilia was silent. "I want you to know, really know, when you say it to me." Warner finished.

Adjusting her on his lap, Lilia felt his body harden again.

"Now, I'm sure we have time for one more." Warner said leaning down to kiss her.

After making love for the second time in his office, they both showered and changed, returning downstairs just as Warner's phone rang.

"Warner Reid," Warner answered and then listened to the person on the other line.

"What's the code word?" Warner questioned and grew silent again.

"Okay," Warner said, pressing a button on his phone.

Warner turned to Lilia saying, "That was the security for the house. Every day and night there will be a different code word for them to gain access to the property. The outside guys will call me, and the inside guys will call you." Warner continued. "I'll download the security app on your phone to give them access to the property, once they've given you the correct code word."

Warner walked up to her taking her hands in his and kissed her on the nose. "It's okay, baby. We'll be fine." Warner continued. "I'll give you and them the code word for the next day the night before. Today they're setting up surveillance cameras, automated lights, alarms, and sensors around the house, and on the doors and windows, so that if any are triggered by movement, everyone is alerted by the sound and, if I'm not here, I'll be notified by that same app."

Warner kissed her again, this time on her lips and said, "Now, are you ready to get to work? I actually do need some of your help on a case."

They went to his office and once she had settled her laptop on her lap, Warner sat at his desk and said, "I should set up a workspace for you in here."

"I'm just fine with the one upstairs. Once you give me what I need, I'll head upstairs and start working on it." Lilia said, "I also have work to do for Carl and Grace. It's best for us to work separately, so there are no distractions." Lilia said with a smile.

"You are very distracting indeed." Warner nodded thoughtfully.

"Okay, stop. Tell me what case you are working on. What do you need help with?" Lilia's tone was all business.

After an hour talking about the case and what research he needed, Lilia excused herself to head to her room to get to work. Within another hour Lilia was hard at it and she didn't even notice how much time had passed before her stomach told her she was hungry.

She went downstairs to the kitchen to find something to eat and found Warner in the kitchen at the stove.

"What are you doing?" Lilia asked in surprise.

"What does it look like I'm doing?" he questioned back. "I'm cooking." He chuckled, "I'm making us dinner, so if you're here to eat your lunch at," Warner checked his watch, "Three o'clock, eat light."

Lilia smiled, "I thought you were ordering out?"

"I changed my mind. Tonight, I decided that I would impress you with my abilities." Warner smiled at her.

"Can I help with anything?"

"You can eat and then leave, so I can concentrate on not burning the kitchen down."

Lilia laughed and went to the fridge to take out the makings for a sandwich. "Did you eat? Do you want me to make you a sandwich?"

"I've been snacking while I'm cooking so I'm fine thanks." Warner smiled at her.

"Did you get in touch with Grace and Carl?" Warner then asked.

"Yes, they were very grateful to have the extra help."

"I'm sure they were. You have this way of processing a case," Warner paused shaking his head, "You go in a direction…access information that would have taken months for us to acquire." Warner continued, "In the three hours you've been upstairs, I'm sure you've made more headway than any of the paralegals."

Lilia sat down at the table and began eating her sandwich. After chewing her first bite she said, "I don't know. I think about what answers I need and work backwards from there."

Warner just looked at her and shook his head. "See you're distracting me. Eat."

Lilia laughed and continued eating her sandwich. When she was finished, she asked, "Has the security team finished placing all of the cameras and alarms and sensors?"

"Yes, and they are in position as well."

"Where is the guy stationed inside?" Lilia asked looking around the room.

"They, two guys, are in here somewhere. Remember, they are invisible, and discreet." Warner said walking over to her. He bent down to place a kiss on her lips, and standing up again, he picked up her plate and carried it over to the sink.

"Since you're cooking, let me clean up." Lilia got up from the table, walked to the sink and began washing up all of the dishes in the sink.

"Thanks." Warner said and they both worked in silence for the next couple of minutes.

Finishing up Lilia excused herself to do more work, and Warner told her to come down for dinner around five o'clock.

Lilia smiled all the way back to her room, thinking of how amazing everything was right now. With Warner, not with her life being in danger. That part was not so good.

At four thirty p.m., Lilia's cell phone alarm went off. She had set it a little early as she wanted to freshen up before joining Warner for dinner. He was putting in an effort by cooking for her, so she wanted to look nice.

When she went down to the kitchen at five o'clock. She entered the kitchen to see Warner standing next to a beautifully set table, decorated with candles and flowers. And there was a delicious scent coming from the oven.

"Oh Warner," Lilia started, "Everything looks beautiful."

"I wanted to make our second date memorable. Even if it is in my kitchen." At that he pulled out her chair and indicated for her to take a seat.

Lilia sat down, glad that she had decided to change her clothes and freshen up, when he said, "You look beautiful." He leaned down to kiss her cheek.

"Thank you, Warner. I can't believe you did all this."

"All for you sweetheart." Warner said and Lilia smiled.

"So," Warner continued, "For dinner we have a medium pan seared New York strip with mushrooms, garlic mashed potatoes, and grilled asparagus."

Warner presented their plates, and brought them to the table, first placing hers in front of her. "I hope you like it."

Sitting down across from her, Warner picked up the bottle of wine and poured them two glasses.

"I'm sure it's delicious. It looks amazing, Warner."

As they both started on their food, they were both silent as they enjoyed each bite. Once they had finished most of it, they begun making small talk, cracking jokes with each other. They continued the evening of just enjoying each other's company and forgetting that the outside world was dangerous.

After cleaning up together, Warner asked her to get her cell phone as he wanted to put the security app on it. He explained again how it would work with the daily generated password that he would give her every morning to allow the next team access to the property.

With that discussion completed, Lilia felt as though she was able to enjoy her day with Warner without thoughts of Wilkins taking over.

"Are you going to the office tomorrow?" She asked Warner.

"Yes. I've got a couple of meetings with clients. I called Susan earlier though. She'll be here at eight thirty, before I leave."

"Are you meeting with the Collins client? I uncovered some stuff which discredits two of the prosecutor's witnesses which should help you with your cross examination."

"I knew you would. Thanks."

"Do you want to go over it now?"

"Sure. I'll meet you in my office. I'm meeting with Collins in the morning, so it'll be great to see what you have."

They went over the Collins case well into the evening, with Lilia helping Warner think of different perspectives of the case, once she gave him the information she had discovered about the witnesses.

Finishing up, Warner leaned back in his chair, staring at Lilia.

"What?"

"You're an amazing woman."

"Warner, come on." Lilia said shyly.

"You've done so much in a couple of hours. I'm going to go over what you've given me tonight," Warner continued, "And I'm serious, you are amazing, and I've known it for a while." Warner paused, "The only good thing that's come out of all of this mess with Wilkins is that we've become closer."

"I do concur, counsellor." Lilia said, "And I will now leave you to your work and see myself to bed."

"Will you stay with me tonight, Lilia? Spend the night in my room."

"I think we should take it as it comes, Warner. I don't want to rush things." Lilia paused, "I mean I... I like where we are, Warner, but with me staying here, I think we should take it slow. Which includes me staying in my room, for the most part."

Warner looked about to speak but Lilia interrupted, "Last night and today... it was wonderful and special and I'm glad we've made it here. I don't want our relationship to stop. I just don't want to put pressure on it by staying in your room with you when I'm living here."

"I understand, Lilia." Warner said reaching across his desk to hold her hand, "I don't want to put pressure on you. I know you need some time to get to where I am and

I can wait until you're ready." Warner continued, "These last couple of months have been a lot for you to deal with," Warner sighed, "And I know that in the past, you haven't allowed people to get too close. I want to be here now. I want to be here next year, and I want to be here in ten years. I see us together, and I will do what you need me to do until you can see it too."

Lilia just stared at him in awe of his surety. "Thank you, Warner." She responded quietly.

"Come give me a goodnight kiss." Warner said smiling.

Lilia stood up and walked around his desk. Sitting on his lap, she placed her lips on his, kissing him softly.

"You better get off my lap and get out of here, before you do end up in my room tonight, and I don't get the rest of my work done."

Lilia kissed him one more time and stood up to walk out of the room. She paused at the door, "Goodnight, Warner. I'll see you in the morning."

"What about me joining you in your room? Is that the same thing?"

"Goodnight, Warner." Lilia stressed, laughing.

Warner chuckled, "Goodnight, Lilia."

# Chapter 28

The next morning, Lilia moved slowly, reluctant to start the day knowing that Warner was leaving the house and going to the office. She wasn't frightened; however, she was feeling quite nervous to be left alone.

She went down to the kitchen to say goodbye before he left, and to say good morning to Susan. Entering the kitchen, Warner immediately looked at her, and, noticing the apprehension on her face, he left the breakfast foods that Susan had left organized on the counter and went to her.

"Good morning." Warner said, kissing her on her lips. Looking deep in her eyes he continued, "You and Susan will be taken care of in this house. There are three men arriving shortly to make sure of that, and countless numbers outside. I wouldn't be surprised if Shawn and Chris have contacts in the military." Warner rubbed his hands down her arms comfortingly. Lilia smiled slightly, trying to show him strength in the smile, to let him know that she was okay.

"Can't you keep your hands off her for one second?" Susan said walking into the kitchen, "This is the first time you've chosen a woman over my food though. Must be special." Susan looked at Lilia and winked.

Warner released Lilia and smiled, "She sure is."

"Ms. Lilia, don't let him distract you from breakfast. You've lost weight since you first arrived here, and I don't want to see you lose any more." Susan fussed over Lilia directing her to the area where the food was laid out.

"Susan, you do spoil us. Cut fruit, poached eggs, bagels, muffins, oatmeal? When did you start preparing? At five o'clock this morning?" Lilia said as she began preparing her plate.

"I never know what Mr. Warner will feel like eating so I like to give him choice. Mr. Warner lets me bring every-thing left over home, and, since my George eats anything, I give it to him for his breakfast for the next day. It makes my life easier."

"I think we'll both have the poached eggs then, right, Warner?" Lilia stated, and then continued, "Susan, you should take oatmeal home for George's breakfast. I'm sure he'd enjoy that."

Lilia took her plate to the table and waited for Warner to begin eating. Once Warner was seated and they had begun eating, he waited for Susan to leave the room before saying, "Acrimony."

"Huh?" Lilia questioned, wondering what he was talking about.

"The security word for you today is 'Acrimony'."

"Do you come up with these words or the security company?" Lilia asked.

"I do, so I know it's legit. I give it to the head of the security company just before the team arrives so there's little chance of a breach."

Lilia nodded her head, "And they are going to call me and say it?"

"Yes, and then you admit them using the app I put on your phone."

"I got it." Lilia said hearing her phone ring.

"Right on time." Warner said while Lilia answered.

"Thank you." Lilia said in response to the person on the other line, saying the password. She then pressed on the app, admitting the team onto the property.

"Easy right?"

"It's weird being protected by people I can't see."

Warner smiled and rose from the table, picking up his plate and hers. "I better get going. You're going to make me late for my meeting, my dear."

"Leave them in the sink, I'll wash up." Lilia said standing.

Warner came over to kiss her, and said, "I'll be back before you've had time to miss me."

"Too late. I already do." Lilia smiled.

"Would you both get out of my kitchen with all of that stuff? I think you have kissed more in two days than George and I have in the last twenty years of marriage."

Lilia's eyes widened at the reminder of exactly how much kissing, and other things, they did over the last two days, and cleared her throat.

Warner chuckled, "Stop, Susan. First off, you certainly cannot compare Lilia and myself to you and George. And, secondly, you are embarrassing Lilia."

Warner stopped at the kitchen door and said, "See you around five o'clock for dinner?"

"See you at five." Lilia responded as Warner smiled and walked out of the door.

"Lunch will be ready by noon, Ms. Lilia; can I expect you downstairs or should I bring it up?" Susan said, taking Lilia's focus off the departing Warner.

"Oh, I was going to do that, Susan." Lilia complained as she noticed that Susan was already washing the dishes.

"Don't you be worried about this. This is my kitchen." Susan said turning her back and dismissing her.

"See you at noon, Susan." Lilia said, walking out, knowing Susan wasn't even listening to her anymore as she was singing a tune to herself.

Lilia walked through the foyer slowly, her eyes darting around to see is she would be able to spot one of the security team. Walking up the stairs and entering her room, she went inside and closed the door, feeling as though her privacy was invaded.

She busied herself with work, checking her email, and then settling in to do some more research.

The morning hours passed by quickly and before she knew it, her phone alarm went off telling her it was noon. As usual, she knew that had she not set the alarm she would have continued working until the hunger made her stop.

As Lilia walked towards the kitchen, she noticed that she didn't hear anything, and wondered if Susan had finished preparing lunch.

"Susan?" Lilia called, entering the kitchen, looking for her.

Walking deeper into the room, Lilia approached the island in the middle of the room. It was then that she noticed Susan's legs sticking out from behind the island.

Rushing around quickly to reach her, Lilia said anxiously, "Susan?" Lilia placed her hands all over her body, checking for injury and blood. Finding none, she said again, "Susan, wake up." Lilia then noticed her back raise and fall, so sure she was breathing, Lilia rose to her feet wondering where the security was before reaching for her cell phone to call 911.

Lilia felt more than heard someone come up behind her. Thinking it must be one of the security guards, Lilia turned, but before she could do anything, her arms were grabbed. Her phone falling from her hands, she opened her mouth to scream when a black sheet was placed over her head.

As she tried to kick and fight her way out of her jailer's arms, Lilia felt a pin prick her on her shoulder. Screaming and kicking as loud and as hard as she could to alert security, Lilia felt suddenly hazy and her legs gave out on her. When she started to feel drowsy, she realized that they had drugged her... *The pin prick...* was her last thought as everything went dark and her body sagged to the floor.

# CHAPTER 29

**W**<i>hat happened?</i> Susan thought as she started to come to, realizing that she way lying on the floor. <i>Oh my… Ms. Lilia!</i> Susan lifted herself up off the floor, her memories coming back to her. Heading for the phone, Susan's first call was to Warner.

"Susan?" Warner answered, "Is everything okay?"

"Mr. Warner, come home. They took her." Susan said, still groggy.

"Are you okay, Susan?" Warner was already out of his office and headed for Shawn's.

"They drugged me."

"I'm calling an ambulance and I'm on my way."

Warner burst into Shawn's office, bypassing his assistant. "Shawn, he got her. Call John. I'm calling 911 right now. I have to go." Warner said, running back out of his office.

"Chris!" Shawn yelled, immediately picking up the phone to call John.

Warner raced to his house with 911 still on the phone, so he knew when they arrived. By the time he got there, John was five seconds behind him, and they entered the house to see the EMTs and the police with Susan.

As soon as Susan saw Warner, she called out to him.

"What happened, Susan?"

"I don't know. I was in the kitchen making lunch and I heard someone come into the kitchen. I thought it was Ms. Lilia, so I turned around and saw a man. I had one second to think that it was probably security, but he grabbed me. He put his hand over my mouth and then I felt him jab me in the arm with a needle. I was knocked out. I'm so sorry, Mr. Warner." Susan began crying.

"You couldn't do anything Susan. Don't blame yourself. That's why we had security. Let the EMTs take care of you Susan." Warner turned to John, "What the hell happened, John?! Where was the security?!"

"I'm going to find out." John picked up his phone and walked towards the security guards.

Warner started walking around the house looking for how they entered when a police officer stopped him, "Sir? I'm sorry. But we need you to remain in the front foyer please?"

Warner picked up his phone to call Shawn. As soon as Shawn picked up the phone he asked, "What happened?"

Warner gave him the details he'd learned from Susan and said, "I'm waiting for John to find out what happened to security. Where the hell were they?!" Warner yelled in anger.

"Calm down, Warner. Your anger isn't going to help find Lilia. We need to think."

Warner calmed down tried to recall any details that might help.

"The cabin!" He shouted. "We need to find out where that cabin is that Sanders got for Wilkins. He could be taking her there."

"That's if he didn't know that Sanders was talking, which he might have.'"

"It doesn't matter—we still have to check. Call Caufield. Find out the address, get the police out there."

"Done. I'll also get him to question Sanders some more. Maybe he knows something about this. What are you going to do, Warner?"

"I'm going to look for her."

After hanging up the phone with Shawn, Warner went to hunt down John.

"What did you find out? Why the hell weren't they doing their job?"

"One of the guys that were posted inside is missing. The other one was found knocked out in the closet. It looks like an inside job, Warner. The company is going to give me his name. I'm going to hack into the security cameras, see if I can see what car they left in."

"Find out who it is. Call me when you have the information."

"Where are you going?"

"I have to find her." Warner said walking out of the door.

\* \* \*

Lilia felt herself slowly coming out of a fog. She felt woozy and tried to get her eyes to focus, but it was very difficult. As she became more lucid, she tried to focus on the room, not understanding why it felt like her bed was moving. Slowly, as the environment became clearer, Lilia realized she was lying down in a dark room, on a hard floor. As she felt her body shake against the hard ground below her, she started to look around, realizing she was in the trunk of a moving car. Instantly, Lilia started to panic, as the memory of what happened came back to her.

Lilia willed herself to get a level head and to think. Her hands and feet were not bound, so her attacker probably thought she'd be knocked out a lot longer than she was. *How am I going to get out of here?* Lilia thought. *Where's my phone?* Lilia began reaching into her pocket for her phone, suddenly remembering that she had dropped it when she was grabbed.

*The trunk release!* Lilia remembered one of the cases that she had helped Melinda with. A kidnapping case where the person could have escaped from the trunk had they known there was a release installed in cars so that people couldn't get locked in.

Lilia started feeling around the trunk in the dark, not knowing where the release would be—not even sure if this model car had one. Lilia began pulling at panel lining, trying to feel for anything to pull on. Unsuccessful,

Lilia decided that she would try to push out the brake lights. She could get her fingers through and hopefully signal to other motorists… Or at least put them out so they could possibly get pulled over by the police for not having brake lights.

Lilia began pulling at the panel lining over the brakes, and then started ripping the wiring out. Accomplishing that, Lilia pushed out one of the brake lights, and tried to peek through. Seeing the blur of other cars passing by, Lilia pushed her hand out of the hole and began waving it as wildly as she was able through the small hole, trying to get as much attention as she could. Lilia looked out of the hole again as she felt the car veer left. The road they were now on didn't have any cars passing them. Lilia started to cry in fear, wondering what would happen to her.

* * *

Warner drove around looking for suspicious cars, drivers, anything out of place, impatiently waiting for a call from John or Shawn. When his phone rang, he answered it.

"Warner, Caufield has the police headed out to the cabin. Detectives are still questioning Sanders to see if he knows anything more about this plan to kidnap Lilia."

"Where's the cabin?"

"Caufield wouldn't tell me, Warner. He knew you would go, and if there's a standoff he didn't want you there. I called John. Caulfield said that Saunders rented it for Wilkins, right? John's going to try to find the paper trail."

"Good."

"If I find out, I'll let you know."

"Did John tell you? Wilkins had one of the inside guys."

"Yeah, he told me. He found out who it is, and the police are on their way to his place too.

"John was supposed to call me!"

"Warner. You have to let the police do this. I know you want to save her, but if you find her, what are you going to do against armed criminals?"

Warner pulled his car over to the side of the road, "I need to do something, Shawn. I can't lose her. I love her." Warner wiped a tear off his cheek.

"I know, Warner. We'll find her. Unharmed. You've got a team behind you looking."

"Thanks." Warner said hanging up and pulling back onto the road continuing his search.

\* \* \*

The car had been driving for a while before Lilia felt it turn again. Looking out, Lilia saw that it looked like they were on a main road. About to stick her arm out of the hole, Lilia waited as she started to feel the car slow down to a stop. Peering through the hole, Lilia thought they were at a gas station. She heard the door open, and slam shut, and a few moments later she could hear gas guzzling into the tank. She stayed as quiet as she could hoping her kidnapper would go inside to pay.

Once she heard the gas stop pumping, she waited a few moments, and when she didn't hear activity, she looked out of the hole again. Seeing another car pull up at the pump behind, Lilia waited until the driver got out of the car, then gave a little shout, "Fire!" She saw the woman look around, to see where the call had come from. Lilia shouted again, "Fire!" At this, the woman faced the car that Lilia was in. Lilia quickly stuck her hand out of the trunk taillight again and waved. Lilia said out of hole again, "Please help me!" The woman shook her head quickly and focused back on her pumping. At that, Lilia realized that the woman was indicating that the driver was coming back, as Lilia heard the door open and slam shut again. Lilia looked out of the hole and as the car started pulling away, saw the woman stop pumping and take her cell phone out. She whispered to the woman, wishing she could hear her, "Thank you."

Lilia then started thinking about what items she had on her that she could take off and throw out the hole. She wanted to leave a trail that hopefully they would find. She quickly decided that her shoes could go first. She took one off and after driving for a little while she threw it out of the hole. Once she felt the car turn another corner, she threw the other shoe out of the hole, and began looking for something to go out next.

Taking off her socks and watch in preparation, to send them all out of the taillight, Lilia waited to feel if they would make another turn. Once they kept on the same straight road, Lilia decided that she would keep waving out the taillight to attract as much attention as she could.

Suddenly, Lilia heard sirens from afar. She pulled her arm back inside and started looking out, hoping to see the police, hoping the sirens were coming for her.

Lilia held her breath as the sirens seemed to be coming closer.

Suddenly, she saw the lights approaching from afar, and felt the car slow down for a split second, before immediately speeding up as the driver must have noticed the sirens as well.

Lilia stopped breathing as she saw the lights get brighter, and then the vehicle coming closer. She felt the car slow down and pull over slightly to the side and her hope died as an ambulance drove past.

Lilia felt the tears fall down her cheeks, as the car took up speed again and she started to feel afraid. *What was going to happen to her?*

Feeling defeated, Lilia placed a sock out the taillight and closed her eyes, waiting for what would happen when the car eventually stopped.

\* \* \*

Warner kept driving around, aimlessly peering into every car, hoping he would see her.

Just as he was peering into another car, Warner's phone rang.

"Warner! A woman just called into the police. She was at a gas station when a woman started yelling at her from the broken taillight, locked in a trunk. They think it's Lilia. They're going after her."

"Where, Shawn?! Where?!"

Shawn told him where the gas station was and said that John and his guys are already en route.

Warner hung up and turned his car around speeding towards the gas station.

* * *

Once again, Lilia heard sirens approach, but she was doubtful as she didn't want to get her hopes up. Lilia raised her head to look out the taillight again, and thought her eyes were deceiving her as she saw police cars racing towards her.

"Please!" Lilia whispered, "Come for me, please."

As the police cars came closer, the driver sped up. Lilia stuck her hand out the broken taillight as far as it would go, so they would know she was there. She felt the car speed up even faster and then swerve. Lilia was tossed about the trunk, cutting her arm, as the driver tried to avoid the police.

*They know I'm here! They're trying to save me!* Lilia thought, while she braced herself from being knocked against the trunk walls.

Lilia then suddenly felt the car skid and come to a stop. Looking again out of the taillight opening, Lilia saw the car surrounded by police cars, with police pointing their guns at the car and driver.

"Please help me!" Lilia yelled franticly so they'd know she was there. "I'm locked in the trunk! PLEASE!" she cried.

"Stick your hands out of the window! Get out of the car with your hands up!" Lilia heard a policeman shout. Lilia grew quiet as she hoped her abductor would listen to their instructions. She didn't want them to shoot at the car.

"Get out of the car with your hands up. NOW!" Lilia heard a policeman yell again.

In the silence, Lilia heard the driver's door open, and hoped that they would be apprehended with no problems.

"Down on your knees! Down on your knees!"

Lilia waited in the darkness, tears running down her cheeks, scared and yet hopeful that she was about to be saved.

"Hands behind your head!"

Lilia looked out the taillight again, and watched the police approach the vehicle with their guns pointed at the driver's side of the car. She closed her eyes and stayed hopeful that she would stay safe, waiting for the trunk to pop open.

When at last it did, Lilia immediately shielded her eyes, blinded by the light after being locked in the dark for so long. She squinted and looked into the eyes of a half a dozen police officers all standing around her. She started to sob and raised her arms to be helped out of the trunk.

"Are you injured?" A policeman asked as he helped her out.

"No." Lilia said weakly, as her legs gave out on her as soon as her feet hit the floor.

"Get the paramedics over here!" Lilia heard someone yell as darkness overtook her again.

When Lilia woke up, she realized she was in the ambulance with an oxygen mask over her face. She tried to speak to the paramedic that was sitting beside her.

"It's okay. We're taking you to the hospital. You have to be checked out."

Remembering that she was injected with some kind of drug, she knew that it was probably a good idea.

Arriving at the hospital, Lilia was being pushed on the stretcher, into the doors, when she heard her name.

"Lilia!" She heard Warner's voice but couldn't call out to him. She raised the arm, that didn't have the IV in it, to signal to him where she was. He ran to her, grabbing a hold of her hand. He rubbed his hand along her hair. "Are you hurt? Did he hurt you?" and then to the paramedic, "Is she okay?"

"She is fine sir, but you have to let us get her admitted so the doctors can keep it that way."

Shawn walked up to Warner, pulling him away from impeding the paramedics, "Come on, Warner, let them take care of her. She'll be fine."

The paramedics spoke to the admitting doctors giving them a rundown of what had occurred. Wheeling her into a private room, the paramedics left and two detectives, a doctor and a nurse entered. The detectives introduced themselves, first letting her know that the person that kidnapped her was apprehended and being questioned. They asked her to tell them in detail everything that had happened, as the doctors conducted a medical assessment on her, and checked out the cuts on her arm.

Lilia explained everything, beginning with finding Susan on the ground. "Do you know if she's okay?" she questioned.

One of the detectives replied that she was fine. "She is receiving medical care here in the hospital as well. We got her statement already."

"Please continue," The other detective stated.

Lilia continued, with tears running down her cheeks as she relived all of the terrifying moments from the time that she was grabbed to being rescued from the trunk.

She told the detectives and the doctors that she had been drugged with something, but the nurse was already taking her blood. The doctors explained they would test for toxins in her system.

The detectives thanked her for her statement and let her know that there would be two police officers stationed outside of her door and that they would be getting in touch with her if they had more questions.

Lilia asked if Warner and Shawn could be let into the room, after the doctor gave permission, the detectives told the police at the door to let them in.

"Lilia!" Warner exclaimed bursting through the door, and coming to her side, taking her hand again.

"I'm okay, Warner. They're just running some tests." Lilia continued, "How did you know I was here?"

"First of all, Lilia," Shawn said, "We are so glad that you are safe."

Lilia smiled, "Me too."

"I have been going out of my mind," Warner started, "Did he hurt you?"

"Besides attacking me, drugging me, and locking me in the trunk?" Lilia continued, "Is Susan okay? The detectives said she's here in the hospital?"

"Yes, she's okay. She was in the kitchen when she heard someone come up behind her. She thought it was you, turned around, and saw a man standing there. He injected her with a drug, and she passed out." Warner continued, "She woke up slightly delirious, but heard him dragging you out of the kitchen." Warner stopped.

"Please tell me," Lilia said.

Warner took a deep breath, "She called me, and I immediately got Shawn, called the police, and sped home…" Warner shook his head and rubbed his thumb over her hand. Looking at the bandage on her arm he said, "He hurt you."

"No. I did that sticking my arm out the broken tail-light." Warner looked at Lilia in wonder.

"I called John," Shawn continued, "John got to the house, delt with the security and hacked into the security footage so we could immediately see who took you, what car and direction he left in. John accessed video surveillance from the surrounding areas to track you, but he lost you."

Warner continued smiling, "The police checked the cabin that Sanders had rented for Wilkins. No one was there so we kept looking for you. Then the call came in from a woman at a gas station. You helped us find you." Warner leaned down to kiss her gently on her lips.

"And they arrested him, right?"

"Yes," Shawn answered, "they have him in custody and are questioning him now. I don't know who he is yet, but John probably already knows and will call us."

"John's also trying to find out how he got out with you. With the amount of security we had, it should have been impossible. You should have been safe." Warner shook his head.

"It's not your fault, Warner." Shawn said, "You—no, we. We did everything we could to keep her safe. Someone penetrated our circle. I know it. We just have to wait for John to tell us who and how."

"I tried to call out. I tried to scream, but it went so fast. When I saw Susan lying there, I thought it was security behind me, trying to help. By the time I realized it wasn't, it was too late. I couldn't scream. He'd already injected me and then I blacked out." Lilia paused, "You're sure Susan is alright?"

"She is. I came here to check in on her, when I knew you were found and on your way here too. I left her with her husband and waited to see you." Warner bent to kiss her hand, "It's only been hours and it feels like it's been days."

Shawn shook his head, "He's been a mess since Susan called him, Lilia. He was driving around looking for you, even though I tried to convince him to leave it to the police." Shawn continued, "I'm going to step out and call John. See what he knows."

With his hand on the doorknob, Shawn turned and said to Warner, "There are two police manning the door, and I've got two of John's guys on the door watching them." Shawn asked Lilia, "Do you need anything? I'll get whatever you need for you. I don't think Warner's leaving your side for a long time."

Lilia didn't want him to.

"Well, I actually threw my shoes and socks out of the taillight. I was leaving a trail for you to hopefully find me."

"So fresh clothes, shoes, and socks." Shawn spoke to Warner, "I'll have some here for Lilia and Susan within the hour."

"Thanks, Shawn," Warner stood to shake his hand, and Shawn pulled him in to hug and clap him on the back. "I appreciate everything you've done."

"Of course. I know you would do the same." Shawn said and Warner nodded. "I'll be back once I have news."

Warner returned to Lilia, sitting beside her on the gurney. "I'm so sorry, Lilia," He said, taking her hand in his again, "I tried to keep you safe, and somehow he still got to you."

"Warner," Lilia caressed his hand, "you did everything you could. If I had been on my own. In my own place…" Lilia's voice trailed off. "You found me."

"Even that." Warner replied, "You saved yourself! Had you not known to remove the paneling and pull out the taillights." Warner shook his head.

Lilia told him about Melinda's kidnapping case that helped her.

"I remember that case. Melinda tried to say that the kidnapper didn't know the kid was in the trunk." Warner shook his head.

Lilia nodded. "Do you think Wilkins got to one of the security team? Like he got to Sanders? With threats?"

"Maybe. We'll know soon enough." Warner paused, "Until then, I am not letting you out of my sight. Probably longer. I hope you're going to be okay with that."

Lilia squeezed Warner's hand gently, "Right now I don't want to be anywhere else but with you, Warner."

At that, Lilia heard a knock on the door. Looking up she acknowledged the doctor at the door.

"Ms. Bennett," he said, entering the room, flipping through the chart in his hands, "We've received the toxicology report back and you were given Rohypnol. It was used to knock you out, but luckily you weren't given too high of a dose, which could have been lethal. You also weren't given enough to keep you unconscious for long, which is why you awoke so quickly."

"Will there be any aftereffects, Doctor?" Lilia asked.

"It stays in your system for about five days, but you could feel aftereffects for up to twelve hours. You could experience blackouts, weakness, memory loss. I'd like to keep you here overnight, so we can keep an eye on you." He continued, "You shouldn't drive, or do anything that could put you in an unsafe position for at least five days. Will you have someone at home with you once you're released?"

"Yes, I'll be with her." Warner said.

"Good, good." the doctor said, making some final notes on the chart.

"Can I stay here with her tonight?" Warner asked the doctor.

"Yes, we have a family room where members can sleep over night if they wish."

"No, I meant here in this room, with her." Warner stated.

The doctor nodded, "Under the circumstances, we can certainly make that happen, if you don't mind sleeping on a gurney."

"I'd sleep in a chair if I needed to." Warner stated.

"Well, no need," the doctor said seriously, "I'll have patient transport bring in a gurney for you."

"Thank you, Doctor." Warner said.

"I'll see you tomorrow, Ms. Bennett. Get lots of rest. You will recover faster."

"I will. Thank you, Doctor."

Once the doctor left, Warner moved over to the chair by Lilia's bedside. He pulled it as close as he could to her and said, "Get some rest. Follow the doctor's orders." Lilia stated to feel a bit anxious, nervous to close her eyes. Warner must have seen the stress on her face, as he then said, "I'll be right here. I'm not going anywhere," he promised. When Lilia opened her mouth to speak, Warner continued as if reading her mind. "If Shawn comes back with news, I'll wake you up. I swear." Lilia smiled at him and reached out for his hand.

Leaning closer to her, while sitting in the chair, Warner reached out and took her hand, slowly caressing the back with his thumb. Only then did Lilia close her eyes and willed a restful sleep to come easily. As peace came over her body, she felt her breathing change and the darkness of sleep take over as she concentrated on the rhythm of Warner's thumb rubbing her hand.

# CHAPTER 30

"Lilia." Lilia heard her name being called. "Lilia." She focused on Warner's voice, trying to pull her out of the darkness. "Sweetheart? Wake up, baby. Shawn's here."

Lilia opened her eyes, "Warner?"

"Hey, honey." Warner smiled at her, still holding her hand, "I didn't want to wake you, your sleep was so deep and peaceful, but Shawn's here. He has some news."

"Lilia. How are you feeling?"

"Hi, Shawn. I'm doing okay. Thanks for coming back."

"What did the doctor say?" Shawn asked.

"He said I was drugged with a small amount of Rohypnol. And basically, I need to rest for at least five days."

"I think rest is a good prescription." Shawn continued, "I've got some news first though. The kidnapper's name is Chris Weston. He got a job with the security company that was hired by you, Warner, two days after you employed them to protect Lilia." Shawn continued, "After Wilkins escaped and you extended the protection to include your property, Warner, he requested the job. Claimed he needed the twelve-hour night shifts."

Warner placed his head in his hands, asking incredulously "He was working for them?"

"Yes. John is digging into his past. To see where he and Wilkins connect. We should have something soon. Until then, the police are still questioning him. Hopefully they get something out of him. I should know what they have by morning." Turning to Warner, Shawn said, "I'll text you if I get anything tonight."

"Thanks, Shawn." Warner said.

"Thanks to John too." Lilia said.

"I left some choices of clothing and shoes in those bags on the chair. Listen to the doctor's instructions okay? We want you back to normal as soon as possible."

Lilia smiled at Shawn, "See you, Shawn. Thanks again."

"Take care." Shawn left the room, nodding at Warner.

Just as Shawn left, he held the door open as a hospital staff pushed in the gurney for Warner. Placing it just on the other side of Lilia's bed, the gentleman nodded at Lilia, "Is this position okay, ma'am?" he asked leaving the bed between Lilia's bed and the window.

"Oh yes. It's just fine. Thank you for bringing it in."

"No problem, ma'am." He nodded again at Warner and left the room.

"Thank you for staying, Warner. I really didn't want to be left alone."

"Please don't thank me, Lilia. If you didn't want me to stay with you, I'd be sitting just on the other side of that door for the whole night."

Lilia smiled, and Warner said, "Go back to sleep, I'm going to sit here for a while."

"Oh, can you call John for me? For that matter, did you find my phone? I think I remember dropping it?"

"Yes. Your phone's at the house. I'll call John while you're sleeping. I'll let him know you said thanks, okay?"

"Okay." Lilia said stifling a yawn, "Can you find out how Susan is doing? If she's staying overnight too? Let her know I'm sorry."

"None of this was your fault, Lilia. I'll call George and find out about Susan. Now go to sleep."

"You should get some rest too. It's been a long day."

"It certainly has. I'll go to sleep in a bit. I just need to watch you for a while." Lilia smiled, as her eyes closed slowly.

"Goodnight, Warner." Lilia's eyes closed.

"Goodnight, baby." Warner responded.

In the darkness, Lilia felt someone grab her. She tried to shake herself free but was unable. Just as her heartbeat started to increase, she shook herself awake. Lilia looked around the room very confused. She tried to focus, and realized she was in a hospital room. Wondering why she was in a hospital again, she noticed Warner was in the bed next to her. *Was Warner injured too?*

"Warner?" Lilia said starting to worry, "Warner?" she said, waking him up.

"Lilia? Are you okay? Is something wrong, honey?"

"Why are we in the hospital?" Lilia questioned.

Sitting up, Warner said, "You don't remember?" Warner went over to Lilia's bed pulling the chair beside her, taking her hand in his. Speaking to her in a calm voice, he said, "You were kidnapped from my house. You were drugged and held in the trunk of a car." Warner continued, staring into her confused face, trying to coax her into remembering.

Memories started to come back to Lilia as, visions of what happened started to peek through the fog in her mind. "I could see through a hole..." She said, slowly remembering.

"Yes. You got the taillight out and you were waving through it to attract attention."

"And then the police came."

Warner smiled nodding, "You remember..."

"Your bed was over there." Lilia said, gesturing to the other side of the room, near the window.

"Yes. I moved it after you fell asleep. I wanted to be in between you and the door."

Lilia smiled at him. "I remember." And her smile faded at the memories. "Do you find out about Susan?"

"Yes. George said she was doing well. She wasn't injected with very much Rohypnol, so she's recovering quickly. He said they should let her go home today." Warner was interrupted by his phone, notifying that he had received a text message.

Looking at his phone, he opened the text, "It's Shawn. John found connections between Wilkins and Chris Weston, the guy that kidnapped you." Warner continued,

"Weston told the police everything. He gave them an address of a place he secured for Wilkins. He was supposed to take you there—apparently Wilkins is in hiding there. They've dispatched a swat team to go get him and his crew."

Lilia breathed a sigh of relief, as Warner continued, "Shawn will let us know when they have him in custody."

"Don't cry, baby." Warner wiped a tear from her cheek. "You're safe, here with me."

Lilia squeezed his hand, "I'll be okay, Warner. I'm just feeling overwhelmed. I'll just be relieved when he's finally caught."

Warner replied, "He will be."

Lilia yawned, and Warner said, "I think you probably need a bit more rest. It's not even morning yet."

"I don't want to sleep." Lilia said, yawning again. "I was dreaming that I was being grabbed again. I was scared."

"You need to sleep, Lilia, or you won't get better. Doctor's orders, remember? I'll be right here holding your hand. If you have a bad dream, I'll be here."

"Okay," Lilia nodded and closed her eyes to accept sleep with Warner at her side.

Waking again, Lilia heard people speaking in the room with her. She opened her eyes to see Warner and the doctor having a conversation.

"She almost slept through the night. She woke once, confused. She forgot what had happened, so I told her bits and pieces to try to get her to remember, and she did." Warner was explaining.

The doctor made notes on his clipboard, "That's good that her memories came back so quickly." The doctor looked up and saw Lilia was awake. "Ms. Bennett, I'm glad to see you awake. I was just hearing how your night went from your roommate here." He smiled, "How are you feeling now?"

"I'm feeling okay, Doctor. I feel much better than yesterday after getting so much rest last night."

"And you remember why you are here?"

"Yes. I do."

"Good," the doctor continued, "I think we can discharge you by this afternoon. I'll write you a prescription for Valium to help you sleep at night. Only take it if you need it—if you are having disturbing dreams or can't sleep. Okay?"

"Thank you, Doctor," Lilia replied.

"Take care of yourself, continue to get lots of rest. If you find you are feeling worse not getting better, either see your doctor or come back here." He finished.

"Yes, Doctor. I will."

"Yes, she will." Warner offered with a smile, while Lilia shook her head at him.

Once the doctor had exited the room, Lilia asked, "Have you heard from Shawn?"

"He texted me about an hour ago saying he'd have an update soon. But I haven't heard from him yet."

Just as Warner had finished the sentence, his phone rang. "It's Shawn," He identified, looking at the screen.

"Shawn," He said, first and then paused listening, "Yes, I'm here with Lilia, she's still in the hospital, but the doctor just left. He said he could discharge her this afternoon." Warner continued, "Do you have news on Wilkins?"

Lilia watched as Warner listened intently. "What?!" Warner exclaimed and listened again.

"What happened, Warner?" Lilia questioned anxiously and Warner looked at her.

"Okay Shawn, I better go, I have to talk to Lilia." Warner said, "Bye." He said and disconnected the phone.

"Warner. What happened? Tell me." Lilia said, "Please."

Warner walked over to her bed, sat down, took her hand in his, and wouldn't make eye contact with her.

"They didn't catch him, did they?" Lilia said as she closed her eyes.

"When the swat team went into the house, they exchanged gun fire with his men. Six were killed. They are still trying to identify all of them, but one man was Wilkins's brother and another one his cousin. John said the rest were probably friends helping with the promise of cash."

Warner took a deep breath and continued, "Wilkins wasn't there. They think he was already gone. When Weston didn't show or make contact, he must have realized that Weston might give him up."

Lilia took a deep breath as Warner said, "John is sending his men over here to escort us to the house when you are released. John's men will stay with us until Wilkins is found." Warner continued, "John will find him. His team is going through the CCTV footage around the property to track him."

"Warner, I'm scared. He's already gotten to me twice. How do we know that the guys that John is sending are safe?"

"Shawn said John was going to call when they arrive to give me a description. They are three guys he absolutely trusts."

Lilia turned away to look out of the window, and Warner rubbed the top of her hand with his thumb. "Hey, babe, look at me." Warner waited to continue until she drew her eyes to his, "I'm not leaving you. This time, I'm not going anywhere. He will be caught, and you will be safe. I promise you."

"You sound so sure." Lilia said.

"I'm certain."

# CHAPTER 31

I t was late afternoon, and the doctor had just finished repeating all of the instructions before releasing Lilia from the hospital, while the nurse handed over all of the paperwork and prescriptions.

"And you are clear to go, Ms. Bennett." The doctor said.

"Thank you, Doctor." Lilia said and nodded at the nurse, thanking her for the paperwork.

"An orderly will be by with a wheelchair to take you to the doors. I have told the officers and they will accompany you and remain with you, Ms. Bennett, until your transportation arrives."

"I'll be driving her." Warner said, "I'll get the car while the police wait with you and connect with John's guys." Warner continued, "I'll tell him that we're leaving soon." He said taking his phone in his hand and excusing himself to call John.

"Do you have any questions for me, Ms. Bennett?'

"No, I don't, Doctor. Thank you for everything."

He nodded and said, "Take care then, Ms. Bennett," He said and then he and the nurse left the room.

Warner returned to Lilia saying that John's men were already outside waiting for them. Lilia just wanted to change and then she'd be ready to go. The orderly and the officers accompanied Lilia and Warner to the front doors of the hospital just as the doctor had promised, and Lilia waited for Warner to bring his car around, to take her to his place. Lilia was on edge while she waited for him, despite the officers and the orderly standing right beside her.

Once Warner pulled up, Lilia noticed a black SUV with tinted windows pull up right behind him, and a man got out of the car to join Warner in helping her into his car.

"Thank you." Lilia said to both the man and Warner. Once Warner was seated beside her, he said, "They'll follow us to my place. There are already three more of John's guys there keeping watch until we arrive. They are going to protect us until Wilkins is caught."

"Has John found him yet?"

"Not yet, but they're on him. They found him on footage so now they are just tracking where he could have gone."

Arriving at his place, Warner looked at her, "Ready to go inside?" Lilia nodded.

All three of the men were already out of the car. While one stood by Lilia's door, the other two had already disappeared.

"Where did the other guys go?" Lilia asked.

"They are securing the property, ma'am." The large man beside her said, "Once I have the okay, then we can move inside."

Lilia stared at him, as Warner joined her on her side of the car. The guard standing beside her, placed his finger on the headset in his ear. "Affirmative." He turned to Warner, "We're clear to move indoors, sir."

Lilia asked, "Thank you, uh, sir? What should we call you?"

"No names, ma'am. We don't exist." He said looking at her seriously, "Now please, ma'am, can we go inside?"

Warner wrapped his arm around her waist, letting her know that she could lean on him if she needed to, and they walked inside together.

"Are you hungry? Do you want to lie down? What can I do?" Warner questioned her.

Lilia smiled, "Warner, I just want a shower right now. That would feel heavenly."

"I think I can make that happen." Warner said coming up close and placing his hands on her face. He kissed her gently on the lips, "Do you want company?"

Lilia kissed him again and then smiled, "I think I'll handle this one on my own. Thanks for the offer though."

"Next time then."

"Maybe." Lilia said playfully as she gazed up at him.

"I'll walk you upstairs and hop in the shower myself. Then I'm going to make you a sandwich. I'll bring it up for after your shower, see if you're ready to eat."

"Thank you, Warner," Lilia said giving him a gentle smile, as he leaned over to kiss her on her forehead.

Warner walked beside her up the stairs and to her room. Once there, he asked her, "Will you stay with me tonight or am I staying in here?"

"Are you asking or telling me?" Lilia asked.

Warner started at her, as Lilia awaited his answer, "Definitely asking."

Lilia smiled, "I'd like to sleep in your room tonight, Warner."

Warner smiled back at her, then pulled her in to give her another gentle kiss on her lips. Lilia heard him moan, as he eased her away from his body. "Enough temptation. I think you should go shower."

Lilia smiled and then looked anxiously at her bedroom. Reading her mind, as she was starting to get used to him doing, Warner said, "John's guys finished checking every nook and cranny of this house just before we got here." He looked at her, "Do you want me to double check?"

Lilia nodded, and Warner entered the room, Lilia standing at the door. Lilia watched as he checked every corner, under every piece of furniture, and behind every door and curtain, in both the bedroom and sitting room. Once Lilia felt secure, Warner left her to shower himself, reminding her that he would return with her sandwich. When Warner left, Lilia locked the door and went to take the steaming hot shower that she'd been longing for.

Lilia spent much longer in the shower than she'd planned and after she finished getting ready, she heard knocking at the door.

"Lilia? It's me, Warner." And Lilia hurriedly went to the door to let him in.

"Sorry."

"It's okay. I understand." Warner smiled, entering the room with a tray full of food.

"There's so much food." Lilia said looking at the sandwiches, bowl of fries, and two bowls of soup.

"I didn't know how hungry you'd be. I, on the other hand, am ravenous." Warner continued, "Whatever you don't eat, I'm sure I can take care of." He finished entering the sitting room and placing the tray on the table. "Come on, let's eat."

After eating in silence for a while, Lilia paused wiping her mouth. "Thank you, Warner. I didn't know I was this hungry." Warner smiled.

"Did Susan go home today too?"

"Yes, George called me and let me know they had gotten home. He said she's doing well, she just needs rest." Warner said, "He said she was really concerned about you too."

"I'm glad she's okay."

"Me too." Warner said, resuming eating his food. Lilia offered him the rest of her fries, and he added them to his, smiling.

Lilia watched Warner finish the rest of his and her dinner, and then he asked her, "Did you want to watch a movie before going to bed?"

"That sounds like a good idea. We can cuddle on the couch."

"I definitely like the sound of that." Warner said with a smile on his face.

Later that evening, as they cuddled on the couch, Lilia snuggled in closer under Warner's arm as the credits rolled.

"Good movie choice, Warner."

"Did you like it? It's one of my favourites."

"A movie about a lawyer, defending a teen on trial for something he didn't do. What's not to like?"

Warner kissed her on the top of her head. "My feelings exactly." He said then yawned.

"You should get to bed. You didn't get much sleep last night, did you?"

"I didn't, but I'm fine. I needed to keep an eye on you."

"I'm glad you stayed with me, Warner."

Warner kissed her on her head again and then eased her off him, "Let's go to bed. I think we could both use some rest."

He got up from the couch, putting his hand out to help her up, bringing her against his body and looking into her eyes, before leaning down to place his lips gently against hers. Lilia's hands rose up his arms and over to his chest. Lilia felt the heat of his hands exploring her body and she leaned back as she felt his hands graze her ribs, giving him access to touch her breasts. As soon as his hand grazed her breast, Warner pulled back, placing his hands on her hips and a kiss upon her forehead.

"Warner?" Lilia questioned.

"You need to rest. I'm just going to hold you close tonight."

"But I'm feeling fine Warner. I…" Lilia started, and Warner interrupted.

"Rest Lilia. Doctors' orders." Warner moaned and closed his eyes as Lilia looked down at his hardened manhood. "No matter what. Rest, Lilia."

Lilia placed her hand on him, massaging him gently. "Really?" Lilia said softly.

Warner reached down and removed her hand, moaning, "Please don't make this difficult Lilia. It's hard enough already."

Sighing, Lilia took a step back from Warner as he said, "Please, go to my room and get ready for bed? I'll be right behind you."

Lilia looked at him, and reading her mind again, Warner said, "It's safe."

Lilia turned and went up to Warner's room, finding one of his t-shirts and climbing under his covers. Lilia left one light on and tried to stifle a yawn as she waited for Warner to come to his room. She didn't realize that she was so tired, she stifled another yawn. Lilia was finding it hard to keep her eyes open and soon gave into the dark slumber of sleep. At some point in her sleep, she felt Warner's warmth wrap around her, providing her comfort as she slept.

"STOP RIGHT THERE!"

Lilia was startled awake, hearing someone yell. She felt arms tighten around her, and she turned to look over at Warner, who was staring at her with his finger on his mouth.

"I SAID STOP!!" They heard again.

Lilia's heart was beating so loudly she almost didn't hear Warner whisper, "Go hide in the closet. Get on the floor." Lilia was so scared she held tightly onto Warner, "Go now Lilia!" Warner whispered loudly, Pushing her gently out of the bed towards the closet. "Go, baby. I love you."

Lilia got up quickly and ran as quietly as she could to the closet and sat on the floor, pulling his clothes off the hangers and covering her body. Lilia was terrified, and she was afraid for Warner.

*Why hadn't he hid with her?* she thought just as she heard yelling again, "Show me your hands!" and then shots being fired.

BANG! BANG! BANG!

Lilia froze, and waited to hear something. Anything. She heard footsteps running around the house, and more shouting. When she heard footsteps approach the closet where she was hiding, Lilia stopped breathing.

"Lilia?" She heard Warner's voice as the closet door opened. "It's safe, baby."

Lilia pushed all of his clothes off of her, leaping out of the closet into Warner's waiting arms. After holding each other tightly, not wanting to let each other go, Warner leaned back to look at her face. He started softly kissing the tears off her face.

"Don't cry, honey. Don't cry." Warner whispered, "It's going to be okay."

Lilia slowly calmed down, still holding tightly to Warner and now hearing sirens approaching the house.

"What happened, Warner? Where did you go?" Lilia asked, finally mustering up her thoughts and words.

"It was Wilkins. He got into the house somehow. John's guys got him." Warner said.

"Wilkins? Was in the house?" Lilia said incredulously. "Is he… Is he dead?" Lilia stuttered.

"Yes, they shot and killed him. The police are on their way."

"Where were you? Why did you leave me?" Lilia said taking a step back from him.

"I didn't leave you. I wanted to be in between you and him, if he got to us. I was standing right in front of the closet door."

Lilia wrapped her arms, tightly around him again, "Warner?"

"Yes, baby?"

"I love you too," Lilia whispered. She was so close to almost losing him, she didn't want another second to go by without him knowing how she was feeling.

She felt Warner's arms hold her even tighter, as she heard him say, "Oh baby, I love you so much." As Lilia laid her cheek against Warner's chest, she felt him laying kisses on top of her head. They paid no attention to the noise and commotion around them, as the police and paramedics arrived and began questioning everyone.

Soon enough one of John's guys knocked on the door interrupting them. Entering the room behind him were three police officers, John, Shawn and Chris.

Shawn approached Warner and Lilia, "Lilia, Warner, are you both okay?"

"Yes, we're fine, Shawn. How did you get here so fast?" Warner asked.

Shawn gestured to John, "John's guys alerted him. They alerted the police and John called me. They think he managed to find a blind spot in the camera coverage along the perimeter. Once he got to the house, he must have watched John's guys waiting for an opportunity to get past them. He must have thought he could get past them to you Lilia, only he didn't know how many guys were inside. He's been obsessed with you for so long that he took the chance. He tried to shoot his way in, past everyone to find you."

The police approached them then. "Mr. Reid?"

"Yes. I'm Warner Reid." Warner stepped forward.

"We just want to clear up some questions on our end. Can we speak with you and Ms. Bennett for a moment?"

Warner held out his hand to Lilia, to bring her closer to them. Answering their questions as thoroughly and as quickly as they could, Warner confirmed all that John's security detail had already told them. That due to the recent attempted kidnapping, they had the security team to protect Lilia from Wilkins who had a warrant out for his arrest. After asking some additional questions, the police told them that they should make arrangements to stay somewhere else as they would have to secure the scene in order to investigate and collect evidence.

As Warner and Lilia began walking over to join John, Chris, and Shawn, Lilia said, "We can go to my place tonight. You can stay with me until you find a place more comfortable, Warner."

"Let's discuss this when we're at your place later, okay?" Warner said, holding his hand out to her.

"Okay," Lilia said placing her hand in his.

"What did they say?" Chris asked.

Warner told them that they had to leave tonight, but that they were going to go to Lilia's condo.

Warner walked over to John, with his hand outstretched. "John, your guys... I can't thank you enough." Lilia joined him, "We." Lilia said, then continued, "If your men hadn't been here..." Lilia went silent, "Did they tell you how it happened?"

John nodded and said, "He came through your office window. There's a blind spot there with your security cameras. Weston apparently told the police that he told him about it along with a layout of your house when they were discussing how to get to you, Ms. Bennett. Luckily, we had more guys inside than outside." John continued, "They spotted him coming out of your office. They told him to stop. When he started shooting at them, they shot back." John finished. "Do you want me to put a couple of guys with you tonight too?" He asked Warner, "Just until you're comfortable?"

Warner looked at Lilia, who nodded her head, "Yes, thanks, John. I think one more night will be good. Thanks."

Lilia turned to one of John's men, "Do you think I can go to my room to collect some things I need?"

"Come with me. We can see if an officer can go in with you." They left the room and found an officer to accompany them. When they got to the door, Lilia hesitated. Guessing at why she was hesitating, the guard said, "It happened downstairs. Not here."

The police officer said, "Ma'am, indicate what you'd like to take with you. I will document it and pick up what you're taking."

"I just need my work stuff and some clothes." Lilia stated and then began showing him the items she wanted to take.

Lilia returned with her bags to Warner's room where a police office and one of Johns men were stationed at the door. Lilia saw Warner speaking with Shawn, though John and Chris were no longer in the room.

"Are you ready to go?" Warner asked. "I just have to pack a couple of bags and then I'll be ready."

"I'd better get going," Shawn said, "Lilia, I'm glad this is finally over. Take care of yourself and take care of Warner. I think both of you could do with about two days of undisturbed sleep. Take it. I don't want to see either of you in the office for at least a week."

"I have cases—"Warner said.

"That you can work on from home. Any meetings that you can't change, Chris or I can take care of." At that, Shawn walked out of the door.

"I'll pack quickly and meet you in the car?" Warner said and Lilia nodded, leaving with the guard.

In the car on the way to Lilia's condo, Warner said, "I was speaking with Shawn."

Lilia waited and when he didn't continue, Lilia asked, "About what?"

"My house." Warner continued, "I can't live there after this. You won't want to live their either. In the future, I mean."

Lilia remained silent.

"What are you thinking?"

"I'm just trying to get through the night and you're thinking of our future? In your house?" Warner glanced quickly over at her.

"I have to think about this now, Lilia. When they release my house, I'm not going back there, and I'll need a place to live." Warner said.

"I'm sorry, Warner. You're absolutely right. You've given up so much to keep me safe already. Now you're giving up your house too." Lilia shook her head.

"I didn't give up anything I didn't want to. I would give up anything to have this same outcome. You. Safe. And here with me." Warner reached his arm over to place his hand on hers.

Lilia instantly turned her hands over in his to hold onto them. "Well, it would now be my pleasure to have you stay with me while we figure it out." Lilia continued. "Although, my place is much smaller than yours… and I don't have a Susan."

Warner smiled as he pulled into the front of the building. He turned to look at her, "I would love to stay with you, no matter how long it takes to figure it out, and no matter how small your place is."

Warner leaned over, taking her head in his hand to bring her closer to him. "While WE," Warner stressed, "figure it out." Looking deep into her eyes, he said, "I love you. And I'll go anywhere you do." Kissing her quickly, Warner smiled, "Now let's go upstairs to your cubicle."

# EPILOGUE

Taking a few days off, Lilia and Warner locked themselves up in Lilia's condo, not leaving once. They even had groceries delivered. They talked about nothing and everything as they took it easy.

Once they went back to work in the office. The first few times, Lilia still felt a little apprehensive and distrustful of everyone around her, considering Sanders, someone who was supposed to protect her, had betrayed her trust and attacked her. Warner tried to make her feel more comfortable, dropping her off at the front entrance and asking Shawn to keep an eye on her whenever he couldn't be in the office with her.

The time finally came when Shawn disclosed to Lilia that his contact in the police department said they had arrested the rest of Wilkins's accomplices. Sanders and Weston were pleading guilty and were testifying against everyone else. Now, Lilia began to feel more secure when leaving the safety of her condo.

After he had come to an agreement with the prosecution, and the plea and sentencing arranged, Lilia got to hear more about what Jeff Sanders had confessed to. She had learned that he had followed her home several times at Wilkins's insistence, reporting back to him. She didn't know when Wilkins became so obsessed with her, but based upon what Sanders had stated, Wilkins wanted her. Sanders said that Wilkins told him that he would break her. Just as he'd broken the other women who thought they were too good for him. He had told Sanders that once he found a woman he wanted, and she dismissed him, he would make sure she'd regret it. She would know she was his and that Lilia would join the rest of them.

Lilia realized that he must have become obsessed with each of his victims, resulting in him attacking them and in some cases, killing them. Had they succeeded in kidnapping her, she would have ended with the same fate as Lucille Diaz and the others.

Chris Weston was Wilkin's cousin, and he shared his sick tendencies. In addition to confessing to all of the horrendous things he had helped Wilkins do, he admitted to raping several women because they "deserved it." Attacking them when they were alone in parks and parking lots. Wilkins had been his mentor, and he had been emulating him. The police were working on identifying the women to include the additional charges.

Warner helped ease Lilia's feelings of apprehension by presenting her with evidence that John's investigation team had conducted unbeknownst to the police. John had IDed all of the men seen with Wilkins and presented a report that each one was either deceased, or arrested and awaiting trial, which proved to her that there were no more accomplices on the loose.

At the firm, to ensure the safety of all, Shawn and Chris had John conduct a background check on everyone employed with Hale, Cross & Associates, starting with security, as they felt that it would help all employees feel safer considering all that had happened to one of their own.

As the days turned into months, Lilia thought that eventually she and Warner would start to be at odds with each other due to working together and living in such a small space, but that didn't happen. Lilia enjoyed the time she spent with Warner and they never seemed to run out of things to talk about. In times sitting in silence, it was never awkward.

After the first couple of weeks of living together in the condo, Warner suggested that they initiate weekly date nights, where they actually went out. They made sure they planned their evenings, each making suggestions so that they could experience new things or something that the other enjoyed.

Lilia was looking forward to this date night, although Warner was being very secretive about it. He would only tell her that Shawn was inviting them to dinner, but he wouldn't tell her what the occasion was. Personal dinner invitations from one of the CEOs of the law firm was definitely not something that she was used to, but that didn't surprise her as she had only recently become an associate. Perhaps this was something Warner was used to, having been a partner for several years.

"Is this Shawn's house? I thought we were going to a restaurant." Lilia questioned Warner as a large, beautiful house appeared after they had driven past security gates and up a long driveway.

"No," Warner said, "It's not."

Warner parked the car and got out of the car, coming over to her side and opening her door.

"Why is he inviting us for dinner here if it's not his house?" She asked as they walked hand in hand to the front door. "And where is everyone?" She asked, noticing that there were no other vehicles parked in the driveway.

Warner didn't answer—he simply opened the door and pulling her behind him into the house. "Warner. Why are we just walking in? Where's Shawn?" Lilia now demanded.

"We were invited here for dinner." Warner said simply, guiding her into an empty room.

"By whom?" Lilia asked noticing the house was empty of furniture, "Does anyone even live here?"

As Warner guided her into another room, Lilia noticed a beautifully set table for two, with flowers and burning candles set in the middle of the table.

"Hopefully us." Warner stated.

"What?" Lilia asked confused. "What do you mean 'us'?" Lilia turned to Warner, confused, when suddenly Warner bent down, kneeling on one knee. "Warner? What are you doing?"

"I'm hoping that we can live here," Warner said, reaching a hand into his pocket and pulling out a ring box, "If you like the house, and if you'll marry me." Warner said opening the box and revealing a beautiful diamond ring.

Lilia's hands raised to her mouth in shock. They had now been living at her condo for a couple of months and she had no idea that he had been planning this.

"What did you say? Warner. When did you do all of this?" Lilia said gesturing to the dressed table.

"I had a little help." Warner answered, then said, "Lilia, I'll happily answer any questions you have, after you please answer mine. Will you marry me?" Warner said earnestly.

"Oh Warner. I will. Of course, I will." Lilia answered, reaching down to guide Warner to his feet.

Once on his feet, Warner took her hand in his and said, "Let's place this where it belongs," Warner said putting the ring on her finger.

Lilia reached up, placing her hands on his face, bringing him down to kiss her. Placing his hands on her hips, Warner first deepened the kiss, then set her away from him gently.

"We need to save some of this. I don't want all of our hard work to go to waste."

"When did you do all of this and who helped you?" Lilia asked as he seated her at the table.

"Shawn and Susan helped me, of course. Finding just the right house was hard. I think I've looked at over twenty. Shawn helped me start looking as soon as my place was sold." Warner answered, smiling as he took his seat.

"Ahem," Lilia heard a voice being cleared, and looked towards the sound.

"Are you ready to be served, sir?" asked the waiter.

"Yes, thank you." Warner said.

Lilia looked in shock as the waiter brought two plates over, "Seafood fettuccini in a white wine sauce, ma'am. Sir." He said putting the plates down in front of each of them and then disappearing into the other room, which Lilia assumed was the kitchen.

Lilia smiled at Warner, knowing he'd chosen this meal for its significance. It had been the first meal they had shared when they had gone to lunch together. She then could not suppress the questions that were in her head.

As she opened her mouth to speak, Warner interrupted her, "Yes. Susan made the food, and helped me with the décor, of course." Warner chuckled as Lilia shook her head smiling.

"Of course, she did." Lilia stated with a smile, "Now Warner. What do you mean this house could be ours?"

"Well," Warner paused, "I bought it. For us." Warner continued, "We can come back tomorrow and do a tour." Warner paused, staring at her tentatively, "If you like it, we can start renovations on it to make it ours. If you don't, we'll put it back on the market and we can look for another, together." Warner finished hurriedly.

Lilia paused dramatically, staring at Warner, then saying, "I love this house, Warner."

Warner looked at her confused, "How do you know you like it? You've seen one room."

"Because I love you. And you chose this house for us. That's how I know, Warner."

"I love you, Lilia." Warner reached over taking her hand in his, "And I can't wait to fill this house with our memories, our laughter, our dreams and our children, if you want them."

"Whatever our life brings, Warner, I'll go anywhere you do."

"I was hoping you'd say that, soon-to-be Mrs. Reid."

Lilia cleared her throat, "Um, Mrs. Bennett-Reid."

Warner laughed, and said, "Your last name can be whatever you want, as long as there is a Mrs. in front and a ring on that finger." He picked up her hand and kissed it. "We better start eating," Warner said picking up his fork, "Susan will claim I'm trying to starve you if I don't feed you."

"I still can't believe you planned all of this." Lilia said picking up her fork again.

"And there's more." Warner said.

"More?" Lilia said incredulously.

"We have an engagement party to attend."

Lilia looked at him stunned, "What?"

"After dinner, there is a party in our honour being held at Shawn's house. My sister and her family are there. I can't wait for you to meet her."

"Warner. What if I'd said no?"

"No?" Warner questioned. "Well, I guess Shawn would be throwing me a 'she said no' party."

"I guess you're glad I said yes then, so you wouldn't be subjected to that."

"I am very glad you said yes, but not for that reason. I'm glad that you love me and want to spend the rest of your life with me." Warner continued, "I'm glad that you choose to be my wife and I choose to honour and protect you always. My lover, my partner, my best friend."

"Oh, I do love you, Warner Reid. I do." Lilia said, getting out of her chair, and walking over to him. Warner pulled her into his lap and placed his arms around her.

"And I love you too, Lilia Bennett." Warner placed his lips against hers and kissed her and Lilia knew he would never let her go.

CPSIA information can be obtained
at www.ICGtesting.com
Printed in the USA
LVHW011925090922
728002LV00002B/95

9 781039 147584